The Darkest Gate

The Descent Series

SM Reine

Other Series by SM Reine
The Ascension Series
Seasons of the Moon
The Cain Chronicles

Copyright © SM Reine
Published by Red Iris Books
1180 Selmi Drive, Suite 102
Reno, NV 89512

The

Darkest

Gate

SM Reine

ONE

HISTORY won't remember one of the most important meetings to ever occur. It was organized over secure phone lines by a third party, who selected a time and public location at random, and gave each attendant a day's notice to travel there—little enough time to ensure they could not prepare surprises in advance.

Nevertheless, James Faulkner was seated at the Pledger Bistro fifteen minutes early. He declined the offer of wine so the waiter wouldn't disturb him, then tipped his head back as though holding it up was too much effort. Even though he had washed and shaved in a train station bathroom, there was no hiding his gaunt cheeks and trembling hands.

The man who approached the table at three o'clock had the slim, dangerous appearance of a concealed pistol. He studied James from beyond arm's reach.

"My name is Alain Daladier. I've come to meet the greatest kopis."

James sat up. "A pleasure to meet you. I'm James Faulkner." The collar of his shirt was loosened to expose a white scar on his chest, and the sleeves were rolled back to show fresh pink skin at his wrist where he had been bitten.

Alain observed these details without changing

1

expression. "Show me the sword."

He flicked back the collar of his shirt. Once Alain leaned forward to glimpse the leather-wrapped handle of a falchion strapped to his back, James concealed it again. "Satisfied?"

"I'm told you have two."

"Not today. Will you sit?"

Alain responded by stepping outside the restaurant. He was replaced by a grizzled man with white hair and a designer watch. "Call me Mr. Black," he greeted, taking the seat beside James. They shook hands. His grip was surprisingly light for someone resembling an aged bodybuilder. "Alain says you're the greatest kopis."

"And I've heard you're not far from the greatest yourself. You went to quite a bit of effort to arrange our meeting today."

"Oh, yes. But it's worth it, to meet the greatest kopis... James Faulkner." Mr. Black covered a smirk with his hand. His brown eyes glowed with mirth. "Faulkner...hmm."

The waiter returned with menus and placed napkins in their laps. "Yes, that's my name," James said once they were alone again.

"What do you know about ethereal artifacts, Mr. Faulkner?"

"As much as anyone else. The information is limited. Angels had only a minimal presence on Earth before the Treaty of Dis was forged, and they're scarce now. Why do you ask?"

"Go on."

James sat back in his chair. "What's the meaning of this?"

"I wouldn't have spent this much time and money tracking you down for a private chat if our conversation wasn't important. Humor me. What else do you know?"

"Very well. Ethereal artifacts have three primary

2

properties: They can be separated, but not broken; they are inviolable; and neither humans nor demons can use their power—which is immense." The scar on James's chest ached. He massaged it with two fingers as he spoke. "Angels don't make them anymore."

"Good, good. I'd bet a lot of cash that you know more about the subject than the average person. Would you recognize one if you saw it?"

"Most likely."

Mr. Black studied his menu. He was still smiling, as though he found James's answer amusing. "I bet you could. I've been searching for one particular ethereal artifact for some years now. It's in the shape of a bowl with notches around the edge. It looks like it's made of ivory, but it's not carved from the bone of any animal I've killed."

"I've never seen it."

"Didn't say you had, did I?"

"Then what are you expecting? If you need a lecture on the properties of ethereal craftsmanship, you could ask someone much easier to reach than I am." He fell silent when the waiter returned to the table with a basket of bread. Mr. Black ordered the duck. James's stomach was a gnawing hole beneath his ribs, but he said, "Nothing for me, thank you."

"Come on, now, you're practically a mummy. I'll pay for your dinner. You're my guest, aren't you?"

"No. Thank you."

"He'll have the fish," Mr. Black said, and the waiter left. "I know you're hurting for money, Mr. Faulkner. It's hard making ends meet sometimes, isn't it? But you don't need to starve." He took a piece of bread from the basket and smeared garlic butter across its surface. "What were we talking about?"

James watched his teeth sink into the baguette. "The bowl."

3

Mr. Black took his time chewing and swallowing. He wiped crumbs from his mouth with the napkin. "Right. I've discovered this bowl's location." He leaned forward and locked gazes with James. "I want it."

"Then you should go get it."

"Not many kopides survive to my age. I'm past my prime. I've left the pursuit of justice and saving humanity to younger men. I bought a nice piece of land down South, I've got a summer home, and I run a few businesses that employ a lot of folks. I'm doing pretty damn good, if I do say so myself."

James realized he was still rubbing his scar and forced himself to stop. Retired? Kopides and aspides never retired. The best anyone could hope for was dying in the service of mankind. The idea of being able to settle down was equally tempting and disappointing, since he knew it was something he couldn't have. He couldn't afford to eat on many days.

"What's your interest in this bowl if you've retired?"

"Call it...sentimentality. This bowl is difficult to reach, as you would expect. I need a young kopis—a great kopis —to retrieve it." Mr. Black's teeth were very white when he grinned. "I said I'm doing well, didn't I? I'll pay a good chunk of cash to have this piece added to my private collection."

"I'm not a mercenary. My services aren't for sale."

"That's fine. I don't want *your* services. You are powerful, Mr. Faulkner, I won't argue that. Alain felt you coming miles off. But you're not the greatest kopis."

James stiffened. "What—?"

"You're wasting my time. I hate having my time wasted." That smile had grown fixed on his face. Without making a single motion, Mr. Black suddenly appeared much more deadly. "Where is he?"

Trying not to glance over Mr. Black's shoulder was

4

pointless. By the time James ducked his head, the motion had already given him away, and Mr. Black turned to point Alain across the street. As soon as he went through the door, a young woman sitting at a table under a tree abandoned her espresso and entered the restaurant, invisible to Alain's searching gaze.

The waiter moved to intercept her, but she pushed past him and dropped into an empty chair at their table. The look of disbelief from Mr. Black as he took in her girlish face and brutally short curls almost made James laugh. She was hollow-cheeked, too young to be out of school, and wouldn't have blended in at a supermarket, much less a fancy restaurant. If James was a mummy, then Elise was barely more than a living skeleton.

"This is Elise Kavanagh," James said. "Elise, this is the man who has gone to so much trouble to find us."

"You can't be serious." Mr. Black wasn't smiling anymore.

The waiter was red-faced. "I tried to stop her, but—"

She kicked her feet up on another chair. Her hiking boots were covered in chunks of dried mud.

James waved the waiter away before he could go apoplectic. "She's with me."

"With all due respect, we do have a dress code, and she's—"

"We won't be long."

Mr. Black snapped out of his reverie. "It's all right." He waited to speak until they were alone again. "Miss… Kavanagh, was it? This must be a joke."

"I'm afraid not," James said.

"But this is a girl."

"Female kopides are uncommon, not nonexistent. I believe there are currently three. She is the strongest of them." James smiled behind a hand. "In fact, she's the strongest of all of you."

5

"How does a teenage girl become known as the greatest demon hunter above hundreds of men? No offense." Which meant, of course, he was absolutely trying to be offensive.

Elise arched an eyebrow split by a white scar. When she didn't reply, Mr. Black looked askance at James, as if they were old friends and she had intruded on their dinner.

In fact, two things had elevated Elise to that status three months prior: Defeating the previous title holder in a formal sparring match, and then outliving him. Those were publicly available facts. The Council of Dis, however, also credited her with the deaths of twelve angels, which no other human had done in recorded history. Nobody else knew this. James thought that was for the best.

"Her father serves on the Council as a touchstone." James shrugged. "He must have recommended her."

Mr. Black gave no sign of hearing him. "All right. If the council thinks you're great, you've got to be pretty good. Are you mute? Dumb?"

James cleared his throat loudly to stop him. "Mr. Black wants to hire you to retrieve a dangerous ethereal artifact. I've explained that we're not mercenaries and not interested."

"We're not?" Elise asked.

"Lord in Heaven, it speaks." Mr. Black rubbed his hands together. "But let's be fair. I wouldn't describe this bowl as 'dangerous,' strictly speaking."

"Anything made by angels is dangerous by virtue of its very nature. Men aren't meant to possess these things, and if you think obtaining one for your 'personal collection' is benign, then you must be an idiot—or think I am. If you want to be fair, let's be fair. You have something planned. We won't have any part of it."

Elise wasn't listening to him. Even though she lounged

6

between her two chairs, there was tension coiled in her muscles. "How much?"

Mr. Black faced her. It was as though James disappeared completely.

"You can walk away from this restaurant with ten thousand dollars. When you bring the bowl to me, I'll round that out to—say, twenty-five thousand? I want this bowl, and I'm willing to pay fairly for its safe deliverance."

"Fifty thousand. Cash."

James reached a hand toward her, but thought better of it. He liked having his limbs intact. "Elise—"

Mr. Black laughed. "Are you trying to negotiate with me, girl?"

She replied in French. James didn't understand the language, and he wasn't sure Mr. Black would, either. Yet the older man's fake smile vanished. When he responded, it was in also in French, and Elise's hands clenched into fists.

James was certain he had just missed something important.

She stood, gave Mr. Black a sharp nod, and left. Both men gaped after her.

"We won't do it," James said weakly.

Mr. Black finished his slice of bread and washed it down with wine. His fingers were shaking as he patted his mouth with a white napkin. "Can I give you some advice, Mr. Faulkner? As a friend."

"No."

"You better get the hell away from that girl. I think she might be the death of you."

And that was how one of the most important meetings in history concluded. James was never quite sure why that was true, but then again, he also never spoke French.

James found Elise waiting on the train platform with a hood pulled up and her hands shoved into her pockets. She could have been any other young traveler commuting home after a day out with friends.

He reached her at the same time the train arrived, and she got on without speaking to him. He took position at the yellow pole behind her.

The train leaped forward. He caught a glimpse inside her hood when she swayed. Elise was usually hyper-alert and watching her surroundings for an attack, but now she was drawn inward. She seemed troubled.

Together, they made several short transfers and walked erratic paths through the city's streets. James thought he saw Alain following them at first, but they lost him after a few blocks. This was nothing surprising. Unholy things often tried to follow Elise and James, so elusiveness was routine.

When they got on the final train, they had an entire car to themselves. James let a moment of dizziness overtake him and sagged against the window. He barely had the energy to lift his head.

His ribs itched, so he reached under his shirt to adjust the straps of the spine sheath. It barely fit. He had lost too much muscle from malnourishment in the last few weeks.

"Elise," he began.

She didn't look at him.

"I know that money must seem like a lot to you, and after all the troubles we've had, I'm not going to pretend I don't find it tempting. But believe me when I say that no sum of money is worth the trouble of Mr. Black's job. This bowl could get us killed…or worse."

His legs wobbled. He sat next to Elise and pretended it was to get her attention, which didn't work.

"Things will change soon," he whispered. "It's going to

get better."

She finally lifted her head. The corners of her mouth were drawn into a frown. "Is it weird that I'm a girl? Mr. Black was surprised when he saw me."

James realized his mouth was hanging open, and he shut it. Two sentences. That must have been a record. "Yes. It's very unusual. Didn't your parents ever tell you?"

She bowed her head against her knees. He saw the hilt of the second falchion—the twin to the one he wore—bulging against the back of her sweater.

They rode on in silence.

TWO

THREE

THERE was blood on the stone.

The column loomed so far overhead that its apex disappeared into night. Looping lines marked its surface like ossified muscle on beams of towering bone. The once-bright sigils ringing the base were lifeless.

The gate was one of a dozen silent scions in a dead city. For endless millennia, they slept over the empty streets waiting for… What?

Elise…

Her bare toes hung over the tip of the world, hair swinging in her face as she craned forward to peer at the water miles below. Tiny stars sparkled in the water, like river stones reflecting moonlight.

The gate hummed at her back. She couldn't look at it. She wouldn't. She would prefer to fall into the abyss and shatter on the shore.

Elise…

There shouldn't have been anything on the other side of the arch. Nothing should have lived in the city.

Yet there was blood on the stone, and something called

her name from the other side, beckoning for her to turn. Invisible fingers clamped on her chin and forced her back from the edge, away from blissful suicide and on toward damnation.

The dry air vibrated. Sinewy stone flushed to life, and a breeze stirred the dead air.

Elise...

She shut her eyes as she turned. She wouldn't look. She wouldn't watch the air darken until it devoured all light, wouldn't see Him reaching through with white hands...

But something peeled her eyelids back, forcing her to look upon the darkest gate.

And she *saw*.

"Elise!"

The tent collapsed on her head. An electric bolt of consciousness shocked through her.

Something heavy smashed into her face and chest, like a bear rolling over the tent. She couldn't inhale. Her neck strained as her head was crushed into the ground.

She felt a bare arm against hers—Anthony's—and elbowed him away.

For a disorienting moment, she was seventeen again, on the run and camping out in whatever bare patch of land she could find. Motels were too expensive and too easy to track. Elise couldn't remember why she was with Anthony instead of James.

A glistening black fang punctured the canvas by her head and brought cold reality with it. Venom gushed from the tip and splattered on her shoulder.

Knife. Where was her knife?

The body shifted enough for her hand to scrabble at the pillow, where she had tucked a blade before sleeping, but the attacker mashed against her again and she didn't have space to grab it.

The fang withdrew and punctured again. Elise twisted

11

her face to the side.

"Anthony! Do something!" she shouted.

His hot skin moved away from hers. He fumbled with the tent. The zipper opened, and chilly night air rushed to fill her lungs.

The weight lifted, but before she could sit up, a foot the size of a trash can slammed into her gut.

Her intestines crushed against her spine. Canvas ripped.

Elise's hand closed on her knife, and she stabbed it into the foot. Something gave an inhuman shriek.

Its weight vanished.

She slashed and stabbed and tore until she could see the stars. Elise scrambled out of the tent's remains, bare skin flushed with goosebumps. It was dark in the desert, much darker than the city, and she could barely make out sagebrush and hills under the sliver of moon.

Her attacker was a hulking black shape perched on top of the Jeep. Each of its eight legs was braced against the roll cage. Glossy black eyes reflected the starlight and shone with a faint red glow, as though fire burned within its furry carapace. It was a spider the size of a small pony.

Anthony brandished two halves of a snapped tent pole at the demon—like going after a tank with a twig.

The spider lunged. A half-second later, Elise jumped too.

She knocked into her boyfriend an instant before the spider would have. They rolled across the desert as the demon hit sagebrush.

Getting up again took too long. She whirled, bringing the knife to bear, but one of those huge legs struck her in the chest again.

Elise was airborne.

Her back hit the Jeep. Her lungs emptied. Her cheek hit dirt.

Anthony cried out. She got to her feet, gasping and wheezing and empty-handed. She had dropped her knife.

The spider darted at him. It moved at a ridiculous speed given its size, blurring through the night to slash with its fangs. He tried to roll out of the way, but a heavy leg pounded into the rock and blocked him. He kicked its face. The pincers caught his leg.

Elise sucked in a hard breath. "Don't let it bite you!"

"Thanks for the suggestion," Anthony grunted, snapping his free foot into its face.

It shrieked and reared. She dived onto its back.

The spider bucked beneath her, and Elise pressed her cheek into its furry carapace and clung tight to its abdomen. When it tried to bite Anthony again, she wrapped a hand around its pincer and yanked.

It ripped free with a wet crunch. Venom sprayed on the dirt.

"Find my knife!"

Anthony squirmed out from beneath them. The spider thrashed. Elise almost went flying again, but she wrapped her fists around its thick black hairs and hung on.

Each of the glistening black eyes rolled around to stare at her.

It flung itself sideways. She lost her grip and rolled across the dirt. The spider pounced, spraying venom and ichor from its open wound, and it stung like sparks of flame where it landed on her skin.

She punched her fist into its clacking mouth as hard as she could. It wasn't hard enough. The spider reared back to bite again, and Elise grabbed the first thing she could reach—the remains of the tent.

Elise flung the canvas in the spider's face. Its pincer tangled in the rope.

"I can't find it!" Anthony shouted.

Her hand fell on a broken piece of tent post.

13

Elise drove the splintered end into the spider's body. At first, she thought it wouldn't be able to pierce the exoskeleton, but then the metal slipped. It buried into the knife wound and kept going.

She silenced its scream by shoving with all her weight. The bar cracked through the other side.

Its legs flailed wildly, and she had to crawl away to avoid getting hit.

Elise picked up the other tent pole and plunged it into the spider's head. She pushed so hard that the tip sank into the earth and pinned the demon to the ground.

It finally stopped moving after that.

Elise let out a long breath. She was soaked in sweat even though it couldn't have been more than sixty degrees in the cool desert night, which quickly approached cool desert morning. A sliver of blue glowed over the hills.

"Hell of a wakeup call," she muttered. The spider's foreleg twitched once.

Anthony crashed through the sagebrush again and grabbed her arms. "Are you okay? I couldn't find your knife."

She gave her body a quick inspection. She was wearing underwear instead of pajamas, so she could see where bruises were developing, which was most of her body. The contact burns from the venom were worse, but none of them were too bad. She would recover quickly.

"I'm fine."

Anthony handed her a flashlight from the Jeep. "Is this the same as the other ones? It seems a lot bigger."

She located her knife by its glimmer in the bushes. He had been searching in the wrong place. "Yeah. It's a daimarachnid. Big fucking spider." Elise rolled the demon onto its back and knelt by its body, pushing the legs away to examine the branded underbelly.

Most demons were like animals with a temper

problem: stupid and directionless. But powerful demons could mark them with brands and control their behavior to some degree. If she could find who "owned" those symbols, she would find out who was responsible, much like a rancher and his cattle.

Elise began slicing along the edge of the brands.

Anthony recoiled. "Jesus! What are you doing?"

She focused on trimming the leathery skin from the shell underneath. It was tough work. She sawed back and forth with the serrated edge of the knife until a strip of flesh two feet long and four inches wide came free.

"Get a plastic bag from the Jeep," Elise said, studying the strip with the flashlight. Someone had slashed crosses through each of the brands and made them hard to distinguish.

He handed a bag to her. Elise sealed the skin inside.

"What are you going to do with that?"

"I'm going to find out who's letting their minions loose and have a talk with them."

"And by 'talk,' you mean…"

"I'll kill them," Elise said. She put the skin in the cooler where they had kept their food all week. There was nothing left except melted ice and a couple cans of beer. "Still want to keep going hunting with me?"

To his credit, Anthony thought about it for a moment before answering. "Yeah. Camping has been fun." He grinned. "And, you know. The attack was kind of hot. Watching you fight in your underwear was…" He pushed her back against the Jeep and growled against her neck. She didn't react. "Aren't you kind of hot?"

"No."

He kissed down her collarbone and traced a finger along the tattoo on her hip. "Are you sure?"

"Getting attacked by demons doesn't excite me." She planted a hand in his chest to prevent his kisses from

15

straying lower. "I'm not going to tell you again." She left the unspoken threat hovering over them.

"Would you stab me? Is that what you're saying?"

The corner of her mouth quirked up. "Would that turn you on, too?"

"You're sick," he murmured into her lips. Elise leaned against the car door with a sigh as he kissed her. His lips traveled to her earlobe. He nipped it lightly with his teeth.

"You think I'm sick?" She stretched her arm back to drop the knife in the Jeep's backseat, and he traced his hand down her exposed ribcage. His fingers found a path under her bra to graze the curve of her breast. "At least demon attacks don't get me horny."

Her cell phone alarmed. She peered over Anthony's shoulder to see it glowing blue underneath the tent canvas. He ignored it and pushed a knee between her legs. She stiffened, but he caught her wrist and pinned it to her side. "Ignore it."

Elise shoved him. He stumbled a few steps back. "It's time to leave," she said, turning off the alarm. Anthony groaned.

"But we were just—"

"I have a meeting with a potential client this morning and it's a four-hour drive from here."

He adjusted the waistband of his sweats. Elise gathered their broken tent and threw it in the back of the Jeep. "I think you like to torture me."

She planted a kiss on his chin as he passed. "It's an unintended bonus."

Anthony tried to glower, but Elise didn't acknowledge him as she finished packing. His mood lost steam without her attention.

After a week of camping, their clothes were crusty with sweat and dust. Elise gritted her teeth as she pulled on dirty jeans.

"What are we going to do with *that*?" Anthony asked when the only thing remaining in their camp was the body of the demon.

Elise kicked it in the side. It didn't move.

"We'll let the coyotes have it. I've got what I need."

They got in the Jeep and drove away, leaving the carcass of the demon to rot.

Elise stopped at home long enough to say goodbye to Anthony, take a shower, and slip into a clean skirt suit. Then she went into the office.

Since scraping together enough credits to graduate from college, Elise had done business as a certified public accountant. Cold, objective numbers were a comforting reprieve from life and death decisions, and there was decent money to be made in handling payroll for demon-owned businesses.

She rented a cheap suite in an old building by the airport, which was primarily occupied by failing businesses and nonprofit organizations that couldn't afford a nicer location. She had fewer neighbors as the months wore on. The economy was killing businesses faster than she killed daimarachnids, and the parking lot was never more than half-full.

Which was why she was confused when she arrived shortly before eight and had to park on the street. The parking lot was crammed with police cars, and a perimeter of emergency tape blocked the entrance. The employees who couldn't get inside were gathered on the sidewalk.

Elise approached a man she recognized as a therapist from the third floor. "What happened here?"

"I think it's a fire. They won't let us in." He dry-washed his hands and glared at the nearest police car. "I've already had to cancel my morning appointments!"

She checked her watch. The meeting with her client was ten minutes away, and she didn't have a number at which she could contact them. They had only emailed each other. She needed her computer.

Pushing through the crowd, Elise waved over a police officer. "Excuse me!"

"We can't let you in," he said, writing something on his clipboard. "It's going to be at least another half hour."

"All I need is my laptop. If one of you could …"

She trailed off. There was a shattered window on the south end of the first floor, where photographers and investigators were working.

It was her office.

Her stomach clenched with dread. The fire was in her room, and police were searching it. They would find the weapons in her desk. She ducked under the police tape and sidestepped the officer's grabbing hand.

"Hey! You can't go in there!"

"It's my office," she snapped as she stomped into the building.

The therapist was right. There had definitely been a fire, and it spread all the way down the back wall from the entryway to her suite. Smoke left brown-gray stains on the yellow wallpaper. The toxic green carpet squished under her heels as she hurried to her door.

Even though the fire had only consumed the left side of her office, her filing cabinet and ficus in the opposite corner were destroyed, too. Her desk had been pushed over. The base of her chair was snapped. The bookshelf was gutted, papers were spilled across the floor, and the nearest pile had something reddish-purple poured on it.

The police and firemen left no standing room inside, but shock rooted her to the doorway anyway.

It wasn't an accidental fire. Someone had ransacked

18

her office.

She picked up a page and sniffed it. The stains were wine.

"Hey there," said a gruff voice from the hall. The officer had followed her into the building. "I have to ask you to step into the hallway. You'll interfere with the investigation."

"Okay," Elise said, letting the paper fall. "It's just—all of this belongs to me."

He studied her with a round, sympathetic face. The badge on his chest said Fred Turner. "You better sit down before you fall down."

"I'm fine."

Ignoring her protestations, he took her elbow, and Elise bit the inside of her cheek trying not to strike him. "Come on, take a seat. I've been robbed before. I was twitching for weeks. Let me get you a cup of coffee."

Robbed. No, it wasn't a robbery.

It was a message.

Elise sat on a chair in the lobby. She didn't want to be inside the building anymore. Hell, she didn't want to be in the state. Her nerves were ringing like a gong and everything was suddenly too loud, from her heartbeat to the footsteps down the hall.

Was it Him? Had they been found?

Her cell phone was in her hands before she realized what she was doing. She rubbed her thumb over the touchpad. James was number two on speed dial. He needed to know. They needed to pack, they needed to run —

She took a steadying breath. No. If James and Elise had been found, it was too late to run.

"Ma'am?"

It took her a moment to focus on the speaker. Officer Turner had returned with a cup of coffee. She took it.

"Thanks."

"Could I see your identification?" he asked. She handed her driver's license to him. He scanned it with a confused furrow of his brow. "Your business is listed as being owned by 'Bruce Kent.'"

"I've filed the paperwork to operate under a pseudonym. It's completely legal. I could show you the documentation, but everything burned."

"Why use a fake name?"

She took her license back. "Do you think I set fire to my own office?"

"You're not a suspect. But considering what's happened, I don't think you'll be leaving town for a few weeks. Right? If we need to interview you later and you're gone, we'll be concerned."

"I'll be around," she said, her voice dead.

"Good."

Fred Turner left, and Elise took a slow sip of her coffee.

Her hand was trembling.

FOUR

THE BODY THUDDED to the floor. A hand whipped the hood off his head, and the man underneath blinked at the sudden light. His bare skin pebbled with cold.

A woman probed his torso for injury, pushing down the shorts that barely shielded his modesty, and then rolled him over to expose his arms. They were bound behind his back. His shoulder blades were red and irritated.

Portia Redmond sniffed as she returned to her seat at the table. "It's wearing an intake bracelet. You said it would be clean."

Mr. Black leaned forward. He was dressed to minimize the physical signs of age, such as a slight paunch to his belly and a sloped back. His hair was wolf-white with accents of gray, and his eyes were blue, very blue, with no hint of warmth.

"Is that an intake bracelet?" he asked, his voice a cool baritone.

Portia's spine straightened. "I think I would recognize the vehicle of my son's death."

A man shifted behind Mr. Black as though to remind Portia of his presence. He was slightly younger than Mr. Black, although he was wiry instead of stocky, and his rust-colored hair was barely touched with white.

There was a gun at his shoulder. He had removed the

strap keeping it in the holster. Portia forced herself to relax.

"Your son was an addict?" Mr. Black asked. "Shame, shame. How old was he?"

"Old enough that I couldn't have another heir."

"What a shame. Miss Redmond—Portia—I don't lie to my customers, particularly those as loyal as you." He smoothed his wrinkled fingers over hers. "You asked for spirited, so I brought the most spirited. That kind of fire doesn't come without cost. Controlling him can be... difficult."

"Lethe is a stimulant."

"For demons, yes. You'll find it has quite a different effect on his type. I'll supply enough to keep him under your gorgeous thumb for a year."

"How much?" she asked.

"Do you think I would nickel-and-dime an old friend? After we've known each other for so many long years?"

She pulled her hand back. "Yes."

"How predictable of me."

"What do you want?"

"I want use of your shipping fleet." Mr. Black waved his hand again, and Alain handed Portia a sheaf of papers. She unfolded them and began to read. Her expression darkened with every line. "I'm bringing in a few archaeological pieces from my personal collection, so I'll require unlimited use of your trucks."

"Unlimited use?" Portia slapped the contract on the table. "What about my needs? What about my suppliers?"

Mr. Black smoothed out the contract and flipped to the third page. "I have accounted for that: I will compensate you for the estimated loss of business. See here?"

She refused to look. "I don't know why you're bothering to ask. I know I have no choice."

"Of course you have a choice." He took a pen from his breast pocket and offered it to her. "Your son had a choice, too."

Her lips trembled.

"Let me inspect them closely. Both the contract and... *that*." Portia indicated the man shivering on her floor.

"He's yours. You can command him."

"The terms of our deal have changed. I won't take custody until I fully agree."

"This is why I love you, Portia. Just *adore* you. You don't tolerate nonsense in your business, and I have to say, I appreciate that." He snapped his fingers. "Nukha'il, stand up and turn around so she can see all of you."

The man picked himself up. Shimmering red-brown hair fell to his back in soft waves. His body was delicate, yet strong, and the top of his head was nearly level with the doorway. Nukha'il spun slowly. He was sheer perfection, despite the fact there might have been no muscles under his olive skin. The lines of his back were unearthly.

He looked a lot like Portia's son.

Her fist tightened, crumpling the contract.

"I'll take him," she said, her voice hoarse. Nukha'il raised his chin, giving her the kind of look that said he wouldn't go down easily.

The moment she signed the last curl on her surname, the papers were gone and the pen was whisked from her hand. Alain tucked the contract into his coat once more. Mr. Black smiled like the Cheshire Cat, his too-white teeth glowing in the lamplight. "It's always a pleasure doing business with you, my dear."

"Yes. Of course. You'll have to tell me your real name one day, Mr. Black."

He placed a kiss on her knuckles. The suit fit him even better when he was standing. Under other circumstances, she might have sought him out to become her third husband. He was wealthy and certainly attractive. But he was also a cold bastard, and he did dangerous business. She didn't want to be witness to the day it caught up with him.

"How do I contact you?" she asked.

"I'll be in town visiting some…shall we say, old friends. I'll be in touch. Don't worry about that."

Portia blinked rapidly, trying to process the information. "You understand if I don't walk you to the door."

"Of course."

She waited until they were gone before letting the shudders overtake her, but once they began, she couldn't stop.

Portia wouldn't look at Nukha'il. His presence nauseated her. She moved short locks of hair into place and dabbed at the sweat in the cleft of her breasts to give her hands something to do. Deep breaths in, slow breaths out.

"What should I do?" Nukha'il asked, making it sound as if he was offering to clean a toilet.

"Don't talk to me," she snapped. Raising her voice, she called, "They're gone."

The door behind her opened, and the Night Hag entered.

Portia had been assured that the overlord of the city was a demon, but she appeared to be a frail, ancient, and entirely human female. Her sagging face was a severe, bony mask that resembled the ancient mummies. Every breath rattled in her chest.

She was shadowed by a man so painfully beautiful that he could have been mistaken for one of Mr. Black's stock. His almond-shaped eyes were black, as though the pupils had overtaken the irises. He had been introduced to Portia as "Thom."

"Mr. Black," the Night Hag muttered. "Bringing his

'collection.' I should have known! And now you've given him your fleet?"

"We can track his movements," Portia said, fighting to keep her voice steady. The Night Hag and her companion *looked* normal, but they terrified her in a deep, primal way. "And you instructed me to cooperate with him."

"We'll kill Mr. Black," the overlord said to herself, stroking claw-like nails down the side of her face. "Yes. We'll have to strike fast." She snapped her fingers. "Tell David Nicholas."

Thom gave a small bow. "Very well." His voice was deep and without accent. He turned to leave, but the Night Hag caught his arm.

"We'll need the kopis, too. Get to her before Mr. Black does."

"What about this...*thing*?" Portia interjected. "You asked for it, and I bought it, but I don't want it in my house."

"Nukha'il," the Night Hag whispered. "Yes. I have plans for you, my new angel."

Two years of client files. All the knives stored in her desk. A safe filled with important documents. Her laptop, her desk phone. Her favorite coffee pot.

Gone. All gone.

The police left after taking pictures, samples, and statements. It felt like her office had been violated a second time, and all that remained after the investigators were done was shattered furniture, smoke stains, and a lingering sense of grief.

She sank to her knees on a clear patch of floor by the window and let the silence engulf her. There was so much to be done. She needed to meet with the landlord, a

25

cleaning company, her insurance agent—not to mention all her clients, whose private files had been stolen.

Elise rested her head in her hands. She had a headache. She never had headaches. It must have been caffeine withdrawal.

"They took my favorite coffee pot," she whispered. That part stung the worst.

She didn't bother locking the door on her way out.

Outside, the day was too hot and too bright. The lack of clouds felt like a personal insult. She jammed sunglasses onto her face, slammed the car door, and went home to start the recovery process. She blew through two stop signs on the way. Elise couldn't seem to focus on the road.

Her roommate greeted her at the door with a feather duster.

"Anthony's looking for you!" Betty announced, plucking a headphone out of one ear. She was a human hurricane of caffeinated enthusiasm, and all that energy was currently directed at cleaning their kitchen in tiny shorts that said "juicy" on the butt.

"Great," Elise said, dropping her satchel on the couch. "Thanks."

"He's probably on his side of the duplex. You can catch him before work if you hurry." Betty frowned. "You okay? You look tired."

It seemed like too much effort to rehash everything she had gone over with the police in exacting detail. "I'll tell you later."

She went into her bedroom and locked the door.

Anthony. He was exactly the person she didn't want to see. He would freak out and expect her to do the same, and then he would try to comfort her, and the thought of having to deal with that much emotion was exhausting.

The endless to-do list kept rolling through her mind: *Landlord. Cleaning company. Insurance agent. All her clients.*

The police. Maybe the security company would have footage, maybe she should…

Elise threw herself on the bed without getting undressed and pressed the heel of her hand to her forehead.

She didn't even know where to begin. Backups? She could restore most of the data to the laptop in her bedroom. That would be the easiest place to start. But thinking of it reminded her that police expected copies of her files as part of the "evidence collection" process, and that got the torrent going again.

Landlord. Cleaning company. Insurance agent. Calling the clients.

"Fuck it," she told her ceiling.

Elise threw on jogging gear, tied her hair into a loose ponytail, and did a few twists in the living room to test her mobility. She felt like hell, emotionally speaking, but her body was in good condition after fighting demon spiders for a week.

"Leaving again?" Betty asked. She was listening to electronica so loudly that Elise could hear the bass through the headphones. "Don't you want to see Anthony first?"

"No."

She sighed. "So what should I tell him?"

Elise stretched a leg in front of her. "Nothing. I don't owe him any explanations."

Betty sighed again, as though that answer put her in physical pain. She was still sighing when Elise rocketed out the door. Sometimes, Betty's antics were cute, but this was not one of those times.

Her feet pounded a rhythm on the pavement that kept time with the incessant thoughts.

Landlord. Cleaning company. Insurance agent. The police, the security company, offsite backups…

She put on her own headphones and blasted Black

Death's latest album from the MP3 player on her arm. It couldn't go loud enough to muffle her thoughts.

Life was so much easier when Elise hadn't owned anything. There was a time she hadn't cared about coffee pots or the nice desk she bought as a treat for surviving her first year as an accountant. All she cared about was sticking close to James—and sometimes, she didn't care much about that, either.

James was the only person she could imagine talking to. He always knew the right things to say. Conveniently, she kept her monthly backups on flash drives in the safe at his dance studio, so that was where she was heading anyway.

He owned a studio called Motion and Dance, which had two classes in progress and a full parking lot when she arrived. Business had been good lately. Demand for his classes spiked when he was contracted to choreograph a casino show, and with another Christmas show in the works, it was only going to keep improving.

But he wasn't downstairs when Elise peeked into the dance hall. One of his employees, Candace, was guiding a group through hip-hop moves. The instructor waved at Elise. She didn't wave back. She jogged upstairs to the apartment over the studio and entered without knocking.

Elise took off her headphones.

"James?"

His apartment was a disaster. The couch was shoved against the wall. The kitchen chairs were stacked on the table. He had pulled everything out of the closets and turned the floor into a cluttered mess. Even the window-mounted air conditioner had been unplugged.

Spring cleaning? He was usually anal about tidiness. It was quiet other than the music downstairs, so he wasn't home to ask.

Disappointed, she went into the bedroom that used to

be hers. Flat pack boxes were leaned against the wall, and everything else was separated into two piles. The belongings she left behind when she moved out had been dumped in a corner. "What are you doing, James?" she muttered, nudging the pile with her foot. She recognized her tattered sweatpants and a bottle of shampoo.

The only thing untouched was the safe against the wall, which had been bolted in place. Elise entered the combination, twisted the key in the lock, and passed her hand over the magical sensor. The door swung open.

She kept a pair of falchions and a back sheath in the safe, as well as a chain of charms she used for exorcisms. The envelope of flash drives nestled next to an old Book of Shadows was laughably mundane amongst everything else.

Elise selected the one labeled with the most recent date and moved to close the door again.

But she hesitated. Her fingers trailed down the long gold chain of her charms, and they whispered to her in a dozen voices, hissing with magic and ancient words. Her finger stopped on a single stone between the ankh and pentacle. It was white and soapy-smooth, like polished bone.

Another voice whispered to her, a voice from her dreams: *Elise…*

A chill rippled down her spine. She locked the safe.

Elise pocketed the flash drive and sat on the laundry to check her cell phone. She had missed three calls while jogging. One was from Anthony, but the other two were from her insurance company and landlord.

Landlord. Cleaning company. Insurance agent. The police, the security company, off-site backups…

She called the remote voicemail service she used for her business.

There were twenty-six messages.

After a week of camping, she expected to find a few things on her answering service, but the majority of clients contacted her by email. She had to brace herself to play the first message. "This is Frederickson Lane. We need to talk about terminating our contract. Call me back at…"

Elise pushed the "next" button.

"I'm looking for Bruce Kent. I'm from Crimson Mark Incorporated, and we need to transfer our accounts from…"

Her heart sped. Transfer?

The next one began. They wanted to discuss ending their business with her, too. More than a dozen of the messages were from different accounts about the same issue.

Elise turned off her phone and set it carefully on the floor as though it had been possessed.

She only had a few clients. Since Elise served a niche market—supernatural creatures with Earth-based businesses—there was no competition, but there also weren't many accounts to take on. And it sounded like she had just lost half of them.

The numbers raced through her mind. Three percent from Crimson—that would mean thousands of dollars if they bailed. A half percent from Plymouth. Another few hundred dollars from Frederickson. She had already been on narrow margins after Craven's took their accounting in house…

Craven's.

Anger bubbled inside her. Who would have the nerve to call Elise's clients and tell them to find a new accountant? Who knew where her office was located, and had motive to vandalize it? The manager and owner of Craven's Casino, David Nicholas, was exactly the kind of bastard who would do both. And more, if given the chance to fuck with her.

Maybe it was time to pay him a visit.

FIVE

CRAVEN'S WAS A cesspool of a casino wedged in a dark corner downtown. Tourists didn't go there. They visited the big hotel casinos that hosted touring Broadway shows and served fancy buffets. The only people who visited Craven's were demons—and angry demon hunters.

Elise had contacts at Craven's that offered a steady stream of information, but she hadn't visited since David Nicholas fired her as their accountant and tried to beat her to death. To be fair, she had beaten him up first, and she ended up killing one of his cronies in his attack. She thought they were even. But apparently he didn't agree.

She still knew the way to his office, which was on the ninth level overlooking the poker tables. She navigated through the dimly-lit casino floor, where people gambled away their savings and drowned in alcohol, and headed up two sets of escalators.

A cocktail waitress spotted her. Her face might have gone pale if it hadn't been caked in so much makeup. She dropped her drink tray and ran in the other direction.

So much for surprising them.

She hurried up the stairs, found the door labeled MANAGER, and shoved it open. David Nicholas looked up from his desk.

"We need to talk," she said.

David Nicholas was a full-blooded, Earth-bound nightmare that hadn't been powerful since the Middle Ages and wasted the centuries since trying to recapture his old glory. He smoked like a factory and usually looked like a greasy scarecrow. But he had filled out in the weeks since Elise had last seen him, as though a layer of fat had developed beneath his papery skin. His yellow hair was cut to the chin and had been washed. His office wasn't even covered in garbage and tobacco ash anymore.

In another time, his strong nose and chin might have been considered handsome. But that foul grin sickened Elise. She would never mistake him as anything but dangerous.

"Yeah, we do need to talk." He returned his attention to the schedule for the cocktail waitresses on his desk. "Heard what happened at your office. I knew you'd come crawling back for a job."

"Is that what you were trying to do? To get me to ask you for work?"

He stabbed the point of his cigarette into the ashtray and opened a desk drawer. Elise tensed, but he only took out another cigarette. "What are you talking about?" he asked out the corner of his mouth as he lit it.

"Someone's been calling my clients and telling them to leave. Likely the same person who started the fire."

"And you think that was me? That's precious."

She drew her knife. "Precious?"

He stood, shoving his sleeves above his elbows. His forearms had the illusion of being muscular now, but a nightmare's strength had nothing to do with its physical form. "You've been away too long, cabbage. The game's changed. You barely matched me last time—think you could take me now?"

"Yes."

He vanished with a swirl of smoke and reappeared

inches in front of her, shoving his beak of a nose into hers. She held her ground.

"Want to try me?" His breath smelled like tobacco and rot.

She grabbed a fistful of his shirt. "You're in my space."

The stress of the morning built in her muscles and desperately wanted to be unleashed on his ugly face. *Give me an excuse. Just give me an excuse…*

His phone rang.

For the first two rings, David Nicholas didn't move. His eyes flicked to the desk and back to Elise.

She released his shirt.

He grabbed the receiver. "What?" he snapped. Whatever response he received wasn't good, because he pulled a face. "Okay." A pause, and then again, "Okay." David Nicholas hung up and held both hands out in a gesture of peace. "Game's up for the night. You've been summoned."

Elise laughed in disbelief. "Summoned? If you're trying to distract me—"

"I want nothing more than to see you broken on my floor, *accountant*." He bit out the last word like an insult. "The day you die is the day I'm a happy demon. I'll throw parties with hats and trumpets and streamers. But today's not that day. *She* wants to see you."

"Who?"

"The Night Hag."

She scoffed. "This bullshit again?" David Nicholas bumped his shoulder into hers as he left the room.

Elise almost didn't follow him. He had been foretelling the return of the Night Hag for as long as she had been in town, but it had always been a lie. And that was a good thing. Part of the reason she had chosen to live in Reno was its lack of a demonic overlord. They didn't like having kopides in their territory.

34

But he walked with confidence, like he expected her to follow, and Elise sheathed her dagger. What did she have to lose?

They took a different path through Craven's than the one she used to find his office. They went down, down, down a set of stairs with walls painted black, and the thump of music began rising around them.

Eloquent Blood was a demon bar in the basement of Craven's, and during the afternoon, it was completely empty. The pit of a dance floor stood bare. All the neon was turned off, and the brimstone droppings were swept into a corner by a cleaning crew. Someone was cutting off the music and switching songs as they ran sound checks. A demon with horned shoulders wiped down the tables. It was…ordinary.

"Where's Neuma?" she asked. Being able to speak without yelling was strange. It felt like a cavern without partiers packing it to the brim.

David Nicholas shot her a sideways look. "You think we live here or something? The dumb bitch has an apartment. If she's not sleeping, she's shooting up."

Elise hadn't given the living situation of local demons much thought. In most cities, overlords kept their subjects close. They stayed in dens and rarely emerged.

The reminder of why they were going into Blood was sobering. She traced the edges of the leather sheath hidden at the small of her back. She had killed an overlord once in a surprise attack, but this time, she was the one taken off-guard. Elise wished she had worn her swords.

Tension built in her skull as they descended to the bottom floor of the club. It wasn't nerves. It was infernal power, and lots of it. "Believe me now?" David Nicholas asked with a sneer when he saw her expression.

She checked her knives for a third time. "Take me down."

They got into an elevator behind the DJ booth. It was an old mine lift, rickety and rusted, and a shaft extended endlessly beyond the grate under Elise's feet.

It rattled, squealed, and began to move.

Rough stone walls slid past them. Lights marked every few feet, but they were weak, and the shadow between them was immense. Every time they slipped into darkness, David Nicholas flickered out of view. But he always reappeared, yellow-haired and sweaty, with one hand on the lever.

The pressure in her skull grew too strong as they dropped, and when they reached the bottom and stepped onto solid ground, there was no ignoring the sensation of eyes on the back of her neck. A dark corridor stretched in front of them.

It looked empty, but they weren't alone. Elise could feel it.

David Nicholas strode ahead, shooting a nasty smile as he passed. She considered knocking the smug look off his face. But she wasn't in her own territory anymore. It was the Warrens—the place demons dwelled far below the city. Even she wasn't confident enough to think she could fight her way out alone.

He led her to a door, but paused before opening it. "Be nice. Or don't. Maybe today can be the day you die after all."

Elise stepped through.

The room beyond was like being inside a hollowed-out ribcage. Webbing as thick as her arms stretched from ceiling to walls to form a low canopy, and the black ground crunched with every step. It was too dark to see what she was walking on.

A man with shimmering brown hair sat on the floor by the door with his ankles chained to the wall. Pieces of white rock were scattered around him, and it looked like he was trying to piece together a puzzle the size of a small car. When he saw Elise, he dropped one of the stones. It rolled across the ground.

David Nicholas delivered a kick to his ribs. "Keep at it!"

He groaned and went back to work.

She moved deeper into the room. Tapestries hung from the supports that kept the sagging mineshaft open. Colorful threads glimmered in the darkness.

"Do you like them?"

Elise hadn't noticed an old hospital bed in the corner. Its sheets were stained, the bars were rusted, and the webs stretched toward it. She approached slowly. "Did you make the tapestries?"

"Yes." Something in the bed was moving. A light flicked on above them.

The Night Hag was illuminated in all her ghastly splendor. She was a skeleton with gray skin stretched over its joints, an IV in one arm, and webs wrapped around the other. Her skull of a face smiled at Elise, making the skin sag at her jowls. The expression was frightening, but not unfriendly.

Power radiated from her like a hand gripping Elise's throat. There was no mistaking that amount of infernal energy.

"I have to apologize for my state. I'm receiving a transfusion."

"Of what?"

Her eyes glinted. "Fluids."

Elise crossed her hands behind her back, resisting the urge to touch her knives again. "I should apologize for moving into the territory without your permission. I was led to believe you had died."

"David Nicholas tells me you had been informed I was merely sleeping."

"He's usually full of shit."

The Night Hag gave a soft, rasping laugh. "I've struggled toward consciousness for the past two months. The delicious scent of power lured me—your power, I hear. Someone's been getting into naughty things."

Elise kept her mouth shut. She had defeated a demon called Death's Hand in the spring, but only after it killed James and possessed his body. She harnessed its necromantic power to resurrect him. Things like that sent waves through all the dimensions, so it was no surprise that it woke up the overlord. But she wouldn't admit that.

When she stayed silent, the Night Hag lifted her chin regally. "I could kill you. You know that, don't you?"

"You could try."

"What an ugly fight that would be. A very ugly fight indeed. I know your reputation, and I'm sure you could kill many of my people before I killed you...and your aspis." The Night Hag paused as though waiting for a reaction. Elise kept her face blank. "My numbers are unfathomable and your loss is certain. But what a waste of time and talent."

"Opinions differ," David Nicholas muttered from the back of the room.

The Night Hag glared and snapped her frail fingers. He vanished in an instant, leaving a hole in Elise's senses where he had been a moment before.

The man by the door cried out.

Elise frowned. "Where—?"

"He has gone to a place of punishment. My men must show respect. Isn't that true, Thom?"

It was only then that Elise realized someone else was in the room.

He sat in the darkness behind the hospital bed. He wore nothing but snug leather pants and a thin black collar. Thom could have been Neuma's human cousin. He was raven-haired and beautiful, but far more elegant than the stripper could dream of becoming. "Yes," he said simply.

"This is my witch. He takes care of things for me. Isn't he lovely?"

The hair rose on the back of Elise's neck. "Lovely" wasn't the word she would have chosen for him. Something about the witch struck her as wrong, like he didn't belong on Earth.

She forced herself to focus on the Night Hag.

"What do you want from me?"

"We share a common enemy. Unfortunately, as you can see, I'm not what I used to be. You are best equipped to kill him for me…with my help."

"Who?" Elise asked. She had a lot of enemies, but none had bothered her since she killed Death's Hand.

The Night Hag waved a hand. Thom stood and held out a photograph.

She didn't reach to take it.

"Look. Look!" the overlord said impatiently. "Before I decide to kill you and have done with it! Don't fear my witch. He's muzzled and harmless."

Harmless? She seriously doubted it.

Thom set the picture on the bedside table. Elise picked it up and turned it over. Cold, unfamiliar fear washed over her.

It had been taken at the house of someone rich. She could tell by the fancy windows, the furniture, the drapes. Judging by the odd angle and grainy quality, the subjects probably hadn't known they were being photographed. But she recognized the men in the picture. They had aged, changed, and grown harder, but there was no mistaking the Southern gentleman and his French bodyguard. The last time she had seen them, Mr. Black's home had been on fire. She had thought—had *hoped*—they died after that.

"Fuck," Elise muttered.

"I'm glad you see the issue."

"Where was this taken?"

"At a home on the southwest side of town. He was conducting a deal with a woman who has been on my payroll for years. I don't know what he wants to accomplish, but it can't be good for anyone."

Elise's legs couldn't seem to support her anymore. She sat down hard in the chair by the bed. But she kept her face blank and her hand steady as she set the photo on the table again.

So the vandalism of her office had been a message, but not from David Nicholas. She should have known he wasn't subtle enough for that anyway. It had been a kind of greeting from Mr. Black—one calculated to remind her of shared animosity and debts owed.

It took her a moment to realize the Night Hag was talking again.

"Worried Mr. Black will kill that handsome aspis of yours? You should be. From what I've learned of your past deals, I'm sure he's positioning his chess pieces to take your favorite pawn as we speak."

Elise clenched her fists. She wasn't a fan of that description. "We'll take care of ourselves."

"By hiding again, like you did for so many years? Where's the fun in that?" She cackled. "Oh yes. I'm familiar with your history. Here is my offer: You may continue to live in the city. I will assign a protective detail to your aspis. And we'll kill Mr. Black together."

"James would never go for that. He hates demons."

"He doesn't have to know, does he?"

Elise studied the overlord with a frown. "What's the catch?"

"During the duration of our agreement, you'll be my employee, and contractually bound to do errands for me—

which may include things around Craven's and my other businesses, as needed—until such a time that Mr. Black is out of the picture and life returns to its usual equilibrium."

"What kind of errands?"

"I haven't decided."

"Can I refuse?"

"Certainly," said the Night Hag. Left unspoken was the condition of that refusal: the termination of their tenuous, momentary truce.

"I want to think about it."

The Night Hag waved a dismissive hand. "Fine. Go. Call me when you're ready to cooperate. But don't take long—we'll have to move fast to stop a man like Mr. Black." She smirked. "Hopefully he hasn't already killed all your friends, hmm? What a shame that would be."

She snapped her fingers again. David Nicholas reappeared, and he didn't look as fleshy and strong as he had earlier. His hair was thinner, his skin was papery, and he had to grab the wall to keep standing.

"You bitch!"

She was surprised to see his insult aimed at the Night Hag instead of her. The overlord wasn't impressed.

"Take the kopis back to the surface. Give her my direct number. We'll be seeing each other again soon—very soon."

Elise stood. "I wouldn't be sure of that."

But the Night Hag only smiled in response.

SIX

"WHAT ARE YOU doing in here?"

Anthony jumped at the sound of Betty's voice, tripped on a pair of shoes, and almost fell over. "Betty!"

She grinned broadly at him. His cousin's hair was pulled into pigtails, which might have made her devilish grin disarming if Anthony hadn't known her too well for that. "You look awfully guilty," she said, propping her shoulder against the doorway. She wore a bikini and had a book tucked under her arm like she was ready for the beach. "What did I catch you doing?"

He snatched his shirt off Elise's dresser and hugged it protectively to his chest. "Nothing."

"You know, Elise is very private. She would hate to find out you were in here." Betty gave an exaggerated sigh. "Fortunately, she never has to know…if I don't tell her. But why would I want to do that?"

"I'm not the only one in her room while she's out of the house. What are *you* up to? I left the door shut, and there's no way you saw me come in."

"Don't try to change the subject. I could waterboard you." She jiggled the water bottle.

"I'm doing laundry, so I was picking up clothes I forgot here. Okay? Laundry is perfectly innocent."

"So there's nothing seditious going on? Too bad. I'm

42

not up to anything innocent, for the record." Betty pushed past him. "In case you were worrying about that."

She set her things on the floor and got on all fours to peek under the bed. He gaped at her. "What…?"

Betty emerged with a shoebox, but she looked disappointed to find nothing but knives in it. She pushed it back under the mattress. "You've spent lots of long, sweaty hours in here. Have you seen anything belonging to James?"

"What? What are you doing?"

She flung open Elise's closet and started digging. Only the professional outfits were hung neatly; all the casual clothes were piled on the floor. Betty dove into the piles first. "I'm looking for magic. Well, okay, I'm looking for spells. James won't let me see his secret stuff. He says I'm not a powerful enough witch to control that kind of magic." She huffed as she sat back on her heels. "Of *course* I'm not powerful enough yet! He won't let me practice!"

Anthony was torn. He didn't like to think of Elise's reaction if she found them riffling through her room, but he also didn't like James, and the idea of defying him was too appealing. "You don't want anything dangerous, do you?"

Betty's eyes became wide circles. "Dangerous? Me?"

She might as well have tattooed her forehead with "full of shit."

"All right," he said. She squealed.

He opened Elise's desk drawers. Her files were more organized than her closet, and a quick scan showed him she wasn't hiding anything there.

"What would it look like?"

"I don't think James would give her his Book of Shadows, so I'm thinking it would be a collection of loose pages with funny symbols. I know she keeps some for him as backup."

"Like this?" He pulled a spiral notebook out of Elise's underwear drawer.

"Ooh!"

He watched over Betty's shoulder as she flipped through it. It was nonsense to him. "What is it?"

"Paper magic. You know, that thing James does where he performs a ritual, and captures it on a page? He's got tons of these at his house. He showed it to the coven last month. But he won't share his secrets." She ran her hand down a page. "These ones aren't activated. This isn't enough. I need instructions or something."

Anthony edged toward the window and peeked at the street. "Maybe we should put it back. Elise will notice it's missing, and it wouldn't be hard to guess who took it."

She ripped out a few pages and tucked them in her paperback before restoring the notebook to the drawer. Then she plucked something red and stringy out of the dresser. "Hello there, sexy undies. I never would have pegged Elise as the lacy thong type."

He snatched it out of Betty's hand.

"I hope you're not going to get in trouble with the paper magic," he said, stuffing the underwear back where it belonged.

Her responding grin wasn't reassuring. But how much damage could she do with a few sheets torn from a notebook?

The doorbell rang.

Anthony jumped and slammed the dresser shut. Betty laughed. "Relax. Elise just walks in, you big dummy."

Cheeks red, he answered the door.

There was a basket on the step, and no signs of a delivery truck. "You've got something, Betty."

"Who's it from?"

He poked around the tissue paper. "No idea. I don't see a card."

Betty set it on the counter and removed everything. There was a bottle of wine, some cheese, and a jewelry box inside. She opened it.

Inside, a delicate silver crucifix pendant was nestled on a bed of cotton. It was plainer than anything she liked to wear, and too religious. "I don't think this is from one of my boyfriends. It must be something Elise ordered."

Anthony dug through the filling, but there was nothing left to find. "Huh. Whatever. I better start my laundry if I want to have something to wear at work." Betty was already searching the drawers for a bottle opener and didn't say goodbye. The pages from the notebook stuck out of her paperback.

He headed back to his apartment, feeling pretty certain he had just helped Betty get into a lot of trouble. But then again, what else was new?

By the time Elise got home from visiting the Night Hag, Betty was sunbathing in the front yard of their duplex. She had stretched out on a checkerboard blanket in an obscenely small bikini, waving a fan in one hand and cradling a paperback in the other.

"Take off your shirt and get down here, Elise! I've saved you some blanket space. And half of this wine." She lifted the bottle and jiggled it.

Elise couldn't find the energy to force a smile. "Maybe later."

All the blinds were closed inside their duplex to shade it from the harsh afternoon sunlight, but it was still nowhere near as dark as the mines below Craven's. Her mood was blackest of all.

She stood in the middle of her living room, looking around at all the things that made it home. Betty had hung

45

a print of a scared cat done in the style of Andy Warhol's Marilyn Monroe portrait, eye shadow and all, over their dining room table. The coffee table was covered in research papers. Empty jugs of protein powder were repurposed as flower pots. And then she tried to imagine leaving it behind and running again.

No. She wouldn't do it.

There was a basket on the counter she didn't recognize. Betty had already ransacked it. Elise cracked the blinds for a little extra light, then picked through the remains.

All that was in it was a small wheel of cheese and a jewelry box, although there was enough room for a bottle of wine, too. Must have been from one of Betty's boyfriends. Elise could watch her sunbathing through the window like they were on a Florida beach, rather than a high-density downtown neighborhood.

She opened the jewelry box. Elise gasped and dropped it in the sink.

That was her necklace. It belonged to her mother, once upon a time. But the chain had snapped during a fight, and she lost it—at Mr. Black's house.

The wine.

She ran outside.

"Changed your mind?" Betty asked, using the book to shade her face from the harsh summer sunlight.

Elise took the bottle from the grass and sniffed its mouth. It was peppery, rich, and woody, with a smoky odor that wasn't typical of wine. She wiped a finger along the edge and tasted it.

Grapes took on the flavor of their environment. The air, the soil, and the amount of sun could have subtle effects on an entire year's harvest. It wasn't common for a vineyard to produce wine after most of it burned, but that one had, and the grapes had taken on the flavor of a fire.

She checked the year on the label. It was from 1999.

"Kind of a weird taste, huh?" Betty asked. "But I like it. Maybe we can go check out the vineyard later. I know you and James love wine tastings, you great big drunkards." Elise marched to the curb and dumped the wine in the gutter. "Wait—wait, what are you doing? Stop!"

She smashed the bottle on the street.

Betty ran over, all her bare parts jiggling in the bikini. She ripped off her sunglasses to gape at the wine mixing with runoff from a garden hose two units down.

"Have you gone nuts?"

Elise scanned the street, positioning herself between Betty and the rest of the world. "If you get any other packages, don't open them."

"That was perfectly good wine!"

She recognized all the cars. A neighbor washed his truck down the street with the help of his ten year old son. A pair of teenagers sat on the corner looking hot and bored. Everything seemed ordinary enough, but there were too many hiding places. Too many houses with closed curtains, too many bushes and trees.

"Get inside," Elise said.

The confusion drained from Betty's face. "What's wrong? Did something happen?"

"Don't argue."

Her roommate's mouth shut. She grabbed her blanket and fan and carried everything into the duplex.

The wine dribbled into the sewer. Bitter anger rose in Elise's throat. The gift of her mother's necklace could only mean one thing.

This was war.

SEVEN

IF JAMES WERE to list "signs of impending apocalypse" from least worrisome to most, he would rank mundane things at the bottom—scrambled eggs, golden retriever puppies, a topiary in the shape of a dinosaur—and move up from there to slightly more worrying indicators. Earthquakes. Locusts. Raining blood. Dead cows.

Finding nine missed calls from Elise might not have been at the top of the list, but it was close. Perhaps directly below "death of all firstborn children in the nation."

He hadn't moved the power cord for his phone to Stephanie's house yet, so when his battery died, he couldn't recharge it. When he finally plugged it in his car to find a single terse text message from Elise ("Get back to the studio"), his stress levels shot through the roof. She had a way of doing that to him.

Twilight was falling when James arrived. Dry heat hung in the air, barely any cooler than it had been at midday. The pavement caught the heat and radiated it long after the sun disappeared behind the mountains. Leaving the air conditioned confines of his car was almost suffocating.

Hints of violet and orange touched the hills, painting the desolation in shades of sunset. Pink clouds faded to blue toward the east, where stars were already beginning to appear. The fading sun made the brick walls of Motion and Dance glow. His neighborhood was quiet that time of evening. The sprinklers kicked on at a dentist's office on the corner, a dog barked a few blocks away, and the illuminated sign for his studio buzzed faintly.

He parked beside Elise's car and jingled his keys in one hand as he headed for the stairs.

The back of his neck itched. He paused at the bottom of the stairs and glanced around the yard. "Elise?" he called. His hand slipped into his pocket where he kept a small notebook. "Is that you?"

A figure stepped from the darkness behind the sign. The light caught Elise's legs and left her a silhouette above the waist.

"I've been waiting for you all afternoon."

"Sorry. My battery died. What's wrong?"

She stepped onto the sidewalk to peer around the street. Elise was dressed for jogging in shorts and a tank top, but her posture made it look more like battle armor.

The street light flickered on and cast her in stark yellow light. She looked tired and grim and about five years older than the last time he saw her. "I've already checked your apartment. It's safe. Let's talk inside."

"Checked it for what?"

"I'll explain when we're off the street."

She tailed him up the stairs like a bodyguard waiting for attack, and watched the parking lot while he unlocked the door. Once they were inside, she put on the deadbolt, peered out the windows, and shut the curtains.

Elise hadn't been subtle about searching his apartment. The doors were open, every light was turned on, and his remaining belongings were more scattered than before. She didn't try to explain what was going on once everything was secured. Instead, she handed him a small blue box.

He tipped the lid open. The cross inside looked

49

familiar, but it took him a few minutes to recognize it. "Isn't this Ariane's necklace? I thought you lost it years ago."

"It was returned to me today."

He tried to remember the last time he saw Elise wearing it. An image of her at a younger age came to mind, when she still had short hair and skeletal features.

And then everything fell into place, and the box slipped from his hand.

Neither of them moved to pick it up.

"Impossible," James said. "We killed them."

He sank onto the couch. Elise took the seat beside him. She didn't have to say anything else. The silence of the night felt heavier than before, and the shadows seemed too dark. He understood why she had turned on all the lights. James had warded every inch of the studio with spells, but it suddenly didn't feel like enough.

James's throat was too dry to swallow. "He'll want to play with us first. That's why we haven't been directly attacked."

She nodded. Lowered her eyes.

"We knew this would happen. When we fought Death's Hand. We knew that would draw attention to us."

Something bothered him about the jewelry box on the floor. He leaned over to pick it up again, and then he saw it: a faint blur of magic around the crucifix. Elise's mother had been a witch, but not the kind that enchanted jewelry. It was something new.

"There's a spell on this," James said.

Elise frowned. "What is it?"

He focused. It certainly felt like the kind of spell Alain would cast. There was no finesse to his magic. It was blunt and raw, almost jagged on the edges, like shattered glass. "It's a locator charm," he said, tracing his fingers in the air over the cross without touching it. "So they can tell where the necklace is at any time."

"That's pointless," she said. "They already know where I live and work. They don't need magic to track me if they have eyeballs."

"And it would do them no good to follow you here anyway. Alain could never get through my barrier spells." James shut the box and set it on the table. "Unless..."

"What?"

"They might have wanted to know when you left your house."

She sucked in a hard breath. "Betty."

They couldn't drive fast enough.

James and Elise raced through the back streets toward her duplex. They saw the plume of smoke before the fire—black, billowing clouds that blotted out the stars.

Sirens screamed. A fire truck blew past them and turned onto Elise's street.

Their building was engulfed in flame. A smoky column rose from the roof on the right side, exposing the building's skeleton. The dry lawn Betty had been sunning on earlier that day had caught fire, too, and was creeping up Anthony's side of the duplex. Even the front door was swallowed by live fire, leaving no way to get inside. Firefighters blasted their hoses at the neighboring houses, which smoldered, but didn't burn—yet.

Elise didn't wait for him to stop the car before leaping out. People had spilled onto the sidewalks to rubberneck, and James had to park at the end of the street. It was too full to get any closer.

James could feel the radiant heat when he jumped out of his car. It slapped him in the face and took his breath away. "Betty!" Elise shouted, shoving through the crowd. He hurried to catch up with her as she snagged a neighbor by the elbow. "Hey! Have you seen Betty?"

The man she had grabbed shook his head. "She was

inside, I saw her cleaning—"

She didn't wait to hear anything more than that. Elise flew up the sidewalk.

A firefighter blocked her path. His gear was black with ash, and his face shield was tilted back to show his grizzled face. "You can't go in there."

"That's my house!"

"It's not safe to enter," he said. "Please step back so we can—"

"You don't understand! My roommate is in there!"

James stepped back while Elise had them distracted. Something was nagging at him—something similar to what he had felt from the necklace, but much more powerful.

Alain must have started the fire. And if that were true, nothing would stop it until the entire place burned.

"Let me go!" Elise yelled, waving her arms in an uncharacteristically panicked way. She caught James's eye over the shoulder of the firefighter and jerked her head toward the house. "I have to help her!"

The firefighter gave a long-suffering sigh as he tried to guide her away. Elise shoved him. It wasn't nearly as hard as she could have.

"Ma'am, I'm going to have to ask you to step away…"

James edged silently around them, slipped behind the neighbor's house, and climbed the fence into Elise's backyard.

The damage wasn't as bad on the other side. The vinyl siding had melted with residual heat in some spots, but there was no active fire. Elise's window was shattered, and smoke poured out of it as flames licked the walls. He felt a pang of fear. There was no recovering from that. She had probably already lost everything.

Alain's aura was so powerful that James knew he must have stood back there to cast the spell on Elise's room, but the witch himself was long gone. He hadn't waited to see the damage. And it hadn't traveled to Betty's room yet.

The other window was cracked. He ripped the screen off and tried to see inside, but even though the air was clear, the power had failed. It was too dark to see anything.

"Goddess help me," he muttered.

James hauled himself over the ledge and squirmed inside.

Her bed was empty. Smoke crept through the cracks around her door and turned the carpet black. "Betty!" he yelled into the hazy air. Shouting made his throat burn. He coughed, hacked, and tried again. "Betty! Where are you?"

She didn't respond.

He felt her doorknob with the back of his hand. It was hot.

He wrapped a pink cotton sheet from her footstool around his face, then grabbed another blanket to open the door.

Smoke erupted into the room with a gust of heat. He staggered back, throwing an arm over his face. His eyes watered. He took a last gulp of clean air through Betty's window, and then pushed through.

Flames had devoured Elise's bedroom door, and he felt his arm hairs scorch as he jumped past it. It was like stepping into a pizza oven. He stepped over a burning patch of carpet to get into the living room—he couldn't see further than a few inches in front of his face—and kicked aside a table that had tipped over. One of Elise's protein powder plants was a shriveled crisp. Their couch smoldered. He glimpsed a burning wall through the smoke.

Hot. So hot.

"Betty!"

No response.

He could barely see or breathe. Their duplex wasn't

large, but there was no sense of direction in the darkness. He had to escape.

James kicked open the bathroom door. Empty.

The change in air pressure sucked smoke toward him. He stumbled over a chair and landed on all fours in their dining nook. He didn't bother getting up. The air was too hot, too close. He could almost breathe on the floor.

He crawled into the kitchen and saw a bare leg.

Betty.

She had collapsed in front of the refrigerator and scattered food across the floor. There was a tub of cream cheese by her head. Her bleach blond hair was thick with ash. The counter next to her was burning—he grabbed her ankle and dragged her away from it.

He would have gasped at seeing her arm in the dim light of the fire if he could breathe better. The skin was raw and peeling from residual heat.

She didn't wake up when he lifted her into his arms and tried to stand.

A mighty crack split the air.

Elise's bedroom wall collapsed, and half the roof went with it. Burning wood exploded around him. The fire swept across the carpet, and a gust of heat swept past him. He fell to his knees again, coughing and wheezing.

He had to set Betty down and lay beside her to keep breathing. "This was a terrible idea," he rasped.

Where were those firefighters?

It was all he could do to pull the notebook out of his pocket and squint at his symbols in the smoke. A spell to stop fever. A spell for broken bones. A spell that created flames—he didn't need more of *that*. And then he found what he was looking for: a spell that made wind.

"Hang on," he gasped to Betty.

He crumpled the page in his fist and spoke a word of power.

54

Magic ripped out of him. A blast rocked the building.

Metal screamed and windows shattered as a massive wind rushed around the room, like the hand of God punching through the walls. Everything on the counters was blasted aside. James threw himself over Betty to shelter her. Pain lanced through his back as a plate shattered against his shoulders.

A second gust followed the first, even more powerful than before. Fire funneled from the back of the duplex toward the front.

Something huge snapped. What remained of the roof crashed into the counters with a groan, and for an instant, the world was impossibly hot. His hair burned. His neck blistered. Coals showered around him, stinging his arms and back.

And then the third wind extinguished it all.

With a whisper of a breeze, the house went silent.

James looked up. The counters had taken the brunt of the collapse, leaving them framed with smoking wood and sheltering him from the worst of the debris. He couldn't get up without moving it, so he didn't try.

Groaning, he rolled onto his side and brushed plaster dust off his shirt. Chunks of wood crumbled at his touch. He could see stars through what was left of the walls, and the summer breeze felt cold on the places his skin had burned. Betty was still unconscious. He pressed fingers to her throat and found a pulse.

"Thank the Goddess," he whispered, and then he let himself go limp, too.

Every breath burned his lungs. The chill on his neck had to be bad. And he didn't care at all.

The voices of men approached as firefighters moved in. James slipped his notebook into his pocket before they grew close.

Then he heard a woman's voice. "James!"

He coughed. "Over here."

The debris on the counter shifted. Elise threw everything aside, forgetting to pretend she wasn't preternaturally strong. "Betty!" She dropped beside them. "Is she...?"

"She's alive."

Elise let out a sigh. "Good." And then she turned on him. "What did you think you were doing? Are you *suicidal*?"

He held out a hand, and Elise helped him sit up. The debris at the back of the house was still burning where Alain's spell had started it, and judging by the amount of smoke, Anthony's side of the duplex was on fire too. "Betty was inside. I had to do something."

"Like dive into a burning building? Why didn't you stop the fire from the outside?"

"Alain's magic—"

"Forget it," Elise interrupted. She threw her arms around him and almost knocked him into one of the smoldering beams. Her grip made his ribs creak and the burned skin on his back ache. "You are such an idiot, James."

"Ouch," he said helpfully.

"I'm thanking you for saving Betty. Shut up."

"Right. Sorry." He patted her on the back.

"Hey! Over here!"

A firefighter had found them, ending the conversation. Elise stood up. "We'll talk about this later. Let's get Betty to the hospital."

EIGHT

THE CHECKER BEHIND the counter swiped Elise's debit card again. "I'm sorry. This one has been denied, too."

She pulled a credit card out of her wallet. "Try this one."

The hospital cafeteria was empty in the middle of the night. Several quiet hours had elapsed since loading Betty into an ambulance, and nothing had happened since the police finished asking questions. The sudden change of pace left her feeling restless, but with her office and home burned, there was nowhere else to go.

Now she was trying to buy a salad for a late dinner, and it was much harder than it should have been. Both her personal and business debit cards had already been denied twice. She could tell by the apologetic look that her credit card wasn't coming up any different.

"Sorry," he said, handing it back. "Maybe it's a problem with our system."

She gave him a ten dollar bill and took her salad back to the waiting room.

The lettuce tasted like tissue in her mouth, dry and flavorless. Maybe it was the dissatisfaction of having her cards denied, or the lingering taste of ash, but she dumped it in the trash after two bites.

She stretched out between two chairs, pillowed her

head on her arms, and tried to focus on the television mounted in the corner. She had never been able to sleep in public before—in fact, she didn't even sleep when Anthony spent the night with her—but fading adrenaline and stress mingled to overtake her.

She could barely find the energy to fill her lungs. Every breath was slower and deeper than the last.

The news was reporting on the fire. Pundits discussed rising crime rates.

Elise's eyes drooped. The figures blurred.

She stretched with a yawn, trying to force her eyelids open. What if someone found her? What if she was attacked?

But she sank into her chair again as the news flickered in front of her, and her eyes fell closed. A dark and endlessly vast space settled around her. It sank into her skin and weighed upon her bones. Air ruffled the hair at the back of her neck.

Someone was calling her name.

Elise...

Fear thrilled through her stomach. She could still see the dim light of the news and hear them discuss investigations and arson. But the room wavered around her.

A pillar grew in front of her like a stone tree sprouting. It was wrapped with thick lines and glowing symbols at the base. It was soapy-white, unnaturally smooth. The pillar arced over her head, and she watched as the other end touched the earth and formed a gateway.

Not here. Not again.

She struggled to focus on the TV, but her eyelashes were glued shut.

"A home in downtown Reno burned last night in an incident the police suspect to be arson..." The newscaster's smile stretched and blurred. Her eyes sank into her skull, leaving black pits in their place. "You deserved it, didn't you? You're going to lose everything."

Her hand reached through the gateway, grin huge and looming. Pale fingers filled her vision.

"I see you, Elise."

Her voice echoed through the air.

I see you...

Elise's eyes flew open as her hand closed on a wrist. She wrenched her attacker off his feet. Her other hand went to the back of her shorts where she kept a knife.

"It's me, Elise, it's me!"

The haze lifted, and she realized the blurry face in front of her belonged to James.

Suddenly, she wasn't in that dark place anymore. She was in a quiet hospital with tan carpeting, bare walls, and murmuring nurses. She released him, sat up, and cradled her head in both palms. "Sorry," she said, blinking hard to clear her vision. Her heart thudded as though she had been running.

James sank to his knees next to the chair. He had ashy smudges on his chin and a bandage across the back of his neck. "Are you okay?"

"Fine." She wiped sweat off her upper lip with the back of her glove. "I'm fine. What do the doctors say?"

"I'm all right, so I've been discharged, but Betty needs to stay the night. She inhaled a lot of smoke and has second-degree burns on ten percent of her body. Anthony will be here soon to stay with her." He offered Elise his hand. She ignored it and got up on her own.

"Will she be okay?"

"Yes, but she's in a lot of pain. They've sedated her so she can sleep." The careful way he spoke told Elise there was more to the story that he didn't want to say. They took the elevator to the first floor and went outside, and he continued once they were alone in the parking lot. "I think

59

she was poisoned. Drugged."

Elise got into the car. "The wine."

"Most likely. That fire was meant to kill her."

"No, it was meant to kill *me*."

"He was surely tracking the cross and knew you weren't there. If Mr. Black wanted us dead, he would be more overt. I think he's trying to—well, punish us."

Her jaw clenched. "Fantastic. Where are we going?"

"The studio. You can't stay at the duplex anymore, and it's one of the only places with strong enough warding to stand up to Mr. Black."

That was optimistic of him. Elise wasn't sure an entire fortress would be strong enough. "Thanks. I'll find a hotel or something tomorrow. There isn't enough room for Betty and Anthony at the studio, and we're all homeless now."

"Actually…" He hesitated. Cleared his throat. "There are two bedrooms in my apartment, and I'm staying with Stephanie. That leaves plenty of room for all of you."

"You should stay with us. Stephanie's house isn't warded, either."

"Her old house wasn't," James agreed.

She shot a sideways look at him. He had always taken their lifestyle with grace. Even covered in soot, he didn't seem as beaten as she did. His black hair looked artfully tousled, while hers was a tangled mess of curls.

"But?"

"She's moved."

The terse response made her uneasy. But it wasn't until they got to the studio again that she realized exactly what it meant.

The last couple of times she had been there, she assumed the disarray meant he was cleaning. But now she saw that his most important belongings were gone. The photography prints, his kitchen utensils, his altar. She followed him into his bedroom and realized half of his bookshelves were empty. She didn't have to check the closet to know his clothes would be gone, too.

It didn't look like a place someone lived. It looked more like long-term storage.

Why hadn't she noticed earlier?

James gathered fresh blankets from the linen closet and tried to get a fitted sheet over the mattress. Elise took the other end and helped him pull it over the corner.

He changed pillowcases and folded the comforter at the foot of the bed. "There you go. Should be comfortable." When she didn't respond, James studied her face with deep furrows carved into his forehead. He misinterpreted her angry silence. "We'll figure this out. We defeated Mr. Black once, and we can do it again."

"I'm not worried about it," she said.

"You don't have to lie to me."

That almost made her laugh. Funny, coming from the man who had moved out of his apartment and hadn't bothered to tell her. "I should rest."

He nodded. "I'll sleep on the couch. I'm too tired to drive, and heaven knows where Mr. Black is right now."

"I can take the couch."

"You need the rest much more than I do." James reached out to tug on one of the curls in her ponytail. "You look terrible, Elise."

"Yeah. Thanks. We can talk more about Mr. Black when sunrise hits."

"A whole two hours of sleep," he said. "I can hardly wait."

Elise watched his retreating back before shutting the door. His room felt strangely vacant without him in it.

She wasn't sure if the tension in her shoulders was from James or Mr. Black. Either way, her urge to sleep had completely vanished. She changed into a spare t-shirt and sweat pants from her laundry pile and splashed water on

61

her face in the bathroom, trying to cool her parched skin.

In the light from the vanity bulbs over the mirror, she really did look terrible. Hollow eyes stared back at her from a face that seemed gaunter than it had the day before. Her auburn hair was fraying from its ponytail. Her tan skin was gray. There was no color to her lips or cheeks. A droplet of water shivered from the hard point of her chin, and she brushed it off.

All those worries crept back in twofold. Insurance company. Landlord—both for her office building and her duplex. The police would have even more questions. Her dwindling client list. All those unpaid bills.

Her gaze traveled to her wallet where she had dropped it on the back of the toilet. Denied credit cards.

A sense of foreboding filled her as she went back to the bedroom and turned on his laptop. She could hear James moving around downstairs, just as restless and unwilling to sleep as she was.

She logged onto her bank's website. Her heart skipped a beat at the account totals.

Two dollars and fifty-three cents.

Impossible.

She should have had hundreds in checking and thousands more in savings. But it was all gone. There were errors where her credit card statements should have shown.

Somehow, she knew if she called the bank, they would have her on record as having made the withdrawals.

"Burning my home wasn't enough?" she whispered.

Of course not. Mr. Black didn't do things halfway.

She stared blankly at a pair of loafers James had left behind. Without money or her home, all she had left was her car—and she could imagine waking up the next morning to find that stolen, too. The only clothes she had were exercise gear, which was now covered in dirt and debris, and some tattered sweats. Besides that, her total assets amounted to two dollars and fifty-three cents and a pair of falchions locked in a gun safe.

No money. No house. No job.

She dialed a number on her cell phone before she realized she made the decision.

"That didn't take long," purred the Night Hag. That hard, ancient voice gave Elise chills.

"I've changed my mind."

"And why is that?"

"It doesn't matter. But if I'm going to work for you, I need a salary. Money isn't a problem for you. I know, I've seen your books. You own all the demon businesses in the city."

A snort. "Greedy, hmm?"

"The bills don't pay themselves."

"And everybody has a price. Apparently I've found yours." The demand didn't seem to anger the Night Hag. If anything, she sounded appreciative. "Consider yourself salaried. But if I'm bleeding money for you, I'll expect you to earn it. And I need a commitment."

Elise braced herself. "I know."

"Excellent."

She heard a *snap* on the other side of the line.

Something whip-cracked through the air, something intangible that reeked of ozone, and Elise felt a hot sting on her shoulder. She pulled down the strap of her shirt and twisted around to peer at the shoulder blade. A brand the size of a penny had appeared, comprised of eight curling lines inside a circle. Blood trickled down her back.

She was marked—just like any demon in the service of a master.

"My witch will be visiting soon. Can't wait to get started."

The Night Hag chuckled as she hung up.

NINE

SHORTLY after meeting with Mr. Black at the Pledger Bistro, Elise told James she needed to see a doctor.

"Have you been injured?" he asked, propping his head up on an arm. James was stretched out on the floor, paralyzed by early summer heat in a hotel room that had no air conditioner.

Elise tossed a knife with a long, slender blade back and forth between her hands. She had just trimmed her hair to an inch short again, and reddish curls stuck to her gloves.

"No."

"It's not going to be easy to see a doctor. We don't have insurance. We don't have *money*."

"It's important," she said, and her strange tone of voice made him give her a second look. Elise was serious. "I need to see a—an obstetrician."

He almost choked. "Are you pregnant?"

"No. Mr. Black said girl kopides are unusual, and I was thinking..." Elise was so stiff that she might have acquired spontaneous rigor mortis. "I've never had a..." She stuttered. Stopped. Tried again. "I've never had a period."

A knot inside of him relaxed. "Ah. In that case, you want a—uh, a gynecologist. I've told you that I danced with a professional ballet company as a teenager, didn't I?"

64

The rapid change in subject made her blink.

"No."

"For three years. Between the stress of touring and low body fat, most of my female counterparts were like you. They didn't...you know. In any case, they were healthy. It's nothing to worry about."

She folded her arms. "I'm going to see someone."

And that was that.

Finding "someone" was easier than expected. There were few doctors who knew anything about kopides, but a phone call to his former coven gave him the number of a nearby practice owned by witches. An appointment was arranged for the next week. The doctor was excited to see one of the only female kopides.

Which was how James ended up with the world's greatest demon hunter in a waiting room decorated with posters of babies.

Elise kept trying to draw her knife. He cleared his throat to remind her to stop. He wished he could have kept her from going to the gynecologist's office with concealed weapons, but he had no control over her—much less her decisions—and she arrived armed in the same way she might while facing a pack of werewolves.

After ten minutes of waiting, and several attempts at pulling a knife on the office staff, he whispered, "The pregnant women aren't going to attack you."

She glared at him. Her cheeks were red.

A nurse came into the waiting room. "Elise Kavanagh," she called.

Elise hesitated by the chair. "Come with me," she whispered to James. Her arms were locked at her sides.

"I don't think they'll let me. I'm not—"

She shifted on her feet, staring at the potted plant furiously as though she could set fire to it with her gaze. "Please." James could tell it pained her to ask. The tendons in her neck were rigid.

She was scared. Elise was *scared*.

Up until that moment, he had never seen her as anything but cold and detached—or, occasionally, furious and blood-thirsty. Yet being subjected to a physical examination petrified her. He couldn't see how his presence would help. She made it clear she didn't trust him. On most days, he thought she didn't even like him.

"Elise," the nurse called again.

Her cheeks burned red.

"Okay," he replied. What else could he say?

They walked into the back together.

The nurse, whose name tag said "Laura," took Elise's height, weight, and blood pressure, asked her to leave a urine sample in the bathroom, then led them into an exam room with a window overlooking the city.

Laura pulled sheets out of a drawer and began setting tools on a wheeled tray. Elise stood by the bed and glared at the room like she was awaiting execution.

"And you are?" the nurse prompted James.

Even though the doctors in the practice were witches, he wasn't sure what the rest of the staff knew, so he didn't try to explain the unusual relationship between a kopis and witch. "I'm her boyfriend."

Whatever Laura thought of a teenage girl dating an obviously older man, she kept it to herself. "I'm going to ask you some personal questions, Elise. Would you like your boyfriend to leave the room?"

She shook her head.

Laura asked about her health and her family's history. She asked about alcohol and drugs, too. When she asked if Elise was sexually active, she shook her head again, and the nurse gave her a skeptical look. She made a note on the clipboard.

"You'll need to strip down, but keep your socks on. It's

chilly in here. This one is a vest," she told Elise, setting one folded sheet on the counter, "and this one is a blanket to cover your hips. Dr. Kingsley will be right in."

She shut the door behind her. Elise picked up the vest. It was made of flimsy blue paper.

James studied the city through the window while she changed. He waited to face her again until the paper on the bed crinkled and Elise said, "Okay." She had pulled extra sheets out of the drawer to protect herself and left her gloves on. She looked frail and childlike on the raised bed, and stared mistrustfully at the waiting stirrups.

"I can leave," he said.

She shook her head again.

They waited together without speaking. James shifted her clothes to the counter, careful to leave her knives concealed, and took the chair by the bed.

When the door opened again, a short man with a bushy beard entered with Elise's chart. He ignored James. "So you're the female kopis," said Dr. Kingsley. "Excellent! I'd say that I've wanted to examine one of your type, but that would sound odd, wouldn't it? The good news is that your pregnancy test came back negative. Can't imagine a pregnant demon hunter, eh?"

Elise looked horrified.

"Let's see what we can find. Lay back and slide to the end of the bed."

He positioned the stirrups and rolled his stool to sit between them. She moved stiffly, settling back against the bed with jerky motions. She was shaking.

"James," she said.

Elise held out a hand. It took him a moment to realize what she was asking, but then he took it and squeezed her fingers.

She didn't let go for the entire examination.

Elise retrieved the bowl that evening.

She didn't want to stay at the hotel with James. It was too hard to face him. On the other hand, finding Mr. Black again was easy. She stood on a street corner until his slender, whip-like aspis appeared on the other side.

She walked to a bakery and looked in the window. His reflection appeared behind hers.

"I'll do it," she said, pretending to study green apple cupcakes. The sight of food made her stomach give a hard cramp, like it was trying to digest itself.

A thick roll of paper was pressed into her hand. By the time she turned around, Alain was gone.

He had given her a note wrapped around a roll of money. She didn't need to count the bills to know that she could buy all the cupcakes in the bakery if she wanted. Elise sat on a bench to read the note while savoring a flaky, buttery croissant.

So glad you came around to my way of thinking. Here's where you can find the bowl. See you tonight.

Numbers were written at the bottom. Coordinates.

She sneaked into the motel where James was showering, grabbed her hiking boots, and stuffed most of the money into the bottom of her backpack. The sound of water traveling through the pipes shut off. She left a handful of twenties on his pillow, tucked her spine sheath and swords under one arm, and slipped out the door.

Using a map from a corner gas station, she pinpointed the coordinates Mr. Black had given her. They were centered on grassy plains bisected by freeways, where great native civilizations had once occupied the land— civilizations that had since been destroyed—and left nothing behind but pottery fragments and earthen mounds.

Elise took a cab to the edge of town. There were no exits from the freeway directly to the mounds, so she climbed over a concrete barrier and walked along the rolling hills.

Cars whispered along the overpass. An occasional horn honked. She moved deeper into the hills without worrying anyone would see. The moon was nothing more than a yellow sliver glowing between wisps of clouds.

The grass grew long and lush as she moved into a valley between mounds. Dew misted on her bare legs. Mud slurped under her soles.

She had brought the map with her, but there wasn't enough light to make out the place she had marked. It didn't matter. A strange quiet settled over her as she approached the eastern mound. It pressed inside her skull like wool. She could tell she was getting close when she found signs of an archaeological dig: leveled ground, a few posted signs, strings stretched between stakes.

Elise hopped a low fence meant to keep tourists away from the excavation and beelined for bushes at the back that hadn't been cleared out yet. She pushed through the branches.

The hole she found was only a few inches narrower than her shoulders. It could have been mistaken for an animal's burrow that had been worn away by rain.

She grabbed fistfuls of mud and threw gobs of it over her shoulder. Once the hole was widened enough for her to fit in with the sheath on her back, she squirmed inside. Mud scraped against her shoulders, her hips. Elise dropped to the bottom of the hole just a few feet down and straightened.

Her vision adjusted to the darkness, but there was nothing to see. Roots dangled from the ceiling. Shards of rock pocked the uneven floor. It was small enough that she couldn't straighten fully. But the pressure inside her skull had worsened, and she knew she was in the right place.

Elise felt along the back wall. Her hand slipped into the

damp soil, and her fingers met something hard.

Blowing her hair out of her face, she dug into the mud. There was smooth stone on the other side. She drew a sword and rapped the hilt against it. Hollow.

She drew back her arm and smashed it into the wall.

The stone crumbled. A few more strikes, and she made a hole. Light glowed on the other side, faint and gray, like early morning.

She returned the falchion to her spine and ripped clay bricks from their moorings. Once she removed enough of it, the wall fell apart on its own, and she soon had a hole as big as her last one. She squeezed inside.

That faint light didn't seem to come from any single source, but the chamber on the other end was obviously manmade. The walls and floor were chiseled, an old stone table stood in the corner, and there were engravings on the walls. A recession had been built into the stones at the opposite end of the room, just eight feet away. It was a different kind of rock than everything else: white and smooth, rather than clay-colored. The platforms and etchings made it look like a monument or altar. And the bowl Mr. Black wanted was trapped inside of it by bars.

The bowl was smaller than she expected—barely any bigger than her fists. It looked mundane, dusty, and boring, but the way it vibrated in her veins told her it was ethereal, which meant it was none of those three things.

Elise tried to jiggle it free. It wouldn't budge.

She scanned the symbols surrounding it. A crucifix formed the center, surrounded by obscure symbols that most educated kopides would have realized were ethereal in origin. There was no other language like it, human or infernal. And no other kopis would have known the symbols were also a lock.

Elise looked at her hands. She wore thick leather gloves with a strap across the back, which she had recently shoplifted from a motorcycle shop.

James would tell her to leave. He would tell her to forget.

He would probably be right.

Her fingers shook as she ripped off the Velcro strap and removed the glove with her teeth, baring her hand to the dry air of the chamber.

Black lines marked her palm, like a freshly-inked tattoo that hadn't had time to heal. The skin was red and swollen around the edges. But Elise had never been under the needle of a tattoo artist, and she never would have chosen the design if she had. The marks didn't match the symbol on the altar, but it was close.

The stone vibrated to life when she stretched out her hand. Silver-blue light traced along the marks at the base.

Elise drew back. The vibrations slowed.

"God help me," she muttered. It was not a prayer. She never prayed.

She pressed her palm to the altar.

A strange singing filled her skull. The vibration vanished in an instant, and so did everything else—the room surrounding her, the stone under her hand, the darkness. A veil of heavy gray light pressed against her.

There was a face on the other side of the veil.

Elise…

That single word made her eardrums ache. The voice was great and terrible, tender and surprised.

She wrenched her hand free with a gasp.

And she was holding the bowl.

Elise blinked at her hands. She hadn't consciously moved the bars aside, but the bowl was no longer captive in the wall, and it was humming. It liked being held by her. There was no sign of breakage or shifting in the altar, so she shouldn't have been able to remove it.

She set the bowl on the ground and took a big step

71

back to study the chamber. It didn't feel so empty anymore. Now the hollows looked like watching eyes, and spider webs swayed in the corner as if ruffled by a passing breeze.

She pulled her glove back on.

"I'm coming for you," she whispered, just to break the silence. "This is going to end."

Shucking her shirt, Elise wrapped the bowl so that none of the stone was exposed. Wearing nothing but a camisole was chilly, but it was better than feeling the ethereal artifact recognize her. It didn't hum so much when it was out of contact with her skin.

It was hard to climb the short, muddy slope to the surface again, but with enough grunting and wiggling, Elise emerged from the hill.

Three men were waiting for her at the top.

Two of them were standing. The other was kneeling with a gun aimed at the back of his skull. Elise probably shouldn't have been surprised to see the one on the ground was James. Alain Daladier's grip was steel on the pistol. Mr. Black stood in front of the others, smiling his most charming smile.

Her hands tensed on the bowl as she straightened. Elise was soaked in mud, and the slight breeze gave her chills. The odds weren't good. Not good at all. Mr. Black may have been old, but he would be fast. Elise didn't like her chances against him. It was an unpleasantly vulnerable position to be caught in.

"You made it," Mr. Black said in a warm voice, like a pleasant older uncle. He wore a fine white suit and leaned on a jeweled cane. "I'd be lying if I said I wasn't surprised, but you have impressed me mightily, young lady."

James was pale. "Elise—"

A nudge from the pistol cut him off.

"I'll take that now," Mr. Black said, stretching his hand

72

out.

She didn't move. "The money."

"Surely you don't think I wouldn't make good on a deal?" He caught her glance toward James and feigned further shock, fluttering his hand at his breast. "Oh, my dear, I realize this must not look good. We spotted Mr. Faulkner trying to follow you underground. We were only concerned he might have been trying to stop you. Don't you see? It was for your safety."

She considered the accusation. As persistent as James had been in following her around, he had never shown an inclination to hurt her. He was taking short, shallow breaths. Not injured. Just afraid. He didn't like having a gun aimed at him. Well, that was his fault for following her where he wasn't wanted.

"The money," Elise said again.

Mr. Black's smile widened with delight. "You don't find having your witch friend at gunpoint motivational? You surprise me again!"

"He's not my friend."

"Well, well. Then I suppose it doesn't matter if we shoot him. What do you think?"

"The money for the bowl."

"Cold, my dear. Very cold. I appreciate that."

Mr. Black gestured. Alain opened his jacket with his free hand, removed a piece of paper, and offered it to Elise. She hugged the bowl tight to her stomach as she stepped up to take it from him. James's features were drawn and grim.

The paper was another set of coordinates.

"I've hidden your money," Mr. Black said. "Couldn't risk having you take it from us without holding up your end of the deal, hmm? Now it appears that wouldn't have been necessary."

Elise thought back to the map. The coordinates weren't

far.

"Goodbye," she said, more to James than the other men.

Then she tucked the bowl under her arm and started toward the lights of the freeway. When Mr. Black called after her, there was no good humor in his voice. "Where do you think you're going?"

"I don't see my money."

Alain moved in the corner of her eye. He was turning the gun on her. In a flash, she grabbed the pistol, slammed her hand into the joint of Alain's elbow, and kicked him to the ground. The bowl didn't even slip.

She aimed the gun at Mr. Black's face. Everyone froze.

He couldn't seem to work up a grin again. It flickered on his lips and was replaced by wary evaluation. Would she shoot him? "You want me to have the bowl as much as I do," he said in a low whisper that only she would be able to hear. "If you want me to kill Him."

"Yes. I also want my money."

He raised his voice. "Alain. Go get it."

The aspis got to his feet, glaring fire at Elise, but he obeyed without argument. He vanished down the hill.

James stood. His knees were wet and he was breathing hard. "You don't want to do that," he said, giving the bowl a look very much like the one he had given Alain's gun. He didn't seem much less nervous without a bullet aimed for his head. "You can still put it back."

Mr. Black wasn't sweating. "A deal's a deal, Mr. Faulkner. You know that better than anyone else."

"What do you know?" James asked, turning pale.

"I've done my research."

Before they could say anything else, Elise released the clip and offered the unloaded gun to Mr. Black. "When you do it, I want to be there," she said.

"Surprises again and again." He tucked the gun in his

74

jacket with a scowl. It twisted his face into hard, frightening lines. "I don't think I like surprises."

Elise pocketed the clip. "I don't like being treated like I'm stupid."

Alain reappeared shortly holding a canvas bag that was almost as muddy as she was. At Elise's gesture, he handed it to James, who looked inside. "It seems to be more than enough," he said hesitantly, thumbing through a stack of money tied together with a rubber band. "But Elise, you shouldn't—"

She gave Alain the bowl. And just like that, Mr. Black was all smiles again. "Wonderful. We'll be in contact."

They walked away. James shook, as though fighting the urge to run after them. "Do you have any idea what they can do with that thing? Don't you realize what could happen?"

"Yes," she said simply.

He waited to speak again until both of the other men had gotten into their car, which was parked on the far end of the hill. The headlights receded into the distance. "I thought you were going to let him kill me."

She turned on him. "What's wrong with you? Why won't you leave me alone?"

"Excuse me?"

"You follow me everywhere. Always. Ever since Russia. There's no reason for it. Go home!" She flung out an arm, gesturing vaguely toward the horizon. "You're not the one who has to run and hide!"

"Your enemies are mine, Elise, and we're safer together than we are apart. You must realize this by now."

"Following me to get an ethereal artifact? That's safe?"

"Perhaps it wasn't the best-conceived plan," he muttered. "You can hardly blame me. I was worried about you."

"Worried. About me."

"Is that so hard to believe?"

She opened her mouth. Closed it again. The breeze lifted, blowing the hair back from his face. James's expression was open and honest, as earnest as it had ever been, and she couldn't think of a response.

She turned to head back to the motel.

As always, he followed.

June 1999

Dr. Kingsley called several days later to say that he had the results of Elise's tests.

They met in his private office, which was decorated with hanging herbs and crystals. He shut the door and locked it behind them. "I don't want anyone to intrude. I haven't discussed your karyotype test with anyone else in the practice," the doctor explained as they sat. "I discovered something unusual."

"Is something wrong?" James asked.

"No, no. Nothing is technically 'wrong.' I had my theories about what could cause a female kopis, but... Well, the tests were informative."

"How so?"

"Some things are not surprising. First of all, you have a myostatin deficiency, which means you build muscle easily. That's an expected trait among kopides. What's more surprising is that you're completely androgen insensitive. Do you know what that means?" he asked. Elise shook her head. "Genetically, you have one X chromosome and one Y chromosome, like a man, but all the physical characteristics of a woman."

Elise's eyes widened. "I'm a man?"

"No. You're a woman with an intersex condition."

"I don't understand."

76

Neither did James. "Is that why she's never…?"

"You'll never menstruate because you don't have a uterus or ovaries, Miss Kavanagh. That means children aren't in your future, either. This explains so much about kopides." Dr. Kingsley rubbed his hands together, face bright with excitement. "We might want to consider surgically removing—"

Sudden motion cut him off. Elise shoved her chair back and stood, face red.

Her mouth opened, like she wanted to say something, but nothing came out. She gave James a helpless look before leaving the room without a word.

Dr. Kingsley blinked rapidly, as though trying to decide what might have upset his new favorite patient. "You couldn't have been more sensitive about that?" James asked.

"What do you mean?"

He had just told a teenage girl that she was not, strictly speaking, a teenage girl, and that she would never have children. And he didn't understand why that might be distressing.

James stood. "Thank you for your assistance. Forward the bill to my coven. I don't think we'll need further help."

"But there are other tests I want to run." The doctor moved in front of the door, preventing him from leaving. "Do you realize what this means? The impact this could have on our scientific understanding of supernatural phenomena? If we could just do exploratory surgery…"

Anger swelled in him. He grabbed the doctor's shirt in a fist and shoved their faces close together. James wasn't imposing, but he had a good six inches on the other man, and the temper to back it up. "We are done with your services."

James dropped him. Dr. Kingsley stumbled back, pale and shaking.

He followed Elise out of the office.

She wasn't waiting for him outside, so he decided not to search for her. Instead, he returned to their motel. Elise had used some of Mr. Black's money to buy food the night before, and there was actual fresh fruit on the table. He passed the time savoring an apple—the first produce he'd eaten in weeks that hadn't been half-rotten and dug from the trash.

Elise returned a few hours later. James didn't bother asking where she had been.

"Thank you. You aren't—I don't—" She bowed her head and cleared her throat. "I don't have anyone else. You didn't have to follow me to the mounds. And you didn't need to go to the doctor with me. So...thank you."

He felt a sudden, foreign burst of affection for her. "You're welcome. I'll always be here, you know. We're in this together now."

She leaned her head on his chest. He almost pushed her away until he realized she was hugging him rather than attacking him. James's hands hovered awkwardly over her shoulders. When several moments passed without Elise moving, he hugged her back.

James wondered what she thought of being unable to have children. It didn't seem right to ask.

A moment later, she stepped back. Her face was expressionless again.

"Well," Elise said. "Guess it's time to go kill Mr. Black."

TEN

ELEVEN

JULY 2009

JULY 2009

FIST connected with bag. Elise grunted. The chain rattled.

Her focus was narrowed on a worn square inch in the center of the punching bag. She struck again and again, feeling the shock all the way up to her shoulders as she rolled her entire body into each hit. The bag swung, and she darted to the side to keep from getting hit. Her chest rose and fell with heaving breaths. Her throat was still raw from breathing in smoke.

Elise had hung her old punching bag from a hook in the back room of Motion and Dance, where the coven usually held esbats. In a past life, it had been a garage, but it was also her personal gym in the year she lived with James. She hoped bringing it out for a beating would make her feel better. Now the bandages wrapped around her palms were soaked with sweat, her hair stuck to her neck, and her jogging bra was drenched. But it wasn't enough.

She leaned back and kicked. Even bare-footed, it was hard enough to make the chain groan and dust explode off the bag.

The door creaked. She spun, fists raised.

Anthony froze in the doorway.

"James said you were down here." He eased into the room and shut the door.

The sight of her boyfriend filled her with exhaustion. She had already spent hours being "interviewed" by the police, and hours more talking with James. She had no more energy for words.

She twisted and lashed out with a foot, hitting the bag again. When it swung back, she punched it once, twice, three times, loosing all her frustrated energy.

Anthony took position at the other side of the bag and held it for her. It was easier hitting it that way, but not as satisfying. She pounded it one more time before stopping. "What do you want?" she snapped. "You should be with Betty in the hospital."

"How can you ask me that? Our apartment burned, Elise. Almost everything is gone. I need answers."

She kicked the bag hard enough to make him take a step back. "I don't have anything for you."

"But you know who did it."

Elise nodded, rolling her shoulders out and digging her fingers into the muscle to try to release tension. She had healed from the bite wound delivered by James when he was possessed by Death's Hand, but it stiffened if she moved her arm too much. Anthony stepped forward like he was going to massage her. She stayed out of reach.

He dropped his hands. "Come on. I've been hunting with you. We killed giant spiders together. If you're trying to protect me—"

"I'm not."

"Then who is it? Let's get him. Let's *kill* him. He's jacked up our lives and we owe somebody serious pain!"

The thought of Anthony going after Mr. Black was laughable. Alain would shoot him on sight. "Go help

James carry everything upstairs," Elise said, even though there was little to move. Not much had survived the fire.

"Let me help you. I'm almost as strong as you are. I have a shotgun. We can do this together."

"No. Drop it."

But he didn't relent. "Are you going after him today? Are you going to—?"

"Anthony," she interrupted. "Shut the hell up."

His mouth clapped shut. "You would take James along. Wouldn't you?"

She went back to abusing the punching bag.

Elise shut him out, shut the room out, shut out all her unpleasant thoughts of empty bank accounts and terminated contracts and burned buildings. All she felt was fury. Retribution. The impact of knuckles against leather.

After a minute of silent watching, Anthony left.

Her cell phone rang. It vibrated on the table by the mirrors hard enough to travel toward the edge. She patted the sweat from her chest with a towel as she picked it up. The phone didn't display a number, but she wasn't surprised when David Nicholas was on the other end.

"Your first job's tonight," he said.

She waited to catch her breath before responding. "Don't tell me I have to work with you."

"Ha. The Night Hag says I'm not allowed near you. She thinks one of us will die."

"She's sharp."

"As a fucking tack," David Nicholas said. "I'm on babysitting duty tonight anyway. Watching every step your witchy friend takes, keeping assassins away, you know how it is. His girlfriend is hot. Perfect tits. Bet you'd like to know what they were doing last night."

Elise didn't take the bait. "What's the plan?"

"Hell if I know. Thom's getting you from your *charming*

81

new apartment at six."

David Nicholas knew she wasn't living at the old duplex anymore. It wasn't surprising, since they had to be watching closely to project James, but it was unsettling to realize she hadn't detected anyone watching them. Somehow, that still didn't unsettle her much as the thought of working with Thom.

"Tell me what you know about Thom," Elise said.

The nightmare snorted. "Sometimes it's better not to know things, and let me tell you, it's better not to know *anything* about that guy. Word of advice? Don't pull your spunky bullshit with him. He's the only person I know more unhinged than you are."

He hung up.

A black SUV pulled into the parking lot the instant Elise's cell phone clock turned to six. She met Thom downstairs.

If she thought the stuffy heat inside the apartment was bad, it was nothing compared to the scalding heat outside. The sun only touched the top of the mountains, but even approaching sunset didn't cool the desert. The pavement rippled.

Thom stepped out of the car, and she got her first good look at him in the sunlight. He was dressed elegantly in a black silk shirt and slacks with a snug leather choker. His skin was copper-brown—darker than she recalled—and his silken black hair was knotted in a ponytail that almost reached his hips.

The witch was so beautiful that she caught herself staring. She *never* stared at hot guys. That was Betty's job.

He ambled toward her, thumbs hooked in his belt loops. As he drew closer, she saw the slacks were made of leather. He didn't seem affected by the heat. "Where are

82

we going?" Elise asked, moving for the SUV. He stepped in her way. She frowned. "What are you doing? Let's go."

"I want to see the studio." But he was looking at her, not the building.

She didn't waver. Elise was all too aware that her uncomfortable alliance with the Night Hag didn't change the fact they were inherently enemies—nor did she harbor the illusion that Thom was under anyone's control but his own.

"You can't get inside. Wards."

"I sense that." Thom circled her. His gaze was not sexual, but analytical. "That outfit will not suffice. Put on a dress." Elise arched an eyebrow. "We are visiting one of the overlord's contacts to gather intelligence about Mr. Black. She's having a formal event tonight. Your current clothing is insufficient."

"I don't fight in dresses," she said. "Or formal shoes, for that matter."

"Then you cannot go to this event."

"Fine. Intelligence won't help us against Mr. Black anyway. It would be much faster if the Night Hag gave me a small army and let me kill him."

Thom's folded his arms. "I'm sure it would, but this is what she has ordered us to do."

The fresh brand on her shoulder itched as though to remind her of the agreement. Scratching it only made the pain worse. She sighed. "Fine. We can do it her way."

"Then you must change your outfit."

The idea of playing by the Night Hag's rules grated at her, but she had already made her decision when she let herself be branded. "Two minutes," she finally said.

Thom nodded.

Even before the fire, Elise didn't have formal clothing (much to Betty's dismay). She never had a reason to wear the quintessential "little black dress." She did, however, have a new red sundress, which she had purchased from a drugstore with one of her last ten dollar bills. It was the only way to survive the summer heat in Nevada. She borrowed a few pieces of Betty's jewelry that had survived the fire and twisted her hair into a loose bun to make it fancier. There was nothing to be done about her plain black gloves, or her exposed scars.

The witch sneered at her feet when she came downstairs. "Sandals."

"My house was burned down. This is what I have."

He dropped the subject, which was as close to acceptance as she expected to get.

The interior of Thom's SUV was plush leather, and it scorched the back of her knees when she sat down. She turned on his air conditioning. He had been driving with the windows rolled up and the fan turned off.

Thom drove like traffic laws didn't exist. He sliced between lanes and blew past every car on the road. Elise studied his profile while his attention was on his driving. Something about the curve of his lips and chin reminded her of ancient statues.

"Where are you from?" she asked.

"Before this, I was in New York City."

"That's not what I meant. Where are you from originally?"

"Originally." Thom rolled the word over his tongue. "I was born in a place currently known as Myanmar."

He didn't look very Asian. In fact, she couldn't have pinned a single ethnicity upon him if she tried. Elise had been all over the world and never seen anyone with his strange mix of features: full lips, sloped nose, wide eyes, chiseled jaw. It was as though each part of his face had been deliberately selected to be as ambiguous as possible.

"Tell me why a witch from Myanmar is working for the Night Hag."

Thom gave an elegant shrug. "It's something to do."

The air grew thick with tension after his seemingly casual response. He watched her from the corner of his eye. It only grew worse as they drove further from the studio. He hadn't done anything to indicate aggression, but the way he looked at her without looking made her skin crawl. And he resonated in her skull like a cracked bell struck by a steel mallet.

She wished the Night Hag had sent David Nicholas instead.

"You are familiar with prophecies," he said, breaking the silence.

"I don't believe in them."

"Elaborate."

They entered the twisting roads in the foothills, and he accelerated instead of slowing down. Elise put on her seatbelt. "By the Treaty of Dis, only humans have the gift of prophecy. They also only see what happens on this earthen plane. That makes them uselessly incomplete."

"True. But you would believe if a prophet could see more."

"That's not possible."

"A man named Benjamin Flynn has foretold the end of the world," Thom said as mildly as though he was sharing a weather report with her.

"That's far from the first time that's been seen." She stared out the window at the passing trees. "A kopis will take care of it. One of us always does."

"So far."

Her fingers twitched at the knife. "Why are you telling me?"

"Benjamin Flynn's prophesies are being logged. There are three volumes to date. I have read them." She caught a glimpse of his gaze reflected in the mirror. His irises were almost black. "The end of the world will be willfully brought about by a kopis. A kopis with magic."

"He's lying."

"Perhaps."

His voice curled around her as though it had substance. She suppressed a shudder.

Elise waited for him to say more, but he didn't speak again until they reached a gated neighborhood at the base of the mountain. He stopped in front of a manor sheltered by so many pine trees that they cast twilight over the property.

She scanned the grounds as Thom rolled down his window. Dozens of cars were parked in front, and she thought she could see valets. There were any number of places armed guards could hide. The ridge would be perfect for snipers, too. But the people she feared wouldn't attack like that. She was much more concerned about magical traps. If only James had been there to sense them.

Thom pushed the intercom button. A woman's voice responded. "Yes?"

His expression didn't change, but his voice became lively and friendly. Almost flirtatious. "Hello! This is Thomas Norrel. I'm here for the party with Ms. Redmond."

"A moment, please."

It fell silent and he sat back.

"Multiple personality disorder?" Elise asked.

The gate opened. Thom pulled forward. "I behave as is prudent for the situation at hand."

She tensed as they rolled onto Portia Redmond's property. People could have been hiding anywhere, watching her unseen. She hated being unable to detect wards. She wished for James again—working without him was like missing one of her hands.

"What do you feel, Thom?" she asked. He gave her a curious look. "This place. Are there any traps? Charms?

86

Spells?"

"That's irrelevant."

Thom stopped at the end of the circular driveway. He got out, handed the keys to an attractive teenage boy with long hair, and then opened the door for Elise. He offered a pale hand to her. Revulsion knotted in her gut.

"Come," he said when she didn't move.

Elise got out on her own and straightened her dress so it fell naturally over the concealed knife. She studied the entrance to the house as they approached. Tiny markings were carved over the doorway. There were crystals in a ceramic bowl at the corner of her porch. A decorative arrangement of flowers was mixed with sprigs of herbs. Portia definitely had a witch on staff. Her skin tingled as she crossed the threshold.

The sounds of laughter drifted through the entryway. Everything was furnished with dark wood and gold, and offset by velvet drapes the color of pine. A haze hung over the room, like dinner had burned in the oven.

"This way, sweetheart," Thom said. He led her to the den.

A man in a black suit played an antique piano in the corner. A double staircase swept around either side of the room, plush red couches had been placed underneath, and hookahs were set on low tables surrounded by pillows so people could lounge on the floor while smoking. They passed what looked like sparkling sugar cubes between them.

She edged around the room, trying to watch everyone at once. The hookah didn't concern her, but the cubes did. Elise had seen lethe parties before. It was a powerful drug designed to give a high to creatures whose bodies ignored most intoxicants—a huge rush for demons, and often fatal for humans.

And everyone on the floor was human. Judging by

their dress, they were businessmen and politicians. Older people. Beautiful people. People who might die if they dropped one too many lethe.

"Drink?"

Elise jerked away from the waitress she hadn't seen approach. She shook her head.

The waitress offered it to Thom instead, who plucked a glass off the tray. Each of them was filled with an unidentifiable green liquid. "Thank you. Tell me, where is the hostess?"

She pointed.

Portia Jericho sat stiffly on one of the red couches with a drink, a polite smile, and a man with a half-unbuttoned shirt hanging off her shoulder. She saw Thom approach and blanched. "I didn't invite you."

"Let's go somewhere private, Portia," Thom said in a suave and husky voice. He winked. Elise's jaw clenched. "Let me assure you, I'll only steal this beautiful creature for a few moments."

"I suppose I don't have a choice," Portia said.

She disentangled herself from the couch and smoothed shaking hands down her blouse. Elise kept an eye on the other alcoves, but nobody was sober enough to move, much less attack.

Portia led them upstairs to an office with a claw-footed desk and turned on a single lamp.

Elise gave the room a quick sweep. There were more enchanted stones by the window, more engravings, and more herbs disguised as floral arrangements. Passive defenses. She positioned herself in the corner so she could watch the door and window simultaneously.

"What do you want this time?" Portia asked, lowering herself into the chair behind the desk. Her hands were in constant motion—adjusting her hair, tugging on the neck of her shirt to hide her considerable cleavage, smoothing down her slacks. "And who are you supposed to be?"

It took Elise a moment to realize Portia was speaking to her.

"This is Elise Kavanagh," Thom said. He wasn't flirty anymore. His changes in mood were fast enough to give her whiplash. "She was once the greatest kopis, but now she is a lapdog of the Night Hag like the rest of us."

She bristled. "Excuse me?"

"Greatest? What made you the greatest?" Portia asked.

Elise opened her mouth, but Thom spoke again before she could get anything out. "They say she's killed a dozen angels."

Portia's face went slack, and she sagged against the back of her chair as if all the strength had suddenly drained from her. "Oh thank *God*," she whispered. Elise flinched. "Then you must have been hired to kill Mr. Black, haven't you? You have to be fast. He's got an army, and he's moving as we speak."

"Indeed. We need your information to take action."

"But I'm the only one who knows anything. If you stop the shipment, he'll know who betrayed him."

"A shipment of what, exactly?" Thom asked.

She fidgeted. "How should I know? Guns? I've given him a truck and a man to drive it. That's it. I'm not privy to his plans."

"Where is this truck going?"

"Thom—the Night Hag—"

He loomed over the desk. He wasn't much taller than Elise, but he suddenly seemed to fill the room. "Tell me."

Portia's lips trembled as she opened a desk drawer, pulled out a map, and began drawing lines. "Here. They're coming from a port in Long Beach and going to a temporary depot. It's been set up in a lake bed...there." Her fingers clutched the map tight. "Giving this to you could mean my death."

89

"Life is a fleeting illusion. Regardless, Mr. Black is not your only danger."

She whispered a prayer as she let go of the map.

At a glance from Thom, Elise stepped forward to take it. She couldn't find any pity within herself. A woman who knowingly dealt with rogue kopides and demonic overlords was no victim.

"Be fast," Portia whispered. "Please. For everyone's sake."

Elise stepped back. Thom opened the door.

"Enjoy your party," he said.

Portia didn't follow them onto the balcony overlooking the lethe party. As soon as the door swung shut, Elise turned on him. "What was the point of that? You didn't need me to help collect information. She's scared shitless. You could have—"

"Silence. Tell me what you see."

She frowned. "Rich people on drugs."

"And?"

Elise gave the room a second look. It was hard to make anything out through the haze of tobacco and lethe beside the occasional flash of a glowing cube, like the flare of a firework. Then a glint of metal caught her eye, and she realized one of the men on the arm of a wealthy socialite was wearing a shackle. It was a bewitched shackle, with no visible chains, but a shackle nonetheless. There was a glimmer in the corner of her eye, a tugging at the back of her neck.

"Magic," she murmured. "That's magic, isn't it?"

Thom leaned over her shoulder, cheek brushing hers. His body was warm at her back. "Why would a kopis sense magic?"

She didn't think he expected an answer, so she didn't try to give one. Once Elise saw the magic around the shackle, she saw it elsewhere, too—twinkling on a

90

woman's earring, haloed around the head of a gray-haired man, on several other wrists. They weren't all in the form of bracelets. Some were necklaces. One was an anklet.

The bound ones weren't smiling, as the others were. All of them had pale blue eyes that were almost silver. And the resemblance didn't end there. Though none had hair or skin of quite the same shade, they all looked similar to the degree that cousins looked similar. Smooth-faced, androgynous, ageless.

None of them were human.

Elise gripped the railing. "Angels," she said, her voice so soft she thought Thom wouldn't hear.

Fingers grazed the back of her neck. "Look closer."

It was like a fog lifted from her mind. She could suddenly sense them the same way she sensed demons, and what was more, she could *see* them. Ghostly stubs glowed at their scapulas. Their wings had been severed, and someone was hiding it. They were enslaved.

"Now you know why I brought you to this party. You had to see—and be seen. Mr. Black will know the sword has come into play."

"He's not the only one who will know. Damn it, Thom, you never should have brought me here."

Even though she whispered, her voice caught the attention of an angel. Recognition sparked between them.

One by one, the slaves fell silent, and a dozen pairs of eyes fixed on her.

Their lips moved in unison to mouth a single word with three syllables. She didn't hear them, but she knew what word it was, and what it meant.

"This was a mistake," Elise said.

"A calculated risk." His hand curled around her wrist. "And now we must run."

Her eyes lifted to the opposite balcony. A gaunt man with shaggy brown hair stood on the other side, and hatred carved furrows into his sagging face. The years hadn't been kind to Alain Daladier. He looked like hell.

Elise retreated into the shadows, but it was too late to hide. He reached into his jacket.

Thom flashed down the stairs, and she ran after him.

A gunshot rang out above them. A bullet smacked into the railing. Wood shattered.

The angels didn't react, but the humans did. Bleary eyes stared around for the source of the gunshot. Someone cried out in surprise as Elise shoved through the room. Her knee bumped a table and sent the hookah crashing to the ground. A man tumbled off his pillow, and she jumped over him.

Still, the angels didn't move. Their eyes tracked her across the room.

Another gunshot cracked like thunder. It shattered a wall sconce as Elise passed it, raining glass into her hair.

Thom ran like the wind blew, shoving open the front door and disappearing into the night. Elise flung herself around the side of the door, drew her knife, and dropped into a crouch.

Her heart wasn't even beating hard. She felt calm, focused, like she was floating apart from her own body.

People screamed inside. She waited.

Footsteps pounded through the entryway. Her fist tightened on the dagger.

Alain took two steps out the door, and Elise jumped on his back, bringing her arm around his throat. His skeletal body buckled under hers. He gave a strangled grunt as they fell down the steps and hit the driveway face-first, tossing her off his back.

She rolled. Got to her feet. Pressed the knife to his belly.

Cold metal pressed into her temple before she could stab.

Alain bared his teeth in a vicious growl as he held the

gun to her skull. "*Va te faire foutre,*" he spat, and she felt his arm tense as he squeezed the trigger.

Elise dropped.

The gunshot blasted over her head and shattered her hearing into a thousand shards of glass. The ringing almost muted Alain's shout.

Thom had appeared, shoving the wrist holding the gun so it aimed skyward. Another shot flashed and filled the air with the metallic tang of gunpowder. Thom twisted Alain's arm around, smashed it into his knee, and forced him to drop the gun.

Even while grappling, Thom looked peaceful. Almost amused.

He shoved Alain to the ground and planted a foot in his chest. Elise grabbed the gun and dropped the magazine.

Mr. Black's aspis looked so much older than he had ten years before. There were burn scars on his neck, purple spots on the backs of his hands, and scruffy white stubble on his jaw. But some things didn't change. His mouth twisted when Elise came to stand over him.

"You burned my office," she said, barely able to hear her own voice over the ringing in her skull. "You stole all my money!"

His mouth moved with a response. She was sure it would have been scathing if she could have heard it.

And then there was suddenly a second gun in his hand.

This time, Elise moved faster than Thom. She threw herself out of the way, instinctively shielding her face with her arms—though there was little that could do about a bullet aimed at her skull.

The bullet hit Thom. He fell to the lawn.

Alain scrambled to his feet and vanished into the trees.

Elise was a heartbeat behind him. She crashed into the

edge of the forest.

His back darted between the tree trunks. Branches scraped against Elise's bare legs. Her strappy sandals caught on a bush, wrenched her ankle to the side, and sent her stumbling. "Shit!"

Her knees smashed against rocks. Pine needles stabbed into her gloves. She righted herself, staggering around a tree to pick up the knife she dropped. By the time she found it, it was too late—the night was dark and complete, and Alain Daladier had vanished.

Elise swore as she ripped the shoes off her feet and flung them into the night.

She limped back to the lawn after a few more minutes of searching, working her jaw around to clear her ringing skull. Kopides had improved healing in comparison to other humans, but the whine in her ears didn't make her optimistic about her ability to hear that pitch ever again.

Thom met her at the end of the driveway. His hair was still in a neat ponytail. There wasn't so much as a single grass stain or a drop of blood on his tidy clothes. "You're alive," Elise said, a little disappointed. "Where did he hit you?"

"You must be confused. I wasn't shot."

She frowned. "But you fell."

"Perhaps I was surprised," Thom said. He kept one eye on the house as though waiting for another attack. "Come. We must hurry to use our brief advantage. If Mr. Black and Alain realize what we've learned, their plans will surely change."

He set a swift pace to the SUV, which was parked with other cars at the side of the house. Elise lengthened her stride to keep up with him even though it made her ankle twinge. "The Night Hag should send someone to protect Portia. When Mr. Black finds out—"

"She's not your concern."

The fluttering of curtains caught her attention, and Elise faltered mid-step.

Angels watched through the windows. They had lined up along the bottom floor shoulder-to-shoulder, silent and calm, and every one of those pale blue eyes was fixed on her. Or, to be more specific, her gloved hands.

Waiting. Expectant.

"Yeah," she muttered. "Fuck you guys, too."

TWELVE

BETTY DOZED IN a drugged haze. Pain kept her on the edge of consciousness. The saline drip was cool where they had taped it against the inside of her arm. The bed hissed and swelled as the mattress inflated, and then sighed as it deflated again. The machines by her head occasionally beeped.

She drifted through dreams of fire and smoke. Occasionally, a nurse would wake her up, but she never opened her eyes. It was too hard. It felt like all the moisture had been sucked from her eyeballs.

A dry cough made her chest hitch. Her fingers twitched for the nurse call button.

Morphine. Her bag had run empty, and she could feel it wearing off.

Metal rattled, and a sliver of light fell on her face. Betty finally peeled open her eyelids. Someone was moving around the foot of her bed, but she couldn't tell who had come to torment her with more diagnostics in the middle of night.

"What time is it?" she rasped.

Footsteps tracked past the sink. Cabinets opened and closed.

She let her eyelids slide shut again.

"Stephanie—Dr. Whyte—said no more tests until

morning. I'm resting 'under sedation.' Supposedly," Betty said. Her irritated throat tickled. Another cough. She stretched a hand toward a glass of water, but couldn't reach. "I'm leaving in a few hours. All I want is sleep and more painkillers and no more shots in my ass."

Plastic crinkled, and then the door to the hallway closed, leaving the room in darkness.

Betty sighed in relief. It burned all the way down her chest.

But the visitor hadn't left. The curtain closed around her, and someone stepped up with a spare pillow from the wardrobe by the window.

Her fingers fell on the remote. She clicked on the overhead light.

The person at her bedside wasn't any of the nurses who paraded through in the last day, though she wore scrubs patterned with red geometric shapes. She was silken-haired with windblown features and delicate hands, which were wrapped around the pillow. Her pupils didn't dilate at the sudden light.

She was sober enough that the strange gaze struck a chord. "You're not here with morphine…are you?"

The nurse lifted her arms.

Betty realized what was about to happen an instant before the pillow mashed against her face and cut off her air supply. Her chest hitched as her lungs struggled to expand, but there was nothing to fill them.

She tried to scream. It came out as a muffled squeal.

The nurse pressed harder. Betty fumbled for the nurse call button and knocked the remote off the bed. Even though she had a full breath of air, sudden adrenaline killed all rationality.

She beat against the arms pinning her down. They felt doughy, boneless, but somehow as immobile as steel. Her hazy head grew thicker. Her pulse pounded in her temples. White noise roared through her ears.

The mattress inflated around her and deflated again.

Betty felt oblivion creeping up on her as her oxygen ran out. If it took her, she didn't think she would ever wake again.

She tried harder to fight, but her arms were heavy and weak. Betty's blood grew sluggish. Her limbs went limp. She screamed and screamed on the inside, but it didn't make a difference—and soon, even that grew faint.

This never would have happened to Elise.

"Hey—*hey*! What are you doing?"

And all that weight was suddenly gone.

Betty shoved the pillow off her face. Color rushed into her vision with a huge gasp of air. She gripped her chest in both hands, making the IV twist in her vein. *Oh God, that hurt.*

Black stars cleared from her vision. The nurse had plastered her back on the wall between two cabinets, and Betty realized with a jolt that her feet weren't on the ground. She was halfway to the ceiling like a bug on a window.

Anthony lunged for her. The nurse scrambled higher on the wall with jerky motions, then leaped and landed behind him.

He spun, swinging a hard right hook. His fist connected with the nurse's jaw.

Her head snapped off.

Betty shrieked, hands flying to her mouth. The nurse's body collapsed like an empty skin suit, and Anthony hollered as he jumped back. "What the *fuck*?"

The head rolled under the cabinet. Empty eyes glimmered at them.

A bulge shifted inside the body, like a balloon inflating inside what used to be the belly, and Anthony grabbed the chair from the bedside. He lifted it over his head and

98

brought it crashing down on the pile of scrubs.

Something squealed and popped. Black fluid gushed out the neck hole.

"Oh, Jesus fucking Christ!" He smashed the chair on it again, and again. And then he slammed his booted foot into it for good measure.

Then he stepped back, shielding Betty with his body, and held the chair in front of him like a lion tamer. But the body didn't move again. He dropped the chair and fell into it, face pale.

"Are you okay?" Anthony asked. He was surprisingly calm, considering he had just decapitated an evil assassin nurse.

"Someone just tried to kill me," gasped Betty. The truth of it sank in, and tremors shuddered through her entire body. "Oh my *God* someone just tried to *kill me*! Why would someone want to kill *me*? I'm just a—I mean—"

"Hey, relax, it's okay."

Betty leaned forward to grab his shirt in both hands, dragging his face close to hers. "You don't get it! Somebody wants to *kill me*!"

"I heard you the first six times. Take a deep breath and lay back before you hurt yourself."

She shook him. "Don't you try to act like this isn't a big deal!"

Anthony gently disengaged her fingers from his shirt. "I *know* it's a big deal, but it *is* okay because they didn't succeed. You're alive. All right?"

"No! Not all right!"

The door opened. Anthony shifted his chair on top of the flesh pile on the floor as a man stepped into the room. Betty saw scrubs and shrieked.

"What's going on?" asked the nurse. He had brown eyes, three chins, and greasy skin. Just like a human should. Totally normal. The empty, rubbery arm of the body was still visible, so Anthony kicked it under the bed.

"Night terrors," he said.

"I thought I heard something fall."

"Nope," Anthony said, his voice an octave too high. "Just night terrors." He plastered a grin on his face. Betty followed suit.

The nurse obviously didn't believe them, but seemed too tired to push it. "Try to keep it down. People in the ward are sleeping."

"I want to check out," Betty said.

"It's after midnight."

"Yeah, but I'm ready to go now. I'm feeling much better!" She was certain her grin must have been manic and ridiculous. "This hospital sure is great!"

He looked dubious. "Let me go talk to the doctor."

The nurse left. Anthony and Betty both sagged.

"I'll call Elise," he said.

Betty snorted. It hurt her raw nasal passage. "Yeah. Obviously."

Anthony half-carried Betty up the stairs to the apartment above Motion and Dance. She was still too woozy from the leftover morphine to navigate the steps herself.

"I must be important," she said again. "They don't try to kill the unimportant people."

He rolled his eyes. "You are very important."

"Maybe I've scared someone. You know, I've been working on my magic." She wiggled her fingers at him, like she was pretending to shoot lightning from her fingertips. "Oh yeah. Bet someone caught wind that there's a powerful new player in town. Wicked witch of the west. Protégé to James Faulkner, the greatest aspis in the world."

"You're about as wicked as a ball of yarn," Anthony

said. He knocked on the door and propped Betty against the railing to wait.

"A ball of yarn who can light a candle *with her brain*."

"I thought you inhaled too much smoke to speak."

Betty stuck her tongue out. "Sure, you're not afraid now, but just wait. Candles today. Whole cities tomorrow."

Elise opened the door. She took one look at them and went rigid. "Get in," she said, grabbing Betty's arm to pull her inside.

"I'll be right back," Anthony said.

He ran downstairs and grabbed the trash bag out of his trunk. Sneaking a boneless corpse out of a hospital had been easy at two in the morning. Getting Betty out had been harder. Finding someone to disconnect her from the IV had taken an hour, and Anthony kept expecting another creepy flesh-sack to attack in the meantime.

The body in the bag had begun to smell on the ride home, and now the entire Jeep reeked of sulfur and rot. His hands slipped on the plastic when he grabbed it.

"Oh man," he groaned. Some of the black fluids had eaten holes in the bag. His skin tingled on contact.

Elise met him at the top of the stairs. "Bathtub."

They dumped it in the bathroom without opening the bag. She turned the on the sink so hot it steamed the mirror and sprayed soap in Anthony's hand. The tingles were starting to become a painful itch. His skin was raw and red underneath.

"Did we wake you up?" he asked, shutting off the faucet with an elbow and drying off using embroidered hand towels cannibalized from the studio downstairs.

"No," Elise said.

He stepped back to take a look at her. She was beautiful with her red-brown curls piled on her head and a dress that hit just above the knees. "I guess we didn't. What were you doing this evening?"

101

"There's a dead body in the tub and you're interested in my night. I'm a bad influence."

Anthony plucked a piece of glass out of her hair and dropped it in the sink. "You look great."

"Uh huh."

Betty was half-asleep on the couch in the living room. "They tried to kill me. I must be important," she mumbled. Her injuries from the fire were covered in some kind of plastic, and the skin beneath it was completely raw.

Elise and Anthony went to a corner of the kitchen to talk without disturbing her. "Tell me what happened."

Anthony whispered a quick and dirty rundown, and by the time he finished, Elise was pacing. Her face was drawn into a grim mask. Her lips were white around the edges. "You'll have to stay here until I take care of this. Both of you. You can't leave the warded perimeter of the studio. It's not safe."

"But my job—" Anthony protested.

"They're watching me. They know who I'm spending time with. You can stay here or die."

"Why? Who is 'they'? What do 'they' want?"

She frowned. "That's not important right now. I have to do an autopsy before the acid destroys my evidence. We still have plastic sheeting from renovating the garage. I'll be right back."

Elise ran downstairs. "Why does she always do that?" Anthony asked the closed door.

Betty hugged a pillow to her chest as she sat up. Her face was still all puffy from the saline drip. "What, pretend you're too dumb to understand what's happening?"

"Yeah. That."

"Maybe because we're too dumb to understand what's happening."

"You're lucky you almost died or I'd kill you myself," Anthony muttered.

When Elise came back, she cut wide swaths of plastic sheeting off the roll and laid them across the kitchen floor. He would have helped, but Betty had become demanding again. She had a whole list of things she "needed," which included a glass of water, Tylenol, and a snack. Preferably cookie dough.

"What do you want now? Your teddy bear?" Anthony asked, exasperated.

"Do you think I'm twelve or something? I'll settle for a shot of tequila." She pressed a hand to her stomach. "Woo, those IV fluids aren't joking around. You could float me over a football stadium right now. I've got to pee like a pregnant woman. Help me up?" Betty stretched her hands toward Anthony. He obediently hauled her to her feet and watched to make sure she arrived safely at the bathroom.

"Two assassination attempts, and Betty's still Betty," Elise said, unrolling another yard of plastic and slicing it with a box cutter. She actually sounded affectionate.

"The entire world could catch fire and Betty would still be Betty."

"Don't tempt fate."

He helped her tape sheeting over the dining room table, which they had positioned in the middle of the kitchen. Once Betty surrendered the bathroom, Elise donned yellow rubber gloves and took the trash bag out of the tub.

The flesh suit spilled onto the table like a hunk of jelly. Anthony covered his nose.

"Jeez. Smells like locker room."

Elise peeled back the eyelids on the head. "Black irises," she muttered.

"What's that mean?"

"On its own, nothing. A lot of ugly things have black eyes." She set the head down. The neck was hollow and couldn't support its weight, so it tipped onto its side. The

103

mouth hung open.

"Turn that away from me," Betty said over the back of the couch. Anthony did as she asked.

"Go to sleep. You don't need to watch this."

"Are you kidding? And miss the show?"

Elise ignored them as she sorted out body parts to make it lay flat. She palpated the bulging abdomen, and fluid squirted from the neck hole. "Interesting," she said, separating the skin and peering inside.

He grimaced. "You're not going to—"

She reached inside. Anthony's stomach churned, but he couldn't seem to make himself turn away.

Elise's hand disappeared first, and then her elbow, and then her entire arm up to the elbow. It was like her arm vanished. The body didn't even bulge. "Interdimensional pouch," she explained when she saw his face. "It's an infernal power."

"Oh. Yeah. Of course."

She extracted something as thick as a tree branch and covered in wiry hair. Elise set it on the table and reached inside for more. She pulled out four of them before Anthony realized that he had seen something like them before. "Those look like spider legs. Like what we found in the desert."

"Mary Poppins would love this," Betty said.

Elise shoved the box cutter into the neck hole. Her face went slack with concentration as her back muscles worked.

A long minute later, she withdrew a strip of flesh covered in glistening black fluid—and demonic brands.

"Bring me the binder on the coffee table," she said.

Anthony flipped it open to the page marked by a sticky note. Elise had drawn a list of brands on the page and labeled them with "desert daimarachnid" and the date they had been camping. He held it up so she could see. Each brand matched, all the way down to the extra marks

104

that obscured them.

"Does this mean the assassin was a giant spider in a human skin suit?"

"I'm saying it's a giant spider in a skin suit owned by the same master demon as the last one." She set down the skin, peeled off the rubber gloves, and scrubbed her arms in the sink. Her skin was red from the venom. "But it's impossible. Mr. Black has angels, not spiders."

Betty sat up. "Angels?"

"Long story." Elise rolled everything up in plastic and duct taped it together so it wouldn't leak. The resulting mummy looked way too much like a small human body. "I'll dump this while I'm in the desert later today. I have to make our new favorite enemy have a very bad day."

Anthony brightened. "You're going to attack the guy who's been after us? This Mr. Black? Then I'm coming too."

"Fine. I can put your mechanic skills to use on this one. But that's not for a couple hours, so you should both sleep while we can."

Ignoring Betty's protests, Elise put her in James's bed, gave her a glass of water, and shut the door. Then she pulled extra sheets out of the linen closet and dropped them on the couch.

"Where are you sleeping?" he asked.

"I'm not."

He pulled his shirt off. Even though he had recovered a few things from his closet at home, including his trusty shotgun, pajamas hadn't been amongst them. "We could sleep on the floor together. There's plenty of room."

"I said I'm not sleeping." Elise's tone was curt, but she softened the delivery by dropping a kiss on his shoulder.

"What do you want to do if you're not sleeping?" he asked, lowering his voice so Betty wouldn't hear if she was still awake. He touched Elise's hip. Her eyebrows lifted.

"Seriously?"

"I don't think I told you how hot you look in that dress," he said, hooking a finger under one of the straps.

"What is it with you and giant spiders?" She spread her gloved hands across his broad chest and kissed his chin. "You've got serious issues."

"Coming from you, that means a lot."

She actually kind of giggled—or at least, what was a giggle for Elise, which was more of a growl. Anthony loved that he could make her do that.

He lifted her onto the back of the couch, pushed the dress up her thighs, and pressed himself between her legs. She was wearing a concealed knife, and she smelled like summer heat and sweat. Anthony wanted to devour her.

Having sex with Elise was never like "making love." Anthony had two girlfriends in high school that had been fun and affectionate and sometimes a little wild, but with Elise, it was more like fighting a forest fire. She didn't know how to surrender or be vulnerable. And she was never affectionate.

When he tried to bend her back for a kiss, she climbed his body and dug her fingernails into his shoulders instead. When he tried to pull off her underwear, she locked her legs around him. He tried to grab her wrists and found himself pushed back against the kitchen table. The plastic sheeting crinkled under him.

It was an unpleasant reminder that they hadn't gotten rid of the body, and that someone was trying to kill Elise's friends. It should have been scary. But maybe she was right about him having issues. The adrenaline only made his blood run hotter.

He tugged the straps of her dress down her shoulders and found she wasn't wearing a bra.

"You did that on purpose," he groaned as he palmed one of breasts, which had a thick ridge of scar tissue down

106

the side.

She ripped his belt out so hard that one of the loops popped.

"Hey!" Anthony protested.

Another little growl of laughter. "Deal with it."

He caught her lips with his and kissed her, long and hard. When he finally pulled back to take a breath, her eyes were lidded and her cheeks were flushed. She really could be so beautiful sometimes. Beautiful, and scary.

"Do you ever think about the future?" Anthony murmured into her neck, trailing his hand down her thigh. His fingers traced along the edge of the knife's sheath.

"No."

"But it can't be like this forever. Giant spiders and assassins." He kissed the soft hairs behind her ear and was rewarded with a shiver.

She still managed to sound stern when she responded, even though her voice had taken a husky edge. "You're optimistic."

Anthony leaned back. He searched her face and found no hint of joking in it. "You retired once. You could do it again."

"I don't think about the future. I'm too busy surviving today." Elise popped his fly open and snaked a hand into his boxers. "Why are you talking?"

Normally, he would have been happy to shut his mouth and enjoy himself. But her resistance to talking irked him. "What about...you know...marriage?" It was too hard to talk while she was stroking him. He caught her wrist. "Children? We're young, and there's lots of time..."

Her whole body went rigid. She pulled her hand out of his pants.

He realized belatedly that he had said something wrong, but he wasn't sure what offended her more: the idea of quitting again, or the idea of a family?

She stepped back and he didn't fight her. "You won't bring that subject up with me again."

Anthony laughed shakily. "We're dating, Elise. This isn't some taboo subject. I know you're not used to any of this stuff, but I can tell you it's normal for people like us to talk about things like that."

She pulled her dress over those gorgeous breasts again. It was like throwing a steel-clad door between them. "I will never have children," Elise said. "Kopides don't do that. And I'm never getting married, either."

It was hardly the coldest thing she had ever said to him, but it still felt a little like getting punched below the belt. "If we don't have a future, then what are we doing? What's the point?"

"We have sex. We spend time together. Isn't that good?"

"But what about a year from now? Five years?"

She fluffed the skirt out where it had become stuck in the thigh sheath. "I've told you what I think. You know what? I have things to do. You need to stay here and watch Betty."

"Yeah, but where—?"

Before he could finish the question, Elise threw the remaining pieces of the daimarachnid's body over her shoulder and went downstairs, leaving Anthony alone.

He tried to get comfortable on the couch, but it was strange being in James's apartment. Everything smelled like sage and jasmine and someone else's aftershave. It didn't help that his feet hung off the edge and that he still had half an erection that was quickly losing all hope.

Pulling the sheets up to his chin, he tried not to imagine the shadows on the ceiling were demons oozing with black pus.

After a few minutes, he heard the chain of the punching bag rattle downstairs.

THIRTEEN

ELISE CALLED JAMES'S cell phone twice and hung up on the first ring both times. She glared at his name on her contact list.

He would want to know about Betty. He deserved to know what was going on. But every time she thought about his loafers at the side of the bed, lonely without the rest of his belongings, she found herself punching the off button again.

Before she could decide if she should try to call again, her phone rang. It was Stephanie on the other end.

"If you're trying to reach James, that's not the way to do it." She sounded exasperated. "He's at a rehearsal downtown and forgot his phone. All you're doing is preventing me from getting enough sleep for my shift tonight."

"Fine," Elise said.

"Why did Betty leave the hospital early?"

She didn't feel like explaining. The good doctor would have only taken it as another sign that she was a bad influence who shouldn't be allowed around normal people. Instead, she turned her phone off.

Hanging up had never been so satisfying.

It was almost eleven, but Anthony and Betty were still sleeping. Her boyfriend was sprawled across the couch with his arms and legs hanging off the side. She stood over him with her arms folded as he slept. Marriage. Kids. Three months together, and he had never once made the mistake of mentioning "the future." It left a foul taste in her mouth.

He didn't even twitch as Elise banged around in search of clothes. She ended up donning one of Anthony's shirts and the same jogging shorts she had been wearing the day before.

Her car smelled of brimstone, even though the body in the trunk was thoroughly wrapped in plastic. She yanked the air freshener off the mirror and tossed it in the back before parking in a garage downtown.

It wasn't hard to find out which theater was holding their dress rehearsals. The show James was choreographing was a major production, so there were signs plastered all over the casino to advertise it. Even so, it took Elise a few minutes to navigate the gloomy floors of the casino. Like all businesses of its type, it was designed to trap tourists among the slot machines with black walls, mirrored ceilings, and confusing signs.

She slipped in the side door behind the box office. It was propped open with an empty water bottle.

The theater smelled like fresh paint and turpentine. Pieces of the set were in place while others were assembled near the orchestra pit by stagehands. She picked a seat in the back of the theater and sat down.

"One more time, from the top," James said from the front row. He wore sweats and a shirt with the studio logo across the back.

When he gestured, a tech in the sound booth started the song again.

Elise watched the dancers, some of whom were in the bulkier pieces of their costumes, with mild bemusement. She had never been a big fan of casino shows. There was

110

far too much glitter for her tastes.

"Having fun playing voyeur?"

David Nicholas had joined her. He draped himself over the chair at her side, reeking of cigarette smoke and filth.

"You're here," she said.

"Where else would I be? Unless you finished the Night Hag's to-do list and stuck that kopis six feet deep, I'm still on babysitting duty."

"You won't be much longer."

"Good. Want a smoke?"

Elise curled her lip at the proffered cigarette. David Nicholas was even fleshier than before. His shoulders were broader, his jaw was squarer, and he was starting to look like a thug instead of a dying addict. "Has anything come near James yet?"

"Nah. Too bad, huh? Sure would make this a hell of a lot more fun. I can only watch this guy bone his girlfriend so many times before it gets boring." At Elise's glare, he gave a helpless shrug. "Gotta keep my eye on him. What if the doctor tried to stab him or something? Sure would be a shame if I missed it."

"If anything happens to James, I will exorcise you to Hell. And then I'll come down, find what remains of your corporeal body, and remove your skin with a rusty potato peeler."

He clucked his tongue. "Naughty, naughty. Remember what the Night Hag said about playing nice."

"Fuck playing nice. You and I both know we'll settle this the instant our truce is over anyway."

"Oh, yes." David Nicholas bared his yellow teeth in a grin that stretched back to flash every molar. It was a coyote grin, inhuman and hungry. "We definitely will."

"But your problem is with me. Don't touch James."

He laid a hand on his heart. "I wouldn't *dream* of it."

The music reached a crescendo. James walked onstage,

111

clapping his hands to attract the attention of the dancers. He all but glided inches off the ground. Of all the things that brought him joy—magic and music and teaching his students—nothing made him radiate like being in his element.

Watching him gather the dancers made jealousy wash over Elise. There was a time he only smiled like that for her, like when they managed to save someone or won a vicious battle.

She realized she was staring and turned back to make a parting shot at David Nicholas, but there was only emptiness beside her. He wouldn't be far away. Nightmares never were. "I mean it," she whispered. "Don't touch him."

If the nightmare was listening, he didn't reply.

Elise found a program left on one of the seats and scrawled a note in the margin: *Anthony and I are making a move against Mr. Black. I'll call you when I'm done.* She didn't bother signing it.

When the music played again, James stayed upstage to watch the chorus line. She sneaked up to his pile of towels and tucked the program at the bottom.

She didn't stick around to watch anything else.

Anthony and Elise stopped at a taco truck to pick up dinner before getting gasoline at the corner station. He ate as she filled a half dozen red jugs and loaded them in the cargo area of the Jeep. They had moved the body of the daimarachnid nurse behind the seats, too, and covered it in sweaters and trash to make it look unremarkable.

Elise paid for their food and gas in cash. She grimaced at the last twenty in her wallet.

"I could pay for some of this," he suggested.

112

She snapped her wallet shut. "Don't worry about it."

They headed north out of the city, beyond the last housing development and into hills filled with wild horses. Evening fell fast in the valleys beyond civilization. The sky caught fire in a desert sunset, striping a violet sky with pink clouds and tinting the sagebrush blue.

Elise spoke on her cell phone for a long time as she drove. Actually, she didn't talk so much as listen, punctuating the conversation with an occasional, "Okay," or "Fine."

"Who was that?" Anthony asked when she hung up without saying goodbye.

"That was the people I'm working with on this raid. They were arranging to pick up the cargo."

"And who is 'they'?"

"A demonic overlord and her court of nightmares. Nobody important."

Anthony couldn't tell if she was joking.

She steered the Jeep off the road, navigating carefully around the largest of rocks. Night sank over them, and soon they could only see within the beam of the headlights.

When they reached the top of a hill overlooking a dry lake bed, she turned the Jeep off and double-checked her map.

"This is it," she said, peering through binoculars to the playa below.

There were lights at the other end of the valley. Wind rustled through the hills, carrying the sweet smell of sagebrush past them. The desert had probably gotten well over a hundred degrees earlier in the day, but the wind was already beginning to cool, and he found himself shivering. "See anything?" he asked.

"The odds aren't good," Elise said, lowering the binoculars. She tucked a dagger into her belt at the small of

113

her back. "Probably a dozen guys out there. One per pickup. No sign of the semi yet."

"What's the plan?"

"I want you to disable the trucks so they can't get away with the shipment."

He held out a hand for the binoculars, and Elise passed them over.

They had assembled a loading bay in the middle of the desert and lit it with a generator-powered floodlight. He could make out the fleet of trucks, but he wasn't sure how Elise deduced the number of people.

"It's going to take a while to disable them all. I have to get into each glove box and pull the fuse for the fuel pump relay."

"My contact said the semi should be due in about..." She checked the map again. "Twenty minutes from now. We need to be in and out before they realize their trucks won't start."

"What if they see us?" Anthony asked.

She just looked at him. Shadows carved her face with deep crags and harsh lines. It was the face of someone who had gone against such odds before and come out alive. He felt immediately stupid for asking.

"We kill them," she said.

Anthony nodded and swallowed hard.

Elise took a moment to roll her shoulders and touch her toes, going through the motions of stretching while Anthony refilled the gas tank for a quick getaway. He dumped the plastic-wrapped body down a ditch, which felt like it had been almost entirely dissolved by venom, then fit his shotgun into his back scabbard and gave her a thumbs up.

She ran, and he hurried to follow.

The desert rushed past him. Elise dodged around the sagebrush and rocks and he followed. *It's just like our camping trip*, he told himself again, and he tried not think about their odds of coming back.

There was no subtlety in their run, no grace. The semi couldn't get to the bay before they did.

When they drew within a hundred meters of the ring of light, Elise stopped. He was breathing hard. He didn't do nearly enough cardio to keep up. "You good?" she asked, and he nodded as he wheezed. "We'll sneak around back." Another nod.

The men talked loudly by the loading bay—something about bitches and liquor—and didn't notice their approach. Elise and Anthony ran to the tall end of the loading bay.

She crouched behind it, pulled him down beside her, and peeked over the top of the wooden platform.

The pickups were parked in two neat rows. Most of the drivers talked and smoked in a cluster by the light, leaving the vehicles unattended. Why worry? They were hours from the city. "Fifteen guards," she whispered. "They're human. And armed."

He opened his mouth to speak, but she put a finger over his lips. Then she slid around the side of the loading bay, and he followed.

One man, a big guy with a tattoo of a kitten on his wrist, stood aloof from the others. Metal glinted under his untucked shirt. A gun. Great.

Elise pointed to the nearest truck. He crawled forward, keeping an eye on Kitten, and reached up to try the passenger door. It was unlocked. He reached in and opened the fuse box on the glove compartment. Removing the fuse for the fuel pump, he shut the door as quietly as possible and slipped back.

He showed her the number on the fuse. She moved for the next truck. Together, they worked their way up the lines. Each pickup drew them closer to Kitten and all the other men.

"My fucking wife just doesn't get it," one of the guards muttered. He offered a joint to the man next to him. "She's gotten fat, sure, but that doesn't mean I don't love her. I don't want anyone else."

"Even Candi?" chuckled a third man with a Disturbed concert t-shirt.

"Candi. Mm hmm. I'd like to stick it in that bitch," said the second, passing the joint back.

Anthony eased another door open and pulled the fuse. He took a quick count of how many he had in his pocket— five. Elise wasn't far behind in the other row.

"Fuck Candi, man. No way some slut makes steak as good as my woman. I'd never trade that in."

Only two vans between Anthony and Kitten. He searched for Elise amongst the other vehicles, but he couldn't see her. He did, however, see a pair of approaching headlights on the horizon.

The semi.

"What are *you*?"

He jerked up just in time to see Kitten looming over the van, an arm braced on the open door. His muscles bulged with veins.

"Uh," Anthony said in a stroke of brilliance.

Kitten clapped a hand on his shoulder and flung him into the crowd of drivers.

Shoulder met playa, and the breath rushed out of his body. Anthony groaned and rolled onto his knees. "What's this? We got a visitor!" crowed Disturbed.

Someone kicked him in the ribs. It was like getting slammed by a sledgehammer, and it shot spikes of pain into his groin.

He fell on his side again. Someone laughed a hyena laugh—a skinny man with a tattoo on his neck that said "Bad" in gothic letters—and he was echoed by others.

Kitten leaned over him. "What are you doing all the way out here? What is that you're wearing, a backpack?" He shoved Anthony's head to the side. "Kid's got a shotgun."

The tone immediately went from jovial to serious. Kitten eased a semi-automatic handgun out of his shoulder rig, and Anthony heard the telltale click of a safety turning off.

"On your knees," Kitten ordered.

He complied, moving slowly even as every nerve in his body begged him to run. He tried not to search for Elise, but he couldn't help but steal a few looks out of the corner of his eye as he got up. Anthony linked his hands behind his head and stared down Kitten's gun.

One of the men took the shotgun out of his scabbard, tossing it aside.

"I'm… I was just…" His mouth was dry, and he couldn't seem to think of the words he wanted to say.

"What are you doing out here?" Kitten asked again.

His mouth moved soundlessly. After a few monosyllabic attempts at speaking, Anthony finally said, "Camping. And…and hunting. Coyotes."

Kitten guffawed. "We look like coyotes to you?"

Following his cue, the other guards laughed as well. Anthony caught a flash of motion out of the corner of his eye. Elise ran from one truck to the next. She wasn't being as subtle now that he had everyone's attention.

"N-no," Anthony stammered. "I thought…uh…"

"Woo-ee! Little boy's going to shit his pants."

"What are we going to do?" another asked, glancing uneasily toward the approaching headlights at the end of the playa. "The boss will be pissed he finds out someone saw us."

"Take him out a half a mile and shoot him," Kitten said. He pointed at Disturbed. "You. Now. Make it fast."

117

The bright lights swirled around Anthony. *Shoot him*? He didn't feel like he was going to "shit his pants," but passing out wasn't off the menu, either.

Elise wouldn't let him get shot. She would save him. Wouldn't she?

Disturbed yanked Anthony to his feet by the back of his shirt and aimed a submachine gun at his midsection. "Walk," he ordered, aiming Anthony toward the nearest edge of the playa.

He briefly contemplated a struggle, but the logistics of an unarmed man against a dozen others wasn't pretty. But the pain was still radiating from his gut to his balls, his heart was about to splatter in his chest, and he thought he was going to lose his taco dinner in the dirt.

"I was just camping," he said.

The gun nudged him in the back.

So Anthony walked.

With every footstep, his head felt lighter. They left the ring of bright lights and Disturbed prodded him again. "Faster," he said, and he didn't sound too confident. Maybe he wasn't much of a killer. Maybe he didn't want to actually hurt Anthony. Maybe he would just let him go…

"Look, man," Anthony said, trying to talk around the cotton balls that seemed to have materialized in his mouth. "I was having fun. I didn't mean any harm, or…Jesus Christ, I won't tell anyone I saw you out here. I swear."

It was probably the most convincing lie he had ever told.

"Nothing should be coming out of your mouth but prayers right now, kid."

Anthony wasn't sure who he should pray to. God? Or his girlfriend, who was—he hoped—a hell of a lot more likely to save him?

The lights behind them faded. The edge of the playa surrendered to sage-filled desert.

Disturbed kicked him behind the knees. Dust ground into his palms as he hit. When he looked up, he stared straight down the barrel of the submachine gun.

"Oh shit," Anthony said.

There was something undignified about pleading. His uncle had a dozen war stories about facing death with stoic silence, and *Tío* Jacob would have chewed him out for being a pussy if he saw the way he was shaking. But at least he wasn't the only one.

"You can do this, dude," Disturbed muttered to himself. "It's not that hard. Just some guy. Come on, let's do this." He shook his shoulders out. The leather strap of the gun creaked. "Okay. You can do this."

Anthony raised his hands behind his head. *Come on, Elise…*

A nearby bush rustled.

He only had time to catch a flash of Elise's thick braid and her pale skin before she struck Disturbed in the side.

The submachine gun fired. They both hit the ground. Anthony flung himself behind the nearest rock.

There was the meaty sound of fist meeting flesh, and Disturbed grunted. Something big scraped against the ground. The submachine gun slid to a stop inches from Anthony's rock.

All his fear fled in a wash of clarity. He grabbed the gun, got to his knees, and spun to face the fight.

But it was already over. Elise crouched over Disturbed's body, one knee on his throat and the other pinning his arm to the ground. He flailed weakly. She shifted, and he went slack.

Disturbed didn't move when she stood.

Anthony joined her, holding the submachine gun awkwardly at his side. "Did you kill him?'

Elise wiped sweat off her upper lip with the back of her wrist. "No. And he's not going to be out for long. Give

119

me your belt." Anthony hurried to strip it off, and she used the strap to bind the guard's wrists and ankles.

The semi's headlights stopped beside the loading bay, and the men began to move.

"Oh man…"

"They can't leave," Elise said. "We have time. Relax."

"They're going to look for this guy when he doesn't come back."

She knotted the belt and stood. "And we'll be gone before they do."

"What's the plan from here, anyway? We have the fuses, but they have the shipment."

"Could you drive a semi?" Elise asked.

"Yeah, my uncle's a truck driver, he—"

She didn't let him finish. "Great. Let's go."

And then she was running again.

"God damn it," Anthony muttered before following her. Every thud of his feet against the dirt jolted through the bruise on his ribs.

They slipped behind the semi. He could hear shouting over the idling engine.

"Why the *fuck* aren't the vans starting?"

"You think I know? They worked on our way out here! Maybe the batteries died…"

"On all twelve of them?"

Anthony peeked around the back end of the truck. The door had been opened to reveal several huge crates stacked in the back, but nothing had been moved yet. Elise climbed onto the side of the cab.

"Fuck this shit," swore a guard on the other side of the semi. "The boss is going to shoot us!"

She eased the door open and gestured to Anthony. He slid across the bench seat to get behind the large wheel. The cab of the semi smelled like leather and fake pine. The radio was on a Christian station, and a young woman sang cheerily about her wonderful relationship with Jesus to a twanging Country background.

He gingerly set the submachine gun he had stolen from Disturbed atop a rosary.

Anthony had been telling the truth when he said he could drive a semi. But he hadn't done it in years, and not on a truck so new. He smoothed his hands over the wheel and checked the gearshift.

"Just like any other car," he muttered as Elise got in and shut the door softly. "Where am I supposed to go?"

"Forward. Preferably very quickly."

Quickly. No problem. He wasn't trying to pass any tests—just escape a whole lot of armed guards.

Footsteps approached the side of the truck.

"Maybe we can jump the pickups or something..."

"Go," she urged. "Now."

Anthony put the semi into gear and hit the gas.

If anyone shouted at them to stop, he wouldn't have been able to hear it. They roared into motion, and seconds later, a spray of bullets ripped into the side of the trailer with a sound like hail.

"Jesus Christ!"

"Go, go, keep going—"

They tore across the desert, and the gunshots cut off fast. The truck shuddered on the rough playa.

"The doors are still open! Are we losing the cargo?" Anthony asked.

Elise rolled down the window and leaned outside. "No boxes behind us. And nobody's chasing. They wouldn't fire again anyway."

"Why?"

"They must not want to hit the cargo." She dropped back into her seat. "Keep going. We need to dump this by the hill for pickup, and we need to do it before they call reinforcements. Maybe a cliff. See any cliffs?"

Anthony laughed. The idea of going over the side of a mountain was hilariously terrifying.

The windshield suddenly exploded inward with a crash. Elise threw herself to the floor an instant before more pellets erupted through the driver's side window. He dropped low to the seat. Safety glass showered around him, catching in his hair and collar.

He gripped the wheel tight, struggling to keep the semi straight. There was nothing in front of him for miles— nothing but the occasional tree—and he could only pray they wouldn't find one on accident.

The sound of a van roared up beside them and pulled in front of the semi.

He peeked over the dash. The back doors popped open. Two men clung to the back, each holding submachine guns. The man in the passenger seat aimed with a shotgun. *Anthony's* shotgun.

Elise grabbed their gun and propped it on the dashboard without looking. Aiming wasn't too important where fully automatics were concerned.

She squeezed the trigger, and it exploded with gunfire. Someone screamed. The van swerved.

"Pull alongside them!" she yelled. "And give me room!"

He squeezed toward the side of the cab without letting go of the wheel. She climbed over him to brace herself against the door. Anthony flanked the van, and the orange needle on the semi's speedometer bounced at the seventy mark.

Elise suddenly ducked.

Shotgun pellets buzzed through the air over Anthony's head like a swarm of angry bees and buried into the roof of the cab.

She got up again, hanging halfway out the window, and Anthony swerved to the left. They hit the side of the van. The semi bucked around him, and Elise's whole body jerked. He grabbed her leg before she was wrenched out of the window.

"Give me that!" she shouted.

Another gunshot.

Elise dove back into the cab with Anthony's shotgun in her hands. Her elbow smacked into the side of his head, and he lost his grip on the wheel. The semi swerved. He scrambled to get a grip on the wheel again as his vision blurred.

She pumped the shotgun.

"I need a clear shot at the driver!"

No time for pain. He sat up enough to see the ground and swung around hard.

The change in direction made the trailer tip. For a breathless instant, it balanced on two wheels. Anthony braced himself for the trailer to unbalance and throw the cab on its side. But a moment later, all four wheels connected with the ground.

Elise rose, aimed at the van, and pulled the trigger.

It clicked. Out of ammo.

The driver of the van aimed a handgun at them.

Anthony hit the air brakes. The truck screamed. Elise gripped the dash to keep from getting tossed out the windshield. "He's coming around!"

He fumbled a couple of shells out of his pocket. Elise flipped the shotgun over to load it, but she dropped the first two. Her fingers weren't as confident on the gun as they were with a blade.

"Here he comes," Anthony warned.

She managed to slip one in the chamber.

The van drew level with them. Elise propped herself up on the window and aimed down. The shotgun discharged with a bang.

The van wasn't next to them anymore.

123

"Did you shoot him?" Anthony asked, and he sounded shrill, even to his own ears. "Did you shoot the driver?"

"Don't stop. Get across the playa."

He made a loop around the sagebrush-filled shore. The bushes scraped and banged against the front of the truck and its bumpers.

"Did we make it?" he asked.

"That won't be the end of it," Elise said. "Too easy."

His pulse beat out a heavy cadence in his chest and throat. "*Easy*? We almost got shot a dozen times!"

She laughed. Elise *laughed*. She sounded as perturbed by the fight as she would have been on a shopping trip with Betty—maybe even less so. "Mr. Black could send an angel as soon as he finds out what happened. If it gets to us before we dump this, you might wish we were facing a whole firing squad."

He stopped in front of the hill with the Jeep on it and cut the engine. They jumped out to check the cargo.

The crates were strapped in, so they had stayed in place despite his stunt driving. He climbed into the truck bed to investigate the boxes. The moonlight was too dim for him to make out any detail.

"Hang on." Elise ran back to the Jeep for a flashlight.

"Let's just go," Anthony said. "We'll let your friends get rid of all this."

"I want to see what's inside first. Hold the light."

He turned on the flashlight and shone it over her head as she pried at the lid off one of the crate. "I don't know much about stuff with demons and angels," he said, "but I don't think those are weapons."

The box was filled by a column of stone. It was the color of ivory, and the end had a slight indent, like it was supposed to fit into another piece. Anthony reached out to caress it. The stone was smooth, almost warm to the touch. It sang against his fingertips.

124

"What *is* that?" he asked.

"Don't touch it!"

Her sharp tone made him freeze. "What? Why?"

She replaced the lid. Elise moved to another crate and ripped it open without responding. It also had a piece of stone, and Anthony went to open a third. All the same.

Something tickled at the back of his skull, like snakes writhing on his brain stem. He slapped the back of his neck and turned to see what had touched him.

But there wasn't anything there.

"Do you feel that?" he asked, scratching the nape of his neck.

A feather drifted past him. They both looked up.

Wings flared, and a man dropped from the sky.

He appeared young—hardly any older than a teenager—and he glowed like a star. His hair was as white as his flesh. It whipped around him like a cloak.

"Get to the Jeep," Elise snapped, drawing her blade.

"But the cargo—"

"Now!"

Anthony scrambled up the rocks, hurrying to reach the Jeep.

He was halfway up when Elise screamed.

A gust of wind blasted his bangs over his face. He flattened his body against the rock. Something hurtled past him, just inches away. The angel had thrown her. Elise's body struck the rocks beside him and bounced off with a crack.

Her fingers dug into a boulder. Anthony yelled, throwing out a hand to grab her by the wrist, but another gust of wind stopped him.

Hands fell on her shoulders. She kicked and shouted as the angel hauled her into the night sky, wheeling toward the stars.

"Elise!"

125

They ascended so quickly that Anthony soon couldn't see them. He hauled himself on top of the hill and searched the black sky for motion.

He spotted a black shape against the moon. They plummeted toward the earth, growing bigger rapidly.

They were falling right at him.

Anthony threw himself out of the way just in time. They struck the dirt like a meteor, angel on the bottom with his massive wings stretched wide.

Soil exploded into the air. He shielded his face with his arms.

One wing swept out as the angel struggled to right himself. Each one was almost as long as a school bus. It clipped Anthony's legs and knocked him onto his back.

Elise rolled off the angel. "Don't—stay back—" she gasped. The wind had been knocked out of her by the impact.

The angel stood, wings folded around him like a cloak. Feathers showered around him. Anthony couldn't breathe. The air had become thick and vibrated with sheer energy. It pinned him to the ground as surely as though one of the boulders had been dropped on his chest.

Elise got to her knees, ripped off a glove, and held out her hand. "Stay back," she said, blood trickling from her nose. "You see this? Don't fucking touch me!"

His wings flared out, catching the wind.

"You!" he hissed.

Air blasted around them as he swept into the sky again.

Elise grabbed Anthony's arm. "Run. Run!"

He leaped into the passenger's seat of the Jeep, but before he could slide over to the driver's side, she climbed behind the wheel. "Sit back!"

She punched the gas, and they tore across the desert. He twisted around to see if the angel would follow, but

Anthony could barely make out its pale shape circling over the semi. "What did you do?" he asked. Elise held her bare hand out to him. There was a tattoo on her palm, and it was bleeding. "What is *that*?"

"A mark."

Anthony didn't get it. "Did you know that—that thing?"

"No. Never seen him before."

"Then why…?"

"Long story."

"It's a long drive back to town."

She shot a look at him from the corner of her eye. "Knowledge can be dangerous. You might change your mind if you knew."

Anthony laughed harshly. "More dangerous than what we just did? I think I can handle anything you throw at me."

So Elise told him.

By the time she was done, he wished she hadn't.

FOURTEEN

STEPHANIE WAS FUMING.

"How in the world is Betty supposed to heal like this?" she hissed, cornering James in the kitchenette. The lights were dimmed in the apartment above Motion and Dance so Betty could sleep, but judging by the wheezing he heard from his bedroom, she wasn't going to get much rest.

"It's all right. I can help her. I have a ritual—"

She cut him off by stabbing a finger into his chest. "She wouldn't need rituals if she was sedated at the hospital the way she should have been!"

"They were attacked. Do you want fights in your hospital?" James asked, setting his glasses on the counter so he could pinch the bridge of his nose. It was a useless gesture. Nothing would stop the tension headache that had lodged between his temples when he found Elise's note at the rehearsal that morning.

Stephanie's voice sounded extra shrill. Every word was like hammering a fresh nail into his skull. "No! But that's another issue entirely. We wouldn't be having fights in my hospital if *that woman*—"

"Who happens to be my oldest and dearest friend."

"—would stop getting into so much trouble! This is why we should have relocated to the Bay Area."

James sighed. *That* discussion again.

In June, Stephanie had been offered a job in California. When James declined to leave Reno with her, she stayed, and insisted they buy a house together instead. He hadn't thought it was a big deal at the time. They spent most nights together anyway. But he was starting to suspect that the issue wasn't Stephanie wanting him to be closer to her. It was Stephanie wanting him to be further from Elise.

"Betty is here for a reason," James said, carefully enunciating each syllable. "She's safest between these walls. She'll be fine with some time and rest, which she can get here just as well as at a hospital. Probably better, actually."

"Magic is no substitute for modern medicine."

"Ordinarily, I would agree. But the magic I cast is not ordinary."

Betty gave a dry, hacking cough that turned into a full-blown fit. She barely had time to breathe between exhales. They both fell silent to listen.

"I should check on her," Stephanie said. She moved to leave the kitchen, but turned back with renewed anger before she made it three steps away. "Elise is dangerous."

He focused on a spot on the ceiling and took a deep breath before answering. James had the same thoughts himself, more than once. And he was angry at her, too, if in a completely different way than his girlfriend was. He had been on the verge of snapping with stress for hours.

But that was his business. Not hers. And he was about ready to slap Stephanie.

When he spoke again, it was in a careful, measured tone. "Yes, she's sometimes in dangerous situations..."

"She almost killed her friends," she interjected.

"You just don't—"

The front door opened.

James grabbed the notebook off the counter. He almost ripped one of the spell cards out before he saw who it was.

129

Anthony entered first, dusty and hollow-eyed. Elise was a step behind him with a fist clenched to her chest.

She wasn't wearing a glove.

The sensation of falling filled his gut, like tripping off a cliff. James crossed the space within them in a flash to grab her wrist. He studied her bleeding knuckles, but she didn't relax her fingers. "What happened?"

Elise shrugged stiffly.

He looked at Anthony, but the younger man was too stunned to string together an entire sentence, much less respond coherently.

Stephanie shot a look at James. "I'll check on Betty."

At the sound of his cousin's renewed coughing, Anthony followed, leaving James and Elise alone. She finally pried her fingers open. There were deep indents where her fingernails had dug into the skin.

James didn't leave her palm exposed for long. He snagged a dish towel out of the drawer and pressed it against the mark.

"Where are your gloves?"

Elise sank onto the couch. "I don't have any other gloves left."

He found a box of cloth bandages over the washing machine and sat down to wrap her hand, but she gripped the dish towel like it was it was a grenade with a loose pin. "Let go," he said. She shook her head. "Please, Elise. We need to cover...that."

"Mr. Black is building a gate."

There was that falling feeling again. "How do you know?"

"He's shipping fragments of angelic ruin into the city. I saw them tonight. I tried to take them from him, but..." She lifted her hand. "He sent an angel to stop me. He has dozens of them."

"But he doesn't have the entire bowl anymore."

"What if he's found a way around that?"

They stared at each other, communicating silently in a way that only partners could after so many years. What if he *had* found a way around needing a complete keystone? Elise's hand clenched tighter on the towel. Her knuckles were white.

He squeezed her wrist gently until she opened her fingers.

James wiped the blood off her skin as quickly as possible and wound the bandages around her palm, careful not to touch the marks. He didn't let go of her when he was done. "Tell me what happened tonight."

Elise gave him the short version: a convoy, stealing the truck, and being stopped by an angel. "When I left, nobody else had arrived to pick up the semi. I don't know if Mr. Black got it or not. The angel was there, so I can only assume we lost tonight."

He frowned. "Who else would have picked up the semi?"

"Friends of mine."

She was a terrible liar. He knew for a fact the only people she considered friends were in the apartment.

"Elise…"

Her phone rang and cut him off. She paced to the kitchen window to answer it. "Hello?"

He returned the first aid kit to the closet and dropped the blood-stained towel in the washing machine. Even though he couldn't hear the other end of the conversation, Elise's terse replies were telling.

She hung up when he joined her in the kitchen. "I have to go. Stay here with Anthony and Betty."

"We can't hole up in the studio forever."

"It won't be forever. Just until I kill Mr. Black." She took a couple knives from James's kitchen and stuck them in her belt. He followed her to the door.

"What are you doing? Where are you going?"

"My contacts recovered the truck, but not all the pieces. I'm going to see what they found."

"You're joking," he said. When she reached for the doorknob, he leaned a hand against the door to keep her from opening it. She didn't fight him.

"Would I be walking around without a glove if I was making a fucking joke? I don't want to visit the Night Hag, but—"

"The *Night Hag*? But she's asleep!"

"Yeah. Funny story. She's not."

He could tell his raised voice carried through the apartment because the murmured conversation in the bedroom died off. James lowered his tone before continuing. "How?"

"Probably the same thing that let Mr. Black find us."

She didn't have to say any more than that. He suddenly understood. "It's because of that damned Death's Hand, isn't it? Every godforsaken creature on this Earth felt my resurrection. You aren't a necromancer, Elise, and by using that magic—"

"It wasn't—"

"By using that, we violated the Treaty of Dis, and everything knows it. If we survive this, Mr. Black could be the least of our worries!" He raked a hand through his hair. "We should have never done that. You should have left me dead."

"No."

That single word was so absolute that he turned on her, ready to argue, but her cold expression stopped his voice in his throat.

"No?" he asked.

"If Death's Hand killed you a thousand times over, I would do the same thing every time. I will always bring you back." Her throat worked as she swallowed. "Fuck magic. Fuck the Treaty. And fuck Mr. Black."

James faced away from her, bracing his hands on either side of the window and letting his head hang between his shoulders. The sidewalks outside were motionless. The street lamp at the corner flickered, but held steady. It was dark enough that there could have been anything outside —an entire army of angels waiting to strike against them— and he never would have seen it coming.

"You know what this means," he said. "The implications…"

Something touched the center of his back. He relaxed when he realized it was Elise's hand.

She slid her arms around him, hugged his ribcage, and rested her cheek between his shoulder blades. He let out a long breath. She was very warm, even through his shirt. "I don't care," she said, softer than before. "I'll always choose you."

"Elise…"

James turned. She took a quick step back. Her face was blank again. "Don't leave. I mean it."

"Wait—Elise—"

She flicked the jacket over her shoulders to hide the daggers and pulled her hair out of the collar. Her cheeks were red. "Lock the deadbolt."

She left, and the apartment was very empty with her absence.

Demons unloaded the semi in the alley behind Craven's. David Nicholas supervised from atop a closed Dumpster lid, arms folded behind his head like he was on a beach chair by the lake.

The casino employed all kinds of local demons. The ones indistinguishable from humans were put to work as cashiers and waitresses—nightmares, incubi, the half-breeds. But the staff that worked in back were the uglier monsters. The ones that couldn't walk outside during the day.

A demon that looked like it was made of raw meat hurried past with a box three times its size when Elise entered the alley. It smelled like an outhouse.

Neuma took notes of the crates as demons lifted them out of the truck and carried them inside. She peeked into every one and wrote a short description before letting them move on. She wore snug jeans that had been attacked by a Bedazzler, a pushup bra that practically made her choke on her own cleavage, and a midriff jacket without a shirt. Considering her usual work uniform, it was downright decent.

Elise's usual revulsion at seeing David Nicholas was pushed aside by her total relief at finding the semi in the alley. She didn't even mind when Neuma greeted her with a hug that lingered a little too long.

"Why aren't you watching James?" Elise asked.

David Nicholas responded from his perch on the trash. "Thom's on babysitting duty today. Rest assured, he's well-supervised."

"And the angel?"

"Killed six brutes before it left. No big loss."

Neuma glowered. "We lost good guys. Manuel—he was just a kid. Jerry has a family."

"Human servants?"

"No, they were Gray, like me," she said. That was what the mixed-blood children of humans and demons called themselves. "But they were good. That fucking angel is going to pay for it."

"Yes. It will."

Neuma leaned her head on Elise's shoulder and let out a sigh. It was such a sweet gesture from someone so

134

aggressively sexual that it didn't occur to her to push Neuma away. Her skin tingled unpleasantly where the half-succubus's cheek rested against it.

"But we got the cargo," Elise said, talking over Neuma's head to David Nicholas.

"Sure. Most of it." He laughed at the alarm in her gaze. "Ooh, nosy little accountant is scared now, isn't she? The angel called in friends before we got there and flew off with a half dozen crates." He inspected his fingernails, which were painted with chipped black polish. "But we got enough to assemble the gate, I think."

Cold fear spiked through her. "You can't do that."

"Take it up with the boss. It's her game."

"Fine. Take me down there."

He sneered. "No."

Between having her boyfriend almost get executed in the desert and losing part of the shipment, Elise's patience was destroyed. She wrapped a hand around David Nicholas's ankle and hauled him off the Dumpster.

The demons scattered when she threw him to the ground. David Nicholas immediately scrambled to his feet.

"You goddamn bitch, I'll cut your—"

She fisted his shirt at the collar. "I wasn't asking," Elise said, breathing hard through her nose. It was all she could do not to throw him again.

"You're fucking unhinged," he spat.

"Take me. Now."

He shoved her off. "Suit yourself."

David Nicholas took the back paths through Craven's. The hallways were unlit. Elise had to keep a hand on the wall and follow the stink of his cigarettes to navigate down the stairs.

When they reached Eloquent Blood, there was no music, and nobody was left at the bar. Like last time, a cleaning crew moved through with mops and disinfectant to scrub off the worst of the encrusted brimstone.

She checked the time on her phone. It was almost sunrise.

"Losing your nerve?" David Nicholas asked, opening the elevator door.

Elise got in without answering.

They went a few levels deeper than the Night Hag's den this time. She watched the ground ascend around them as the elevator sank deeper and deeper into the earth, where noise could not touch them and the air grew motionless and cold.

When it finally came to a grinding halt and David Nicholas pushed open the cage, nothing greeted them on the other side but darkness.

He darted into the shadows without waiting for her.

"Hey!" Elise called.

His chuckle came from everywhere and nowhere at once. "Not afraid, are you?"

Elise turned on her cell phone's flashlight mode, which made the screen white. It wasn't powerful enough to break the tangible darkness, but it illuminated a small circle in front of her feet. Enough to see rough stone floor.

There was only one way to go—forward.

A powerful presence grew as she moved through the hall. It wasn't just David Nicholas as he flitted in and out of the shadows. There was something else. Something immense, and not demonic.

She came to a crossroads. She had to stop to let a line of demons pass, carrying crates between them on litters. They flinched at seeing her cell phone light. Their eyes were wide and bulging with huge black irises—perfect for seeing in dark mines. The demons were marching deeper into the earth, treading a dusty path split by footprints.

"What is this?" she asked, raising her cell phone to see the boarded-up walls. It looked like an old mine, but there

136

wasn't stone beyond the boards.

"Top levels of the Warrens, of course," David Nicholas whispered. "Don't you want to see where the worst of us lurk? Like turning over a river stone and finding leeches and cockroaches and all sorts of slime."

"I just want to talk to the Night Hag."

"You will. Almost there."

The last of the demons walked on. Elise fell in step behind them.

"Almost there" was subjective. It felt like hours passed as she followed them through the twisting hall. Her breath fogged from her mouth and her skin rose in goose bumps. Then a dim light appeared at the end. A pair of tall doors stood open, leading into a dim cavern. The demons scurried off with eyes lowered.

Elise started to follow them—but she stopped when she stepped through the doors and emerged on a platform near the top of a cavern.

The room was so impossibly tall that the ceiling stretched up into shadows like an underground cathedral. Dim blue light emanated from stones in the walls, turning the shuffling line of demons into silhouettes as they stacked the crates. Several tapestries were hung in the back of the room, framing the room with images of alien forests and cemeteries.

Other demons unpacked the boxes beside a tall dais. And at the center stood a gate.

It was only halfway completed, but Elise already knew she had seen that gateway before. It wasn't quite like the ones in her dreams, but it was cast of the same soapy-white stone with brands around the base. It was thrice her height and wide enough to accommodate a train. She knew it because Mr. Black had built one just like it years before.

Someone moved through the demons to check their

137

work—someone tall and beautiful and ageless. Even in the dim light, Elise recognized the man who had been chained in the Night Hag's cavern on her last visit. But now she recognized the glimmer of magic around his necklace and the silvery stumps at his back.

The Night Hag had one of Mr. Black's angels.

Elise moved down the ramp toward the gate. The angel caught her looking and stopped. The expression on his face was a mix of recognition and fear, just like the one the angel in the desert had looked when he saw her palm. How had she not known what he was before?

"Like it?" David Nicholas purred, reappearing from with a whiff of brimstone. "I'd be lying if I said your shock wasn't delicious."

"You people are making a huge mistake. You don't understand what that does."

"It's a gateway to a city."

Elise turned. The Night Hag had sneaked up behind her. She stood straight-backed and strong, arms folded and chin lifted regally. Her breasts and hips had become plump, with a tight-cinched waist, and her black hair was shot with gray. Instead of looking like a woman of ninety, she might have been James's age. But it was her. There was no mistaking the way the brand on Elise's shoulder burned when she saw her.

"I thought you were only trying to defend the Reno territory from Mr. Black," Elise said. "You have his gate. You have one of his angel slaves, which you need to operate the gate. You realize what this looks like to me?"

The Night Hag waved a dismissive hand. "Yes, yes. But we must be proactive. Mr. Black won't be the only one to come after the ruins."

"Do you know what can come through that?" Elise asked, stabbing the air with a finger.

The gate reacted to her motion. It hummed as the

138

symbols glowed, then faded.

"Nothing. It's only a doorway to the real threat—the angelic city, which I suspect is buried deeper still beneath the Warrens. If we don't get there first, someone else will. Don't you see? The angelic city to which this gate opens is what makes Reno a powerful territory—and to keep control of the city above, we must control the city below."

"All of you will die if you go to that city," Elise said.

"It's a risk we've got to take. There are nine doors in the angelic city—*nine*. If we finish it and cross through before Mr. Black builds his, we can destroy all entrances to the city. Nobody will ever be able to seize it."

"You think you can control it—"

The Night Hag snapped her fingers. Bright pain flared in Elise's shoulder, and she cut off with a groan.

"Petulant worm," she said.

David Nicholas cackled.

"No. We can't control it. I am not suicidal, Elise Kavanagh, and I did not ascend to the position of overlord by foolishness. The only way I can keep my position is to destroy the gates at the source. This is my plan and you've agreed to work with me, so you'll deal with it."

Elise glared at the Night Hag, David Nicholas, and the gateway. Her fingers itched for her daggers. But she kept her hands at her sides. "Nothing good will come from the city."

"I've made my decision. Have you? Is our truce finished?"

"Please say yes." David Nicholas bared all those yellow teeth in a grin that literally stretched to his ears.

It took all of Elise's strength to say, "No."

"Good."

Elise was obviously dismissed. The Night Hag glided toward the angel, turning her back to the kopis as though she was no threat at all. But Elise called out to her.

139

"I stopped the convoy. I got the parts for your gateway. When are you paying me?"

"Payment. Money." The overlord snorted. "Petty things."

"If it's petty, then paying me isn't a problem."

"Fine. David Nicholas will take care of it. Now get out of my sight—I have work to do."

FIFTEEN

THOM WAS WAITING outside the studio when Elise got back. He sat on the Motion and Dance sign, awake and bright-eyed, and he acknowledged her with a nod. "You will be pleased to know that someone attempted to cast a remote spell on the studio and failed."

She was too tired to care. "Great. Fine. Good job."

Elise started to march upstairs. Thom hopped off the sign.

"Quite a greeting for the person safeguarding your aspis. You appear displeased."

"It's four-thirty," she snapped. "The sun's coming up soon and I haven't slept. David Nicholas said he's going to pay me 'later' and I have nothing in my bank account in the meantime. Sorry if I'm not chipper enough for you."

Thom tilted his head to study her. "You saw the gate. Then you know the whole story. What will you do about it?"

She spread her hands wide. "What am I supposed to do? I'm branded by the overlord. My options are limited."

"Hmm."

"Save your pragmatic bullshit," Elise said. "Get out of here. Take a break. I'll keep an eye on my friends for a couple of hours."

"If you wish." He vanished, immediately and silently.

She stumbled upstairs, went to her old room, closed the curtains on the sunrise, and didn't sleep.

The air mattress she had dragged into the room for her and Anthony to use must have been leaking. It was almost flat to the floor. Her boyfriend snored without stirring when she climbed in with him. She never slept on the rare nights she allowed him to stay over, so she knew he was always terrible about that. It sounded like he was sawing wood. Must have been nice to sleep so deeply.

Something scraped against the side of the building. At first, she thought it was a tree branch. But then it scraped again, and again, in a rhythm that sounded deliberate.

Elise stood and moved to the window.

She saw nothing in the street outside. The only motion came from shifting clouds a paler shade of gray than the dawning sky of morning.

Another scrape.

The dose of adrenaline put her body on high alert. Elise stretched out with her other sense—the one that would have let her track a demon blindfolded.

There was something downstairs.

Elise felt for the knife at her back on reflex, but there was, of course, nothing there. Nor were there any weapons in the bedroom. She had dropped her swords in the kitchen.

She slid into the hall silently. James's bedroom door was open, where Betty slept propped up by pillows. She wheezed in her sleep. Stephanie had dosed her with enough Vicodin to let her sleep through an attack from a horde of angels.

Elise sneaked around James—unconscious on the couch with an arm thrown over his face—and found her spine sheath on the kitchen table. She took one of the falchions. Its engraved blade gleamed dully.

She snagged James's keys off the coffee table before

142

slipping out the front door.

Nerves singing, she crouch-walked down the stairs. The breeze made her sweat go cold. Grass crunched under her bare toes. She eased around the corner of the building, alert for signs of attack.

Nothing outside. Not even cars on the street.

She levered herself up to one of the windows in the main dance hall using her fingertips. The lights weren't on, so it was hard to see. Figures moved among the mirrors.

Nothing should have been able to get through the wards. Nothing.

She cupped the keys in her hand to keep them from jingling as she unlocked the front door and sneaked into the reception area. The footsteps were louder inside. It sounded like there were a dozen people stomping through the hall.

Elise set the keys on the table and peeked through the door.

One of the back windows was broken, but the magic seals James placed over the frames should have still been in place. Yet a trio of hulking forms moved between the mirrors. Their two-segmented bodies were suspending above the ground by long legs.

Spiders. Giant, Malamute-sized spiders.

They weren't the same breed as the demons Elise had been fighting out in the desert. These were sleek and mean-looking, with boxing-glove mouth parts and shiny black flesh. One turned in her direction, and she had a glimpse of six glimmering eyes before she pulled back into the shadows.

She pressed her back against the wall to collect her thoughts. Elise wasn't scared of spiders, but these looked like dogfighters, fast and sleek, and three was two more than she wanted to fight at once.

A sense of calm settled over her. A challenge.

The spiders moved into the secondary hall, where Elise's punching bag waited.

She tried to follow, but her foot caught on something dry and clinging. Thick gray webbing tore free of a mass that stretched from wall to floor. She tried to wipe it off, but it only stuck to her fingers instead.

Spider webs. They had trapped the doorway.

The spider-demons stopped moving in the other room.

She crawled to the closet by the desk, trying not to make any noise or brush against the wall. Daimarachnids had poor eyesight and hunted by vibration. She was slower than usual, a little clumsier. Her foot was numb where it had been caked in webbing.

Their stomping steps picked up pace as they approached. She ducked into the closet.

Before she shut the door, a trap door in the ceiling caught her eye. An idea struck her. The crawl space between floors wasn't big, but it let out in the other room. She could get behind them.

Elise climbed on a box of records to push it open. There was a crawl space just tall enough for her to belly-crawl through on the other side.

She threw her falchion into the crawl space.

Something rubbed against the other side of the closet door. It sounded like a claw-footed bathtub come to life.

A demon struck the door and shoved it open. She came face to face with six glistening black eyes. Its mouthparts clacked.

She grabbed the sides of the trap door and hauled herself up just as the demon barreled into the box, knocking it over with a thunderous crash. Elise struggled to pull herself through the trapdoor.

It reached for her with its boxing-glove mouth. She pulled her legs inside. It knocked into the ceiling instead, and its thick, hairy forelegs scraped against the crawl space.

Elise pulled her elbows underneath her and wriggled forward as quickly as she could. Dust tickled her nose as she squeezed under the beams. Her falchion's blade was only two feet long, but it got in the way and made her crawl much too slowly.

Spider-demons scrabbled on the floor below. Spotting her had thrown them into a frenzy. But even if they were twice as smart as the spiders she fought in the desert, they would still be half too dumb to realize where she was going. She moved faster, dragging herself along with her free hand as wood scraped at her bare back and stomach. Elise was certain she had splinters in her arms. She could barely breathe.

Her hand slipped into an indentation.

Another trap door.

Elise shoved it open and maneuvered to exit feet-first. Her arm and back muscles flexed as she sank into a controlled drop, waiting in a chin-up position to gauge the distance to the floor.

The spiders had coated the room in webbing.

She froze, fingers trembling as she studied the mess they had left behind. It was stuck to the mirrors, the curtains over the garage door, and formed a net over the parquet flooring. The only bare spot was on the floor by the exit—a good ten feet to her right.

Okay. Maybe they weren't so stupid.

Elise aimed carefully and swung her legs in a wide arc. And then she let go.

She landed by the door, but her foot sank into a mass of web. The sticky strands held fast, refusing to relinquish her leg. It burned against her bare flesh. Vibrations spread through the web as she fought to pull free.

Hacking at the web with the falchion helped her rip away from the greater mass, but it stuck to her skin, forming a sticky gray stocking from foot to hip. It made her muscles prick and spasm.

Thudding in the dance hall.

They were coming.

Elise clambered over the webbing, her left leg immobilized at the knee, and carefully climbed under a thick strand that stretched from one side of the doorframe to the other.

A shadow rushed at her.

She dived and rolled, coming up with the sword above her head to bury the blade in the spider-demon's body.

Its legs thrashed. A meaty limb connected with her midsection. It was like getting struck by a baseball bat, and all the air rushed from her lungs as she fell to her knees.

Elise wrenched the sword free and drove it under the daimarachnid's mouth.

The point of the blade burst out of a liquid red eye. She stabbed again and again. The exoskeleton cracked. Fluid gushed from its body as the eight long legs curled inward.

With a final twitch, the spider died.

Elise took a moment to examine what remained of the spider in the moonlight: the red marks on its belly, the fine hairs on its legs, and the brands down its sides. Every mark had been scored to render them unreadable. "Damn," she whispered.

She heard motion in the lobby. There were still two others.

Need to move.

Elise climbed awkwardly out the open window, dragging her stiff leg behind her, and dropped to the grass. She couldn't get both feet under her. She sank to her knees in the yellow grass, and her useless leg barely bent. The web was hardening. "Shit," she muttered. Two more spiders. She couldn't be immobilized.

Crawling to the corner, she peeked around the wall.

One spider dragged its spinneret along the lawn as it moved for the stairs on the side of the building. Gossamer stretched between its posterior and the wall, shiny and moist on the end closest to its body.

She slipped under the stairs and waited until it anchored the silken strand to the bottom step before moving. Elise stepped over the trip line it had created at the bottom and followed it silently up the stairs on her toes.

When it reached the landing, she struck.

The spider was too fast. It saw her and twisted. What she intended to be a death blow glanced off its side.

It smashed her into the railing and nearly threw them both off the side. She tangled her free hand in the hairs on its back and hung on. Unbalanced, her shoulders tipped over the rail. The world spun and flipped as she dangled. The ground was at least twelve feet down.

She hooked her ankle on the spider's leg, holding tight. Slimy pincers snapped over her face. She slammed her elbow into one of its eyes. It squealed.

Upside-down, she saw the third spider reach the bottom of the stairs.

Hauling herself upright, Elise threw her weight into the second spider and shoved them away from the edge. It crashed into the door. She slashed. Blood splattered on her face. It keened and fell.

And then the third one was there.

It slammed into her with its glossy body and knocked her onto her back. The hairs on its belly scraped against Elise. She drew her one good leg up to shield her stomach as fangs dropped out of its mouth. They came down on her knees instead of her ribs, and she twisted to the side before they could puncture.

Pincers rushed at her face. She flung her arm up. The sword caught in its mouth.

147

Red eyes bored into her from inches away as it pressed into her. Her arm trembled as she struggled to force it back. The angle was poor and it was too strong—a line of venom dripped onto her neck and slid into her hair.

She pulled her fist back, and for an instant, hairy feelers scraped against her face.

Then Elise shoved the blade straight into its mouth.

It screamed as it thrashed, twisting from side to side above her. The contortions seemed to only pull the blade deeper into its body. Her slippery fingers lost grip on the hilt.

One of its feet smashed into her leg, and another into her shoulder. Elise flung her arms over her head, trying to curl into a ball to protect her vital organs from its death throes, but its weight was too much.

With a final rasping sigh, the air left its lungs. It stopped moving.

The door opened.

"What—*Elise*?"

James stared at her through the tangle of legs.

"Help?"

He lifted the daimarachnid, and Elise wiggled free of the carcass. Venom and other, unidentifiable bodily fluids seeped out of its stab wounds. She looked down at herself. There was an imprint on her leg where it had almost managed to break the skin, at which point her blood would have been pumped full of all that poison.

"What happened?" he asked. His cheek was imprinted with the pattern of the couch fabric, but his eyes were alert as he took in the two bodies of the spiders.

"They were downstairs. I don't think they wanted to attack us. Hold this."

She picked at the web on her leg with her fingernails. It wouldn't come off, and she couldn't feel her skin beneath it.

"The wards," he said. "How—?"

"They're broken. I don't know how."

She shivered as she limped back into the apartment. Elise suddenly felt very, very vulnerable in her underwear and wanted nothing more than an actual pair of pants.

"Impossible," James said, staring at the doorway where he had etched tiny marks of warding. "These are the strongest wards possible. Petty daimarachnids couldn't have broken them."

Anthony staggered into the hallway wearing nothing but his boxers. He had found a knife somewhere. "What's going on? Was it an angel?"

"Wake Betty up," Elise ordered, grabbing a clean pair of James's jeans from the laundry cubby. She pulled them over her stiff leg, threaded a belt through the loops, and pulled it tight. They were so long that they bunched over her feet. "We're not safe here anymore. We've got to move."

"I'll take them to my—" James stuttered. "To Stephanie's house. The wards aren't as strong, but nobody should know where it is."

Anger surged through Elise. Stephanie's house? She would have preferred to take everyone to the Night Hag's den. Biting back a nasty comment, she nodded sharply. "Fine. Let's get going."

Morrighan arrived at the studio exactly two hours later. Nobody in the coven approached James's skill with magic, but she was unusually good at protective charms—with the added bonus that Mr. Black wouldn't be out to kill her.

"Thanks for this," Elise said, stifling a yawn. "How long do you think it will take?"

The witch surveyed the studio with a binder hugged to

149

her chest. "You want the entire perimeter redone? At least three hours. I'll have to do some measurements."

"Thanks."

Elise rolled her pant leg up to the knee and picked at the spider webbing stuck to her calf. Instead of sleeping, she had spent the last hour in a hot bath trying to separate the web from her flesh. She had peeled most of it off, along with half her skin, and was slowly regaining sensation above the knee. There was still a thick sock of slime over her ankle.

A car pulled up behind her. She prepared herself to turn away yet another dancer who hadn't gotten the message that classes were canceled for the day, and then realized it was Anthony's Jeep. And Betty was driving.

"Hey, what are you doing here?" Elise asked, offering her a hand out of the car. "You don't drive."

"I came to help redo the wards," Betty said. She still sounded like she had smoked an entire pack of cigarettes in one sitting, but the bandages on her shoulders were gone, and her skin was completely unmarked by burns. "I got coffee. Check the passenger seat."

"You should be somewhere safe. You can't be here until Morrighan finishes."

"There's nowhere safer than with you. Besides, Stephanie's house radiates bitch vibes. Didn't I tell you to grab the coffee?"

She found a cardboard container with four huge cups of plain coffee. "There's only three of us here."

"Those are all for you. I already drank mine, and Morr doesn't imbibe."

Elise had to smile. "Thanks. What happened to your burns? Did James take care of them?"

Betty grinned. "Something like that."

She took a sip to test the temperature. It was perfect. Elise tipping her head back and drank until nothing but

150

dregs remained. She sighed and rolled her shoulders, enjoying the familiar warmth she had missed since losing her coffee pot. Betty's smile grew.

"Five hours," Morrighan announced, joining them at the Jeep. "Hi, Betty."

"Hey there."

"Whatever James did here originally is powerful. I'm going to have to cast three levels of charms to fix them. Do you have some touchstones so I can rebind the wards to him?"

"Sure," Elise said.

She went inside to gather some of James's remaining belongings. He kept a few broken things around for spell fodder—cracked coffee mugs, old bed sheets, jeans that had worn thin at the knees. Belongings James had used a lot but no longer needed. The wards would be tied to him and him alone.

Other than watching for attack, Elise could do little to help. She gave James's belongings to Morrighan, then finished cleaning up spider-demon corpses and the web they left behind. The bodies were easy—she skinned the brands off one, gathered as much of its venom as she could in a Tupperware for later, and then stuck their corpses in trash bags.

The webbing was much more difficult. Elise donned rubber gloves to remove it, but it was too tacky. It wouldn't come off.

She connected a hose to the tap in front of the house and power-washed the dance hall. It broke down most of the mess and left a blurry residue on the mirrors. James wouldn't be thrilled, but at least his workspace was clean. It was a start.

Elise paused to study herself in one of the wall of mirrors. She still didn't have any money to buy clean clothes and James's hand-me-downs were ridiculously

151

baggy on her. She twisted around to look at her shoulder, bared by a wife beater that she had knotted at the waist. The Night Hag's brand was angry and red.

"What is that?" Betty came inside, sweaty and pink-cheeked from the summer heat.

"Nothing," she said, fluffing her hair over the mark to hide it. "How are you feeling?"

"I'm on so much Vicodin that I could be an amputee and I wouldn't know it. So I'm fine. When it wears off, though..." Betty's smile was wan. "The attempts on my life are not my favorite."

Elise clenched her jaw. "I know."

"You must have really pissed this guy off."

"Yeah."

"I'm sure he deserved it."

She nodded again, and Betty didn't ask any more questions. There was a reason they were such good friends.

They went outside and sat on the front step to watch Morrighan work. She was so focused on burying objects around the yard that she didn't seem to notice how hot it was becoming.

"I wouldn't blame you if you wanted to leave," Elise said suddenly.

Betty blinked. "Where would I go?"

"You could visit your family in Canada for a few weeks. At least until everything settles down."

"You're trying to protect me, right? It's sweet. But I'm a big girl. I understand the consequences."

"This isn't a game. You could die. The fact you haven't already is miraculous."

"Trust me. I'm getting to be a better witch." Betty glanced around the street, as though she expected someone to be listening, and then she pulled a notebook out of the back pocket of her jeans. "Check this out. I finally figured it out last night, when I couldn't sleep. James didn't heal me. I did, using copies of his spells."

Elise flipped through the pad of paper. Each page was labeled in Betty's looping, girly handwriting with a single word, like "candlelight" or "wind." The rest of each page was covered in huge black marks.

Paper magic. It was James's specialty, and he had never taught anyone how to do it.

"How did you make this?"

"I've been peeking at James's private Books of Shadows. They don't all work. I haven't figured out how to activate everything. But think about it! Imagine going into a fight with two witches who do battle magic!"

Elise's fist clenched on the notebook. "Betty…"

"I can make fires," she said, yanking the paper back. "See this one? It makes a big noise—sounds dumb, but I can think of some clever uses for it, and—"

"James can handle this magic because he's unusually powerful. It could kill you."

"I could be powerful. I just need practice. Maybe someday I could even bind to a kopis as aspis. Wouldn't that be awesome?"

Elise touched her friend's arm. "Promise me you won't use these. Not without James's guidance."

"Oh, come on."

"Promise. Or I'll take this from you right now."

Betty groaned. "Fine. I promise. Unless someone tries to burn me to death or smother me again—then all bets are off. I'm not going to be defenseless. Okay?"

"Fine."

She grinned. "Fabulous."

Elise didn't like the enthusiasm in her voice. Betty had always been too excited by life-and-death situations, but she thought if anything would put a damper on that enthusiasm, it would be assassination attempts. "Can I say

153

anything to convince you to throw out that notebook?"

"Nope. You could tell me how amazing I am for healing myself, though."

"That is difficult magic," she conceded.

"Hell yeah it is. Say I'm amazing."

Elise shook her head and sighed. "You're amazing."

"That's what I thought." Betty leaped up to join Morrighan again, swaying on her feet as she ran over to help dig a hole for one of James's old sweaters.

"Damn it," Elise muttered.

There was a dark form beyond the witches. Someone stood under the trees near the fence. His back was turned, but something about the slant of the shoulders told Elise it was no stranger.

By the time she reached the trees, the man had climbed into the lowest branches with his feet dangling off the side. He lounged against the trunk, comfortable and casual as a cat. Thom was dressed in all black and a thick shirt that was almost woolen. He wasn't even sweating.

He plucked a petite apple from a branch and turned it in his fingers. "These will make a good pie soon," he remarked.

Elise didn't bake, and she definitely wasn't interested in casual conversation. "What do you want? You're supposed to be watching James."

"There are others watching him." He dropped the apple. "I have something for you." Thom swung his legs over the side of the branch and slipped to the ground in front of her. He held up what appeared to be a credit card.

"What is that?"

"This is a key to a penthouse in a downtown casino." Thom flicked it against his fingers. "A very fine penthouse. The kind of place where very rich men stay. You must have a key card to operate the elevator and reach that floor."

"Mr. Black is staying at a casino?"

The witch shrugged. "If you're not interested in getting the key…" Elise held out her hand. Thom didn't immediately give it to her. "The Night Hag does not know I am going to give this to you."

Her eyes narrowed. "How did you get it?"

"You would be amazed at what I can do." He waved it through the air to taunt her. "The Night Hag doesn't want you to confront Mr. Black directly. There is sense in that."

"Then maybe you shouldn't give me access to his penthouse."

"Hmm. Maybe." He held out the key. After a moment, Elise took it. The room number was written on the logo in permanent marker. "There's beauty in the spontaneity of chaos. Too few people appreciate it."

She stuck it in her back pocket. "Thanks."

"You were right when you told your friend she should leave, you know, but she is not the only one. You and all your friends would be wise to escape."

"And break my pact with the Night Hag? That would go over great."

Thom rested his hand on her shoulder. It was heavy, and her brand ached. The pain radiated through her arm, her chest, hot and cold all at once. It wasn't threatening, like when David Nicholas had done it. It was almost… possessive.

His eyes bored into Elise. "Leave now and you may prolong your fleeting days on this Earth."

"Is that a threat?" she asked in a low voice.

His fingers flexed. The pain traveled through her body, heating her skin, quickening her pulse. Thom's face suddenly didn't make sense, as though it wasn't a human face—he was alien, unnatural, his eyes too large and his skin nearly transparent.

"I am not your enemy, Elise Kavanagh."

"You're not my ally."

The corner of his mouth lifted. A smile. Thom was actually smiling. His lips were a shade pinker than the rest of his skin, and Elise had the strange urge to reach up and touch them. "The world is permeable. Every day, it changes." His hand slid from her shoulder to collarbone, brushing up to her throat. "I am not your ally today."

A shudder rolled down Elise's spine. She took a quick step back.

"Don't touch me."

"Yes," he said. Thom hooked his thumbs in the waist of his pants, dragging them down an inch. Only an inch, baring a pale strip of skin and the lines of his hips. A fine brush of black hair disappeared behind his belt. "I suppose it is too late for you to leave. You will need help soon. When you do, you may summon me."

"Summon you? I thought you weren't my ally."

"Not today."

Elise glanced over at Betty and Morrighan. They were still working on the hole they had been digging minutes before. "Look, I'm not in the mood for—"

But when she turned back to face Thom, he was gone.

She turned in a circle, searching for him on the street, but there was nothing. Not even a hint of swaying grass to indicate a person's passage. Somehow, Elise wasn't surprised.

"Great," she muttered at nothing.

Betty was leaning on her shovel again when Elise returned. Her shirt was plastered to her chest and back by sweat. Morrighan wasn't much better, even though she hadn't been doing any of the physical labor herself.

"Do I even want to know what that guy wanted?" Betty asked, and Elise shook her head.

"No. You don't." She took the shovel from her friend. "Come on. I'll finish digging."

156

An hour later, Elise told Betty that she was going to run an errand and left for the penthouse.

She watched the hotel elevators from a bank of penny slot machines, where nobody would bother her as long as she continued feeding what little cash she still had into the slot. She lost five times as often as she won, but the free drinks helped make up for it.

There was no sign of Mr. Black as Elise emptied the change out of her wallet. But an hour and two Long Island Iced Teas later, Alain emerged from the elevator.

He wore sunglasses and a tan suit, and didn't look in her direction as he breezed toward the lobby. People gave him a wide berth even though he wasn't especially imposing. It must have been all the burn scars.

Elise stood once his back faced her and contemplated attacking. She had worn the red sundress again, since she had a habit of tripping over James's jeans, and there was no way to conceal her swords in it. She wasn't sure the daggers would be enough to take Alain down.

So she let him pass. He spoke on his cell phone in French with no mind for his volume—most likely confident that nobody else would understand him. But Elise did.

"I have a map of the mine shafts," he said. "I'll bring the car to you."

He disappeared into the lobby. She set her half-empty glass on top of the slots and ducked into an elevator.

There was no button for the top floors. Where the numbers for the five highest levels should have been, a card reader had been installed. It was obviously much newer than the rest of the sixties-era building. She swiped the penthouse key, the light flashed green, and the elevator doors closed.

157

Each of the walls was mirrored, so she could see her back and sides as she made a slow ascent. Even with her hair down, the Night Hag's brand was conspicuous on her back. Dim yellow light washed out her skin and made her curls the same color as the dress.

She double-checked the position of her knife.

The doors chimed and slid open.

A short hall terminated in the penthouse door, from which a "Do Not Disturb" sign hung. She pressed her ear to it. No sound.

She unlocked it and slid inside.

Mr. Black's penthouse was fashionable and impersonal. A spacious entryway filled with a cubist's idea of furniture led into another sitting room. There were two bedrooms with sliding doors and a kitchenette. The tinted windows had a perfect view of the mountains and the city that stretched between them.

The air hummed. Elise didn't see anything to cause it and assumed it was the air conditioning.

With her ears perked, she moved to the papers stacked on the desk. Mr. Black had an old Royal Deluxe typewriter under a plastic cover and stacks of pages that he had annotated in red ink. She shuffled through them.

They were mostly business letters and invoices. The letters were stamped unevenly across the page, like the mechanisms on the type ball were out of alignment.

"Why a typewriter?" she muttered.

On a hunch, she tried to turn on the plasma TV. It wouldn't work. Electronics often failed around ethereal energy.

So the hum wasn't air conditioning.

She found a map that showed the route of the hijacked semi from Los Angeles to Reno. He had drawn a big red line through the segment that led away from the lakebed and circled the downtown area instead—not far from

Craven's.

Elise pushed the map aside to find another one that indicated entrances to abandoned mines. Most of them were crossed out. One had been marked with more arrows than the others.

At the very bottom of the stack, she found a leather-bound journal. Elise opened it. It was new enough that he had only filled the first dozen pages, but she didn't have time to read it. She tucked it under an arm, put the papers back the way she found them, and went into the bedroom.

The bed was unmade, towels were piled on the floor, and the open walk-in closet was filled with Mr. Black and Alain's suits. A maid obviously hadn't been through since they began occupying the penthouse. But why? Elise would have expected it if they were storing fragments of angelic ruin, but there was nothing out of ordinary in the bedroom.

Long loops of ribbon on the bed caught her attention. Elise lifted one to inspect it. Someone—most likely Alain—had been drawing icons on them in black ink. They were similar to the symbols that had been marked around the gate at Mr. Black's vineyard. Symbols of warding and protection. They sparked silver-gray in the corner of her vision, like the magic around the angels' shackles.

It looked a lot like paper spells.

A door opened in the other room. Her pulse sped. Someone was home.

Elise drew her knife. Where could she hide? The bathroom? The closet?

Her eyes fell on the balcony.

Elise slid the glass door open and slipped out silently, closing it again behind her. It had high rails and was sheltered from the wind by the building's angle, but the floor-to-ceiling glass left her little space to hide. Far below, cars crept silently along the road, like bits of flotsam on a paved river. Above, there was nothing but an endless stretch of white-blue sky.

She pressed her back against the opaque wall panel between the bedroom and living room, clutching the journal to her chest. The beating sun made the concrete burn against her shoulder blades. Even in a cotton dress, she sweltered.

No noise made it through the windows. Someone could emerge onto the balcony at any moment and she would have no idea they were coming.

Was it Alain or Mr. Black inside? She could surprise them. Sneak up from behind, drive a dagger into his back, watch him bleed out on the carpet. It would be beautiful justice.

But a powerful urge to not get shot held her back. If it was Alain, he would have a gun. And if it was Mr. Black... even worse.

Elise peered around the corner into the bedroom.

Alain was staring through the window.

She hid again, heart pounding, but he hadn't seen her. He gazed at the mountains with his cell phone to his ear.

Elise opened the living room door.

Alain spoke loudly in the bedroom, discussing mine shafts and elevators. She crept toward the front door.

The handle turned. Someone else was coming.

Instead, she darted into the spare bedroom, careful not to make a sound. But the second room wasn't empty.

A dozen pairs of pale eyes stared at her. Angels stood shoulder-to-shoulder in rows and packed every square foot of the floor, from the wall to the bed and to the mirrors. All of them were shackled at the throat or wrist. None of them had wings.

Elise froze, hands raised to her shoulders. She recognized the angel from the desert, but they didn't attack her. They didn't move at all.

160

They just…stared.

Outside, she heard Alain speak again. This time, he was addressing Mr. Black, who responded in his Southern drawl. They were both just outside her door. She couldn't make out the specifics of their conversation through the wall, but she would have known that baritone anywhere.

A mix of anger and fear twisted in her. He was *right there*. She could kill him and end it all.

But if Elise wasn't certain she could take one of them with nothing but a knife, she was definitely sure she couldn't kill both. She stepped toward the angels. "I need to hide," she whispered.

They stepped apart without a sound.

Elise swallowed down her nausea and moved between them. They shifted their arms aside so she wouldn't accidentally brush them.

It had been years since Elise was so close to an angel outside of combat. They pulsed with energy so thick it was tangible, like trying to push through a steel curtain. Ants marched from her spine to her hairline. Her palms itched. Her mouth filled with the iron taste of blood.

Once she passed the first line, the second moved, and the third, and then she was at the back of the room.

The angels continued to face the door as she sank to a crouch behind them. Her muscles wouldn't support her for a moment longer.

The angel that was closest to her turned. It was a female-looking creature with thick brown hair, brown skin, and expressive lips. Her nose was almost flat to her face. "If you see Nukha'il, tell him that Itra'il lives. Please." She was so beautiful, but the idea of helping her made Elise's skin feel like it was trying to crawl off her bones.

Mr. Black's voice rose outside the door.

"Someone's been here."

Itra'il faced forward again. Elise's hand tightened on

161

her dagger.

The men spoke in quieter voices that faded away. No words, no footsteps, no motion.

Then the door opened.

Through the legs of the angels, she could see gray slacks, leather loafers, and the base of a jeweled cane. The hand that gripped it wore a silver cuff bracelet that glimmered with magic similar to that of the angels' shackles. But this was far more powerful.

Mr. Black.

"Has someone been here?" he asked. His voice was so much harsher than Elise remembered. "You. Speak."

A feminine voice rose from the front of the room. "No."

"Then who touched my papers?" No response. "None of you are supposed to leave this room. You understand that, don't you?"

When they remained silent, he dropped his cane.

A cry rose from the front of the room. Elise saw one of them hit the floor, and a fist swung into view. The angel didn't make a noise when the blow landed on its jaw.

"Talk to me, you useless piece of shit. My journal didn't disappear on its own!"

"Mercy," whispered the angel.

Mr. Black fisted a clump of long blond hair and dragged it out of the bedroom. The other angels moved to the doorway, leaving Elise feeling exposed in her corner.

"Tell me where it is!"

She couldn't see what was happening, but even without a single noise of pain from the angel, she recognized the sounds of someone being beaten. The angels fanned out around Mr. Black to form a loose circle.

Alain was there, too. She could just see the top of his head. His back faced her. "Let me shoot this one. Perhaps that will help the others speak."

An angel glanced at her, then the door. A path to the

162

exit was open.

"We can't kill any of them," Mr. Black said. "I need them all—for now."

Elise crept toward the door, keeping an eye on the kopis and aspis, but they didn't seem to notice her. They were too focused on beating the angel. It wasn't fighting back—she didn't think it could, with those shackles on—and the others weren't moving to help.

She held her breath as she opened the door a crack and crawled into the hall.

When she shut the door, the angel finally screamed.

SIXTEEN

WHEN ELISE RETURNED to the studio, Betty greeted Elise with a shovel and a smudge of dirt on the bridge of her nose. "Mission successful?"

It took Elise a moment to realize she was being spoken to. "Yeah," she said, bumping the car door closed with a hip. She was carrying her dagger and Mr. Black's journal, which Betty eyeballed with way too much interest. "Are you finished?"

"I think so. Morrighan's taking a last look to make sure. Want to help?"

"It's probably fine. I'll take you back to Stephanie's house once you're done."

Betty frowned. "You're kind of pale."

"I'm fine. Check the wards."

Elise sat in the shade under the Motion and Dance sign as Morrighan and Betty made a last lap around the studio. She turned Mr. Black's journal over in her hands, considering the smooth leather and gold foil pages. It shouldn't have bothered her to see him beating his slaves; they were hardly her problem, and far from allies. But she couldn't seem to shake the sound of him punching the shit out of an angel on his carpet.

She shook her head and opened the journal. Much of it was handwritten, but he had inserted a few loose pages from the typewriter. Every entry was signed with the letter "P." She wondered what that name was supposed to indicate. A quick flip through the pages didn't give her any answers.

The first two entries were dull. He had written a short description of his initial deals with Portia, and outlined plans to assemble his gate in one of her warehouses.

The third entry was much more interesting.

Goddamn bitch, it said, as well as, *She stole my collection.* He could barely put together a complete sentence, and his anger turned into a rambling diatribe about legacy, failure, and dying. *What makes a kopis great? Or the greatest? What is my legacy? Nothing left behind…can't die…*

She skimmed the long, unbroken paragraphs of ranting until she reached something more coherent.

I have the artifacts. I have the angels to operate them. Why don't I have the power to summon Him?

"Looks good!" Betty chirped from across the yard. "Thanks so much, Morr!"

"No problem. I'll see you at the next esbat," said the other witch. She raised her voice. "Bye, Elise!"

She didn't look up from the journal. Elise turned to the very last entry, where a folded paper had been inserted between pages. She opened it. A single word was typed across the top in all caps: *GODSLAYER.*

A hot breeze ruffled the page. She smoothed it down with a shaking hand.

If I can't have the gate, I'll use the hag's. And I'll use that Godslayer bitch as God-bait. Maybe then it will work.

A shadow fell across the entry. "Why the sour puss?" Betty asked, flopping to the grass. When Elise didn't immediately respond, she lost her grin. "Okay, you can't fool me. What's wrong? What are you reading?"

Elise snapped the journal shut.

"Nothing. Are you ready to leave?"

Betty sighed. "Yeah. Sure."

Elise took her chain of charms and twin falchions from the safe before leaving. She didn't trust Morrighan's new wards to protect them.

Betty was smart enough not to ask any questions as they drove out to Stephanie's suburb. Elise brooded in silence, knuckles white on the steering wheel.

While waiting at a stoplight on Vista Boulevard, the brand on her shoulder flared with white-hot pain, startling her from her reverie.

An instant later, her cell phone rang. She answered it.

"Get to Eloquent Blood," David Nicholas said.

"Why the fuck should I? You still haven't paid me."

"Night Hag said it's my job to handle your payment. Yeah? You want money, you get down here now."

He hung up before she could ask anything else.

"Who was that?" Betty asked.

Elise set the cell phone on the dash of her car. "Nobody important."

Stephanie's house was exactly what Elise expected. She lived in an unfinished development bordered by golf courses, where the water traps doubled as duck ponds and biking trails wove in and out of each carefully-manicured garden.

James enjoyed the cooling air of sunset from the front step of a house at the end of a cul-de-sac, which had perfect green grass and a white picket fence. Elise felt something unpleasant clench in her throat, like being choked from the inside. It looked like the kind of place people raised kids. Big yard. Quiet street. And James fit in perfectly.

He stood when they pulled into the driveway, brow pinched with concern.

"Don't leave here until I get back. You hear me?" Elise told Betty. She didn't bother turning off the car. There was

166

no way in hell she would go inside that house.

Betty climbed out. "Yeah, yeah. I get it."

She shifted into reverse, but James stepped into the drive before she could leave. He had a book tucked under one arm. The Book of Shadows didn't fit his cozy domestic image. "Are you making another move against Mr. Black?"

"No."

He leaned on her door. "I should come with you." There was a faint hint of scarring near his hairline. Where did he get that one? Elise couldn't remember. They had gotten too many scars together to distinguish them.

She snagged the journal out of the backseat. "Take this."

"What is it?"

"You'll see. Anyway, I'm just running an errand. I'll call you later." She waited, and he didn't move. "Let go of my door."

He stepped back. Elise turned the car around and gunned it.

She couldn't get out of suburbia fast enough.

Downtown Reno was dirty and cramped, as though every casino rejected by Las Vegas had banded together to struggle for survival on the banks of the Truckee River. Even at night, when the neon overwhelmed the stained faces of aging buildings, it didn't look like somewhere that fun things could happen. But whether it was the sticky heat or Elise's black mood, it looked even bleaker than usual.

She parked in a half-empty garage and walked down to Craven's. Elise left her swords in the car, but wore her charms like a necklace. They jingled as she passed through a casino and down the alley to Eloquent Blood.

Blood's layout had been changed that night. Not only had the dance floor been cleared out and replaced with a huge iron cage, there were none of the usual humans

167

hanging around seeking a quick thrill with an incubus. The patronage was distinctly infernal. The demons that hid in the Warrens had come out for a night of fun—the ones that looked like mutated sheep, the amorphous black masses of flesh, and even a Fury so tall that its head would have hit the top of the cage.

Inside, a succubus stripped to the waist took blows from a half-snake demon. It was an ugly, mundane fight. Knuckles connected with face. Blood spattered. They grunted, ducked, dodged, and struck again. Fist against flesh made a sound like pounding into a hunk of meat.

The snake flung the succubus against the bars. The cage rattled, and the crowd roared.

Moving through the crowd, which occupied every floor of Blood, Elise watched money exchange hands with envy. A nightmare threw a wad of cash at his companion when the succubus dropped to the floor with watery blood pouring from her nose. Waitresses hurried around to take formal bets. So much cash in one place.

For once, there was nobody at the bar except Neuma, who wore liquid latex smeared across her breasts. She hurried to fill drinks and drop them on the trays of passing waitresses. Her eyes lit up when she saw Elise.

"Hey, hot stuff! I have something for you! Jump on over."

Elise climbed over the bar. "What's going on?"

"It's our monthly cage fight night," Neuma said, blasting beer into a stein and passing it to one of her waitresses.

"How did I not know about this?"

"You're a human. No humans allowed." She pinched Elise's shoulder gently. "Now you've got the Night Hag's mark, it's an all-access pass to our events. Fun, huh? Here, pour a few drinks and I'll grab your paycheck."

Neuma passed a bottle of tequila to her, leaving Elise to

168

quickly fill a few shots. She could see the edge of the stage from her position back against the wall, and another scream from the crowd cued her to look down and see David Nicholas throw the unconscious succubus over his shoulder. She was completely limp and bleeding freely from the face. Half-demon Gray were fragile creatures with virtually no ability to heal. That broken nose was probably a mortal wound.

The bartender bounced back with an envelope a minute later and stuffed it down Elise's waistband. "Here you go. Gimme that back."

Elise handed her the alcohol, fished the envelope out of her shorts, and broke the seal.

The check was written out in David Nicholas's distinctively hideous handwriting. There was a cigarette burn on the corner. And the amount was for two hundred dollars—barely enough to fill Elise's car with gas all month.

David Nicholas strutted on stage with a microphone. "That useless cunt is down for the count!" he announced to renewed shouts as the snake demon pumped her fists in the air. "Anyone want to take the lamia? Can you beat this bitch?" A scuffle broke out on the bottom floor. Someone shoved a red-fleshed aatxegorri to the front of the line, and he scaled the steps to the cage with a cackle.

David Nicholas thumbed through a roll of cash before flinging it on the crowd. It showered like confetti.

"I'm going to kill him," Elise said.

Neuma's eyes widened. "What? No—no! Don't go down there!"

She ignored the bartender and vaulted over the bar, shoving her way downstairs as David Nicholas returned to his perch in the DJ booth.

He stepped in Elise's path. "The fuck are you doing in my club? You got your money. Get out of here."

"Where's the rest?"

"What you see is what you get. Not happy? Then you should have negotiated terms. No agreement about pay, you get what I give you."

Elise shoved her face into his. "I deserve more than this, and you know it."

David Nicholas gripped her shoulder, digging a bony finger into the brand. It felt like having a knife driven into the bone. "Challenging me? Again?"

She hauled back and knocked him across the booth with her fist.

He sprawled atop the sound board. David Nicholas scowled without getting up. "I'll tell the Night Hag," he hissed, upper lip curling to bare teeth yellowed by time and tobacco.

"Tell her what? That you're skimping out on my pay?"

"I'll tell her that you're violating the contract. The part that says you and me aren't allowed to kill each other."

"I got you those ruins, I made an appearance at that party, and if you don't pay me—"

He sneered. "Nobody ever said how much money you get. You deal with it, or you don't get paid at all. No complaints from me if you want to call this truce off. I'll kill your aspis myself."

She grabbed his shirt in both fists and dragged him to his feet, then slammed his back against the panel. Elise shoved her face close to his. "Say that again."

"Whoa! Hang on there!" Neuma grabbed Elise's arm. "Let him go, doll." She lowered her voice. "People are watching. Calm down. Have a drink." She pried one of Elise's hands off of David Nicholas's shirt so she could shove a bottle of vodka into it.

Elise released him. She itched to turn his face into a pulpy mess, but it wasn't the time or the place. And he was right. She should have known better than to not declare

170

the terms of her contract in the beginning. But two hundred dollars wasn't going to cut it.

She glanced at all the money exchanging hands below. The aatxegorri was completely destroying the lamia, and people were getting rich on it. The snake demon wasn't fast enough to withstand his bull-like strength, and he had already ripped open her tail with one of his horns. Elise had fought an aatxegorri before. They were hideous, but slow. She could outmaneuver them in her sleep.

She turned on David Nicholas. He raised his hands to defend himself, but she didn't attack. "Let me take the next fight. Hell, the next dozen fights."

He grinned. His split lip bled something black. "Why? Is it my birthday or something?"

"No, Elise, you don't know what you're volunteering for," Neuma said. "Drink. Drink!"

She took a swig. It burned hot all the way into her stomach. "I'll take the next few fights. You know I'll kick ass. Nobody expects a female kopis, so you guys can collect on all the bets against me—and I get a percentage."

"Deal!" David Nicholas said before Neuma could open her mouth again. "Here's the rules: You get in the pen and fight until one of you isn't standing. No killing." His mouth twisted. "Unfortunately. You keep at it for five rounds, or until you're kicked shitless and can't get up. I'll send you home alive with a cushy paycheck. A thousand bucks, if you win them all."

A thousand dollars. Her head buzzed, and she wasn't sure if it was alcohol or excitement.

"Neuma, get cloth bandages. Now," she said, taking another drink. "And I want to take you in the ring, David Nicholas."

Neuma ran off. He dragged on a cigarette she hadn't noticed him lighting. "Fuck no. My life's worth more than that. You can have five percent of the bets."

171

"Fifty. I'm the one fighting."

"Employees got to get paid. Ten."

"Twenty-five, or I'll go to the Night Hag and let her pick an amount. I wonder what she would think of this."

His mouth twitched. He smashed the tip of his cigarette on the sound board. "Fine."

She stripped off her jacket. Neuma returned, and Elise took her gloves off one at a time, replacing them with bandages around her knuckles. In the cage, the lamia crumpled, and a waitress dragged her out by the tail.

The crowd started to cheer as soon as David Nicholas leaped onto the stage.

"Ladies and gentlemen, we have a fight!"

"No humans."

James squinted at the bouncer blocking the door to Eloquent Blood. It was almost twice his height and had to stoop to fit in the doorway. Thick tusks protruded from either side of its mouth. He thought it was a female, but it was hard to tell if sagging breasts were a sexual characteristic on demons or a racial feature.

"Pardon me?" he said, realizing he had been analyzing its exposed breasts for too long.

"No humans," it repeated, barely able to articulate English words. It crossed its massive arms over its chest. Each one was as thick as his waist.

"But this is the human entrance to Eloquent Blood. It even says 'humans.'"

"It's a cage fight night. No humans. Too dangerous."

James stepped back with a frown, tipping his glasses over his nose to study the alley entrance to Craven's again. If there were no humans allowed in Eloquent Blood on the night of a cage fight, then what was Elise doing?

He had left Stephanie's house five minutes after she did and followed her downtown. He didn't have to track her car to find her. James had a sixth sense for Elise in the same way she had a sixth sense for demons, and he could have found her anywhere on the planet. Her car was parked in a nearby garage, and he was certain he could feel her inside.

"I could pay you," he suggested.

The bouncer rolled its beady black eyes, backed into the hallway, and slammed the door. The rusted sign that said "humans" bounced and rattled.

He took a deep breath, tamping down on his frustration.

Knowing Elise, she was in mortal peril right that second, which was her idea of "running errands." He wouldn't have had to chase her down if she had just let him come along.

"Damn it, Elise," he muttered to the closed door.

He took the street entrance to Craven's. Since that was the door to the human entrance, there had to be one for demon patrons as well. And hopefully it wouldn't be guarded by some kind of troll.

Craven's was especially labyrinthine, even for a casino. Finding his way to the back was difficult, and it didn't do any favors for his mood.

He spotted a pale figure darting behind a row of slot machines with bare shoulders and a crate in her arms. She looked like some kind of waitress. James tailed her through the winding paths until she ducked in a back hallway. He made sure nobody was watching before following.

Now that he saw her unobstructed, he realized with dull shock that she wasn't just another cocktail waitress. She was a pale, voluptuous woman wearing nothing but liquid latex. Definitely one of the strippers from Blood.

There was a black handprint on one of her otherwise bare ass cheeks. He caught her arm.

"Are you going down to the club?"

She didn't snap at him for grabbing her. Her eyes illuminated with delight, and she set the crate down as easily as though it was filled by feathers instead of jingling bottles of alcohol. Once her arms were free, she melted against his body, warm and soft and pliant.

"Well *hello*, handsome. What can I do for you?" she purred, rubbing a thigh against his. "I have a few ideas if you don't. My name is Neuma."

Bile crept up his throat. Demons. Mindless animal urges wrapped in something resembling flesh. Yet another thing he hadn't missed since retiring.

"I need to get to Blood—*without* the succubus charm, thank you. I'm looking for a kopis. Elise Kavanagh. About this height, kind of wavy hair…" He gestured at chest level.

"You're Elise's, huh? Ooh. She sure likes 'em tall. And mature." Neuma trailed her hand up the hem of James's shirt and stroked his hip bone. He caught her wrist to prevent her from dipping her fingers behind his belt. That didn't seem to actually discourage her. She circled around to plaster herself against his back. "Maybe she'll share if I ask nice."

She traced her fingernails over the white streaks at his temples and down the line of his jaw. He swatted at her.

"Stop that."

"I could be just as much fun as she is. Even more fun. Why d'you want her?"

Where a succubus was concerned, his mind was not in charge. It was hard to think when all the blood was being redirected from his skull to his pelvic region. "I'm her aspis," he said stiffly.

His arousal vanished in an instant, like a switch had

174

been flipped.

Neuma took a big step back. "Oh." She heaved a big sigh. "Sorry. I didn't realize you're *James*. I never would have…heck." She glanced around as though she expected to see someone else in the hall, but they were alone. "I don't think I should take you down there."

"I'm asking politely. For now."

"All right, handsome. Don't blame me if you don't like what you see. But you get to carry the booze with those big ol' hands of yours."

Before he could protest, she shoved the crate into his arms and started down the hall again. He staggered under the weight of it as he hurried to follow her swaying hips.

"How do you know my name?"

She bat her eyelashes at him over her shoulder. "I read minds. You're having dirty thoughts about me, you bad boy."

"The hell you do."

"I like a temper on a man. Makes him tastier." She sighed, giving him a long look that said she was mentally undressing him. "Crying shame. Come on, keep up with me."

Neuma led him down several flights of stairs. When she pushed through a door marked "Employees Only," the sound of a roaring crowd spilled into the stairwell. She led him to a dressing room. There was an entire wall occupied by shelves of alcohol.

She started to unload the crate as he held it, but James dropped the box on one of the vanity counters.

"Where is she?" he asked.

Neuma jerked a thumb at the door. "Out there. You can't miss her, if she's still standing. Don't come complaining to me when you see what's what. You got it?"

James ducked out of the room. The end of the hall opened up behind the bar. It was mostly empty, but what

175

was there almost made his eyes fall out of his head. He had only ever heard of Blood from Elise before, but she failed to mention that they didn't bother clothing their waitresses, all of whom appeared to be half-demon Gray. These ones wore nothing but panties, boots, and reflective electrical tape over their nipples.

The women gave him a few strange looks when he exited the bar, but nobody stopped him as he moved up to the rail to scan the crowd. He searched for Elise's auburn hair amongst all the motion. No humans. Most of them didn't even have hair.

And then he saw the cage.

"Oh hell," he muttered.

Elise faced off against two demons: an aatxegorri and a brand new nightmare, semi-transparent skin and all. She had a half-empty bottle of vodka and a swollen eye that dripped blood down her cheek. Her clear eye blazed. Her lips were peeled back in a grin. Every time her fist or foot connected, something like satisfaction surfaced in her expression before fading into the drunken haze again.

Intoxication hardly slowed her down. If anything, it kept her from holding back.

She *brutalized* her attackers.

Knuckles met face with a wet crunch. Her legs were a blur of kicks and lunges. She stopped only to throw back another swig of vodka, then twirled to backhand someone as they jumped at her.

The crowd loved it. They screamed, they cheered.

James was horrified.

He rushed down the steps and shoved through the crowd. It was hardly less violent in the audience. He took an elbow to the face and a hard shove on his way down, but he managed to fight his way to the front row and grip the bars of the cage.

"Elise!" he shouted. "Elise!"

176

She didn't hear him. The crowd was too noisy.

Elise snapped a high kick into the jaw of the nightmare. It cracked so loudly that the audience was shocked into a moment of silence, and then they cheered again with new vigor. The nightmare crumpled against the side of the cage. It didn't look like he was getting up again.

She pumped her arms into the air victoriously.

"Who's next? Who can take down this machine?" shouted an announcer.

The aatxegorri took the moment of distraction to jump at her again, but there was no surprising her. She whipped around, grabbed his neck, and smashed his face into the bars.

Clawed hands shoved wads of money through the cage. Elise grabbed a fistful and kissed it. "Oh dear Lord," James groaned. He couldn't even hear himself over all the shouting.

A demon wrenched the door open, and only the succubus bartender leaping in the way prevented half the crowd from spilling inside. But when a Fury twice James's height stomped through the crowd, Neuma didn't even try to fight him. It stooped low and climbed into the cage.

Elise grinned when she saw what joined her. She shoved the money down her shirt, threw back another drink of vodka, and beckoned for the Fury to attack.

James's anger was forgotten in a wash of fear. Elise had killed a Fury before—and a multitude of other large and nasty creatures—but that was when she was armed, sober, and free to move around the landscape. Her remaining eye could barely focus on her attacker.

The Fury rushed her. Two pale, meaty fists seized her by the shoulders and slammed her into the bars in front of James.

The crowd roared and jostled him against the barrier.

"Elise!" he yelled again. She didn't see him. She kicked

the Fury away.

The aatxegorri clambered to his hooves. With a snap of his wrist, a switchblade flashed in the stage lights. She was too busy with the Fury to notice.

"Watch out!"

She still couldn't hear him.

The aatxegorri inched to the side, waiting for an opening.

James leaped onto the steps, pushed Neuma away from the door, and got in. There were protesting shouts from the audience. He ran forward and punched the aatxegorri in the back of the head.

He hadn't thrown a good punch in years. The force of it radiated all the way up his arm and into his spine. One of his knuckles split open with a flaming shock of pain.

The demon whirled on him as he shook out his fist. He raised his hands to indicate no desire to fight. "I'm not—" he began to say, but it didn't wait for him to finish. It lowered its horned head and rushed him.

James knocked the knife out of its hands and took the full brunt of its body.

Getting hit by a bull-demon was a lot like getting struck by a car on the highway. James's back hit the bars, blinding him with pain so powerful that it took a good five seconds for him to really feel it.

What he *did* feel was the tip of a horn ripping his sleeve open and burying in his bicep. He seized the horns on instinct and wrenched them away, throwing the aatxegorri into the Fury.

They both dropped. The impact made the entire cage rock.

Elise's eye met his over the bodies. Her jaw dropped. "*James*?"

He jumped over the Fury and grabbed her elbow. He was about ready to give her a good shake, but she was so pummeled that he wasn't sure she would remain conscious through it. "What were you thinking? A *cage fight*?"

But it wasn't time for an argument. The Fury pushed itself onto all fours.

Elise shoved James out of the way. "Move it!"

She drove her knee into the Fury's face, and it fell again with a splatter of yellow blood.

Demons were yelling, the stage lights were blindingly bright, and James regretted jumping in. Neuma alone wasn't enough to hold the crowd back for long, and the entire bar was about to start fighting. The announcer seemed to love it. He shouted incoherently over the speakers.

The aatxegorri charged again. James dived for the knife. He clutched it in his fist and blindly jabbed.

It sank into flesh and jerked free of his hand.

An instant later, all the yelling outside the cage changed from excitement to panic.

The crowd shifted. Footsteps thudded. James ran to the bars to squint outside. The demons were feeling for the doors to the Warrens. Even the aatxegorri and the Fury shared in the panic—they both scrambled out the door and down the steps.

Elise chugged the last of the vodka and flung the bottle to the stage.

"Hey! David Nicholas!" she shouted, shielding her eyes from the spotlights. "What the hell's going on?"

It was Neuma who replied. She appeared in the open doorway again, breathless and wide-eyed. "There's a whole freaking army of cops. We gotta clear."

James's heart dropped.

Elise snatched his hand and dragged him off the stage with a pronounced limp. She scrubbed furiously at her blood-crusted eye. "Where are they?"

179

Neuma hung back on the steps, visibly torn between following Elise or the other demons. "The girls are trying to hold them off upstairs in Craven's, but I don't know—how would they know how to find the door to Blood anyway?"

"Mr. Black," Elise said, spitting his name like an insult. "Get out of here. Go!"

The bartender ran after the others. Where there had easily been two hundred bodies clustered around the stage moments before, there was nobody left a few moments later. David Nicholas was gone. One of the basandere waitresses darted up to the hall behind the bar and vanished.

Elise hauled James up the stairs to the human entrance. "Shouldn't we follow—?" he began.

"No. Can't go into the Warrens. We have to make a break for it." She stumbled over her own feet. He caught her.

"Jesus, Elise, you can't even run! How much did you drink?"

"Enough."

James propped her upright, but she sagged on him. "I think you and I need to have a talk."

"Lecture later. Move now."

She shoved him toward the door, and they broke into the long hallway back to the alley on the surface. The tusked bouncer was long gone. Nothing kept them from rushing out of blood and into the hot night air.

On the other side, someone had opened the gate blocking off the alley. Three police cruisers with flashing lights waited on the other side.

Elise tripped on a bag of trash and sprawled across the pavement.

"Don't move!" someone shouted. The spotlights mounted above the windshields blasted right at them, and

James could only make out blurred shapes on the other side. He froze in mid-crouch with his hands on Elise's arm.

"A very serious talk," he muttered. Louder, he said, "I'll comply! We're not going to run, we're just—"

A man in uniform emerged from the light to take James's arm. Elise chose that moment to roll over and focus her bleary eye on them. Rage instantly filled her face at the sight of someone grabbing her aspis.

Elise lunged to her feet and swung one of her best punches.

The cop took it in the jaw. Out in a heartbeat.

"Don't fight, don't fight!" James cried, but it was much too late. Three of the others descended on her with pepper spray and batons.

He didn't get a chance to watch. The last officer was too busy shoving him against the police car and handcuffing him. He got into the enclosed backseat of the cruiser without arguing.

Elise put up a good fight, as always, but even she had her limits. Facing down four trained police officers after a long cage fight was apparently hers. They pinned her down, cuffed her, and tossed her in the cruiser with him. Her good eye was streaming from the pepper spray.

"What were you thinking?" he hissed when she drooped against him, coughing weakly. "Attacking a *police officer*?"

She responded by passing out drunk on his side.

SEVENTEEN

JAMES AND ELISE were fingerprinted, photographed, and thrown into jail.

He rested on his side to keep his swollen cheekbone against the concrete floor of his cell. The chill felt good against the heat of his bruises. His head throbbed and his arm ached, but the worst part was imagining what Stephanie would say when she realized that Elise had gotten him into a fight. Again.

"This is not one of my best days," he groaned.

Elise reclined against the wall in an adjacent cell, pinching her nose with her head tipped back. "I've had worse." Her voice came out tinny and nasal. She pulled the tissue off to examine what had come out of her nostrils, grimaced, and put it back.

"Do you want to tell me what that was?"

"That was a cage fight gone wrong. Or gone right. It's hard to tell."

He swore under his breath. "Yes. I saw that. The question is, *how* did you end up in a cage fight?"

"Long story. Not worth telling."

"We've been incarcerated for public intoxication and assaulting a police officer. You damn well better have a good reason for it. What is going on, Elise?"

"My office got trashed. Mr. Black has driven off my

clientele, burned down my house, and destroyed my savings. I don't have clean clothes to wear. I can't buy anything new. I have no money."

He rolled over to glare at her. "And how was a cage fight supposed to help?"

"Percentage of bets. And..." She snorted into the tissue. Blood dribbled down her wrist. "I cut a deal with the Night Hag. I'm kind of working for her now."

"Good Lord, you couldn't have found something *safer* to do? Something less bloody?"

"I'm sure they would let me strip on the bar."

James's headache tripled in an instant. He mashed his bruised face against the concrete again to try to block out the mental image of Elise as a latex-clad bartender. "Why didn't you just ask me for help?" He managed to sound exhausted instead of angry. "I have plenty of money."

"Even though you just bought a house with Stephanie?"

The sharpness in her tone made him flinch, but he wasn't sure why. There was nothing to feel guilty about. "You know you've always been my first priority," he said in a measured voice.

"You didn't even tell me you were moving. I found out because all your stuff was gone." Elise's words were slurred. He wasn't sure if it was the bloody nose or the alcohol. "If that's first priority, I don't want to see second."

James gathered his willpower and sat up. All the blood rushed to his head. He groaned and pressed the heels of his palms to his temples. "This conversation isn't about me. This is about you becoming some kind of... I don't know what in the world you're becoming. A mercenary?"

"I did it for you."

She was quiet enough that he wasn't sure he heard her right. "What?"

"I said..." She snorted again. There was less blood this

183

time, but pain furrowed her brow. "I did it for you. Jackass." Elise dropped the tissue and rubbed blood off her chin with a wrist. "Mr. Black is out to get us. Killing you would be the fastest way to get back at me. I can't go after him and protect you at the same time, and I needed money anyway, so I agreed to work with the Night Hag. She's had guys watching you."

"You've had demons following me? *Demons*?"

"You're welcome," she said, resting her head against the wall again. This time, it wasn't to keep blood from flowing out of her nose. She appeared to be on the verge of passing out. A fifteen-minute blackout had probably been the most sleep she'd gotten in days.

"I can't believe you've allied with an overlord."

"I ally with no one."

His fists gripped the bars. Now that she was beginning to sober, her chilly calm grated on him. "Then what do you call this?"

"Survival."

James laughed harshly. "Survival? Getting drunk and fighting for money is survival? Getting thrown in jail is survival?"

"Yeah, well." Elise gave a half-hearted shrug with one shoulder.

The only thing that calmed his temper—slightly—was when she moved her hand away so he could see that her face was practically hamburger. That damned sense of pity he always harbored for her had a habit of winning out over everything else.

She spoke again before he could find inner calm. "Did you read the journal?"

"No, I didn't have time. What's in it?"

"It belongs to Mr. Black. It says he wants to use me as bait for…for Him."

And in an instant, all the anger vanished from James.

184

"Jesus."

"Yeah. He seems to think it will give him power." She sounded calm, but he could see the fear in her expression. Even Elise wasn't good enough to hide that. "I won't let Mr. Black do it. There's no way in hell I'm going through one of those gates."

"Why don't I call Stephanie? She can post bail. We'll discuss Mr. Black and decide how to address him. There must be a better way than working with demons."

"Yeah, the good doctor's going to love this," Elise said. "Have fun with that."

He threw his hands in the air. "Do you think those new *friends* of yours are going to help us? I seriously doubt that!"

"Hmm. Such cynicism."

That wasn't Elise's voice.

James turned. There was a strange man outside his cell, with hair like night and darkly glimmering eyes. He set every one of James's instincts alarming, but it was hard to tell why. The un-tucked black shirt and slacks were hardly threatening. James found himself backing into the corner of his cell anyway.

"Who are you?"

The stranger gave James a languorous look from feet to face. Silver rings with heavy black stones glimmered at each of his fingers. "You may call me Thom. I am known as a witch in the service of the Night Hag. There's no need to introduce yourself; I am very familiar with you, James Faulkner."

"Did you come to laugh at me?" Elise asked, utterly unsurprised at his silent entrance.

"No. I am here to take you away. The overlord wishes to see you."

"I'm already going in front of a judge for assault. I don't need a jailbreak on my record, too. But tell the Night

185

Hag thanks."

"You will have nothing on your record, and no officer will remember bringing you here," Thom said.

James squared his shoulders. "We won't go."

The other witch surveyed him expressionlessly. "You will owe us nothing, James Faulkner. The debt from this release falls solely on the shoulders of your kopis."

Even worse.

Elise tossed her tissues to the floor and climbed off the bench. "Fine. Let's go." She showed no sign of her earlier intoxication aside from flushed cheeks. James searched for something to say that might convince her, but words failed him.

"Don't," James said. Thom laid a hand on the lock to her door. It sizzled and filled the air with the smell of hot iron. Molten metal dripped to the concrete. "Elise—listen to me. Don't do this."

The cell sprung open with a whine. Thom offered his hand to her—the same hand that had just melted a lock.

Elise met James's eyes and laid her fingers in Thom's.

"This is your last chance," said the other witch.

"Go to hell," James said.

Thom grinned a disarming grin.

He took a step to the side, and without so much as a sound or a flash of light, they both vanished.

Instantaneous teleportation was not all it was cracked up to be. Elise's mind was unprepared to process the shift. She didn't black out and her vision didn't fade, so she had no frame of reference for a transition from the jail to Eloquent Blood. James's face watched her from the other side of the iron bars one moment, and then she was staring at a mirrored wall illuminated by blue neon the next. The air went from warm to cool. The smells shifted.

And then, too, did the contents of her stomach.

She doubled over. Her shoulders heaved, and with two short jerks of her abs, bile spattered at her feet. It tasted like vodka. Tears blurred her vision.

A smooth hand cupped her elbow, keeping her on her feet. "Don't worry. Your head will clear shortly."

Elise had to spit another mouthful of acid onto the floor before she could speak. Good thing she hadn't eaten anything in days. "That's impossible. How do you...?"

"Your aspis possesses magic of which other witches cannot dream. It is not inconceivable that there are greater and older magicks beyond that." Thom stood back and she righted herself with a hand on the bar.

All the house lights were on in Eloquent Blood. The paint was dull and boring without the mystery afforded by strobe and fog machines. Broken bottles and scraps of paper littered the floor by the empty cage.

It wasn't an illusion or a dream. She had really been transported.

"I believe this is yours."

Thom held up her chain of charms. They had been confiscated by the police before they put her in a cell to sober up.

She took them. "Don't touch these ever again."

"You're welcome. This is yours as well."

Where had he gotten her falchions and spine sheath? It seemed like a stupid question, considering he had magically whisked her out of jail. Of course he could get into the trunk of her car. She pulled the scabbard on like a backpack and pulled her hair out from under it. "Why am I back here?"

"You've been summoned to the Warrens. I prefer not to substantiate where demons will see me for now, and the walk will help you ground yourself. I thought you might

187

also like to clean up."

He swept a hand toward the dressing rooms. Elise climbed over the bar and went inside—alone—to flick on the lights over the vanities.

Her reflection blazed in the mirror, and she grimaced to see herself. Blood caked her hair to her scalp. Her face was one big bruise from chin to forehead, and her left eye barely opened. There were lines on her brow she didn't think had been there before.

No wonder James had been so disgusted with her. She looked like she was dying.

Elise turned on the sink and stuck her head under the faucet, scrubbing her hair until the steaming water ran clear. Then she rinsed off her cracked knuckles, patted her face dry with a towel, and bound her hands in fresh bandages. The damage almost looked worse once she was clean.

Either Thom was too polite to remark on her appearance when she returned to the bar, or he genuinely didn't care. "Come." He strode off, ponytail floating behind him, and she realized belatedly that he wasn't wearing shoes.

Elise's head spun as she followed him, unsteady from the transition. The floor tipped under her feet as she walked.

The long, slow elevator ride and journey through the mines left her nothing to think about but James's guilt trip. She couldn't push away the memory of his last plea: *Don't do this.*

Ungrateful bastard.

"He will come around," Thom said, stopping in front of the doors to the Night Hag's chambers.

"What, is mind reading another one of your super-witch skills?"

"I don't need to read your mind when I can read your

hormones. The cortisol, the oxytocin—not to mention your heart rate. The flush in the cheeks. The longing stares." He sneered. The lines on either side of his mouth were strange on his blank, beautiful face. "Always the same, you people. So predictable."

Elise realized her jaw was hanging and clapped her teeth shut. "What are you talking about?"

He pushed the doors open.

"As you requested," Thom said, entering the room like a herald in front of royalty.

The Night Hag was in bed again, but she wasn't propped up by pillows anymore. Instead, she sat with a straight back and her arms resting on the bars like it was a throne.

Thom moved to attend to a bag of saline on her right, regarding the valve with the same impassive gaze he used on everything else. The rubber tubes on the overlord's other arm led to metal drums tucked behind the bed, where a whirring motor pumped something sludgy and black through the needle. There was no way her veins should have been able to accommodate so much fluid. Her skin was flushed with crimson.

She snapped her fingers. "You. Come here."

Heat stabbed through Elise's shoulder brand. Clenching her jaw, she limped to the chair at which the Night Hag pointed.

As she moved to the other side of the bed, a bloody pile writhing on the floor came into view. It looked like several thick, twisted worms draped in shreds of cloth.

A daimarachnid? She froze.

"Sit. Sit!"

Elise sank into the chair. "The payment…"

"Yes, I've heard what David Nicholas did, even though I explicitly told him not to fuck with you. I also heard about his little game with the cage. Funny. Very funny."

Her lips peeled back in a grimace. "Unfortunately for his sake, I have no sense of humor."

She glanced at the pile of flesh when she spoke.

Oh no.

Elise's stomach flipped. She could see it now: the yellow hairs, the leather jacket, the shredded black jeans. It was as though David Nicholas had been turned inside out. Nightmares didn't have bones and organs and muscle the way humans did, so he was barely more than a rubbery mess of skin.

He moaned from a hole that might have once been his mouth. A ruined black tongue lashed between shattered fragments of teeth.

"Kill him," Elise said. "This is…"

"Lose the sentimentality. He knew the consequences of challenging me."

Sentimental? That was one adjective Elise had never heard used to describe her before. Was it sentimental to find the destroyed nightmare's agony nauseating? Was it sentimental to prefer quick, clean deaths to…*that*?

"You should know I volunteered for the cage fight."

The Night Hag's skin shivered. The flesh over her shoulders rippled as though something pressed against it from the inside. "And *you* should be thanking your beloved God that I need you more than David Nicholas, or I would do the same to you."

Elise gripped her chain of charms. "You're awfully confident you would win."

"Keep that mouth shut, kopis, or I'll rip it from your face. Remember who is branded by who! Now. We have two things to take care of. Firstly…" She lifted a hand. Elise tensed.

Thom stepped forward to offer Elise an envelope. Her skin crawled when she took it.

There was cash inside. She took the time to count it

without caring if it was rude to do so. "Five hundred dollars? I brought you a semi full of angelic artifacts."

"No, you brought a semi *partly* filled with angelic artifacts. That's a failure in my book. Don't pull faces; you can earn more—much more. I'm not done with you yet."

Elise stuffed the money in her back pocket. At least it was more than David Nicholas had tried to pay her. "What else?"

A smile grew on the Night Hag's lips. It wasn't a happy smile, and it made her gut clench like she was going to throw up again. "The second thing, yes. Finish David Nicholas."

The pile on the floor groaned.

"Nightmares can't be killed," Elise said.

"Exorcise him. Send him back to Hell. Let him float in a mire of souls for a few hundred years."

Even though Thom didn't move or speak, Elise suddenly felt compelled to look at him. Indeed, his absolute stillness was what drew her attention. His eyes glimmered. They were completely black, from pupil to iris and consuming the whites.

She had exorcised nightmares before and would do it again. But she didn't want Thom to see her do it.

Elise thought of her empty checking account. The insurance company. Her landlords.

"Fine," she said, unspooling the charms from around her neck as she stood.

She considered David Nicholas at her feet. This was the creature that had irritated her like a fly she couldn't swat for months. He had refused to pay her. Treated her like shit. Abused his employees. Gathered his friends, jumped her in a parking lot, and tried to beat her to death.

He twisted, rolled over, and oozed a few inches to the right. His body left an imprint of blood and ichor. A fingerprint of misery. A single eyeball rolled in the mass

191

that was his skull, and she thought it was glaring at her.

"Hurry up," snapped the Night Hag. "I have better things to do than watch this."

Elise wrapped the chains around her fist, then drew one of the falchions on her back and rested the flat of the blade against him. He thrashed weakly. *"Crux sacra sit mihi lux,"* she said, closing her eyes and focusing on her other sense. Those shattered yellow teeth were burned in her skull. *"Non draco sit mihi dux."*

A light flared through her eyelids. The St. Benedict charm had illuminated.

She reached out with her mind to grasp the sense of the nightmare in front of her—a once-powerful demonic force that had begun fading like a dying heartbeat. He fought, of course. They always did.

Elise gripped him tighter. The mass on the floor grunted, bubbled, and fell silent.

"Vade retro, Satana, nunquam suade mihi vana." A shriek. A twitch. *"Sunt mala quae libas. Ipse venena bibas."* Elise envisioned the gates to the infernal planes, and all the pain that would be waiting for him there. "Return to the Hell in which you belong, David Nicholas. Begone."

It wasn't as much of a struggle as it should have been. The light flared brighter for an instant, blotting out the shadow David Nicholas cast upon her senses. But when she opened her eyes, all that remained in front of her was the ichor stain. Her charms were smoking.

He was gone.

"The flame of a thousand years quenched in an instant." The Night Hag grinned. "Fantastic."

Elise sheathed her sword and stood, trying not to look at Thom even though she could feel him watching. She shook the charms loose from her hand and hung them around her neck again. "Five hundred dollars won't last long."

"Yes, yes. David Nicholas's suffering has put me in a good mood, so I'll send along your winnings from the cage fight. Does that mollify your greedy soul?" She didn't wait for an answer before waving her hand again. "Get out of my sight."

Thom glided to the door, and Elise followed him. She felt odd without David Nicholas's taunts to follow her—odd, but satisfied.

The Night Hag called out. "Remember, kopis. If you piss me off, that will be you next time."

And with that friendly reminder, Thom closed the doors.

Elise strode briskly toward the elevator.

Thom stepped close, blocked her path, and stared at her with gleaming eyes. No, not at her—at her charms. "Interesting," he said.

"I want to go home." She took a quick step back when he reached for the chains. "I told you not to touch those again."

His hand dropped. "I suppose I would be defensive if I had a critical piece of angelic ruin around my neck as well."

Elise clenched her fists.

He knew.

The soapy white stone was the size of her thumbnail, suspended between an ankh and a Star of David, and completely innocuous. There was no way to tell that it was part of the bowl she had retrieved for Mr. Black a decade before. A kopis might have recognized it, if he knew what he was looking at, but a witch?

"Have you told her?" she asked.

"No. But she will seek it when her gate does not work."

"You know, when I was in Mr. Black's penthouse, there was a map of old mine shafts," Elise said. "He's found a

193

way into the Warrens. The gate isn't safe here. She shouldn't assemble it."

"Interesting. But hardly my concern."

"Why did you send me there if you don't care?"

He bent down to whisper in her ear. "Because I wanted to see what you would do." His mild tone sent shivers down her spine.

She stepped around him and set a fast pace to the elevator. She hated having that witch behind her, but her urge to leave overruled everything else. He was so quiet at her back that she thought he had fallen behind, but when she turned to shut the elevator door, he side-stepped in before she could close it.

Thom pulled the lever. The elevator lurched into motion. He never stopped staring at her.

They ascended slowly, inch by inch, and the rock slid past them outside the cage. The lone bulb flickered. It cast strange shadows on Thom's face, making him look more like a statue than a human.

Her back hit the railing. She didn't realize she had moved away from him.

"Careful," he said in that mild voice.

"Stop looking at me like that."

"Like what?"

Elise's hand tightened on her mother's cross, where it dangled beside the charm of St. Benedict. "Like you're going to eat me."

He hooked his thumbs in the loops of his slacks. Jutted his hip to the side. Tilted his chin. It was a look of pure seduction, but those eyes—those black eyes—completely ruined it. "Would you prefer this?"

She drew her sword in response as the elevator shuddered. The light went out. Her heart pounded and her nerves rang like a cracked bell struck with a mallet. The darkness lasted only a second, maybe two.

When the light came back on, Thom had vanished.

Elise whirled, searching for him in the little six foot by six foot box. There was nowhere to hide. He had transported himself away again.

The lift stopped, and she kept her sword at the ready as she opened the door and moved into the hall behind the DJ booth. Someone had turned off the house lights in Blood again. Only a thin neon strip by the floor lit her path.

She couldn't see Thom, but he spoke. His voice came from the end of the hall. The only way out.

"Accelerated heartbeat. Vasoconstriction. Auditory exclusion. Loss of complex motor control." He gave a low chuckle. "I see how you move, hunter, I read your body signs. That is fear. Arousal."

Another step forward. There was nowhere else to go.

"Don't touch me," she said. "I said I'm leaving, and I'll go through you if I have to."

"It takes so little to disturb humans. Nothing more than a few tricks of light. After what I heard of you, I expected you to be different."

Elise reached the end of the hall. She eased around the corner, back to the wall, and faced the DJ booth.

Nothing.

"But you are what you are. There's no mistaking that." Thom's voice dropped, assuming that husky tone again. "I need you, and I will have you."

She didn't bother responding. Instead, she drew her other sword and stepped around the DJ booth.

Thom lounged by the cage, studying his fingernails. He didn't look the same as he had in the earth below. The shift was subtle, but distinct. A strange glow had come over his flesh, and his hair had turned to ink. It was as though he was airbrushed smooth, a dream walking on earth, and it was hard to look at him for very long.

195

"What the hell are you?" she whispered.

"That isn't relevant. What matters is that I know who you are." He pointed to her gloved hand without touching it, and his lips formed a single word: "*Godslayer*."

Elise stiffened. "Where did you hear that?"

Thom pointed to the sky.

There was nothing above him but a roof painted black, smeared with sticky fluids that might have been cooking grease or blood or both. But she knew what he meant. And she felt cold, so horribly cold, like the chill that accompanied death had settled upon her.

Such knowledge was dangerous. Too dangerous.

Elise lunged.

The blade sliced through empty air. Thom darted to the side, and she spun and swung the sword again in a wide arc. But he was gone again, and again. Elise twisted and jabbed, sinking her falchion into nothing every time.

When she missed her third thrust, she unbalanced and staggered. Her left knee connected with the ground. The impact jolted up her hip.

Thom stood just out of reach, arms folded, completely composed. "You would kill someone for simply speaking that name."

"I have before."

"You could never kill me. You are weak."

Elise gritted her teeth. She threw her entire body into her dive, slashing and swinging. Thom stepped aside. The breeze ruffled his hair. Jerking her second sword free, she brought them both in a high arc. Elise cut across his body.

He was suddenly on the bar, and she hadn't seen him climb it. Elise leaped onto a chair, a stool, and onto his level.

Elise was a blur of motion as she moved on instinct. She had never been so fast in her life. But Thom was faster. She kicked glasses out of the way and they shattered on the floor. Another thrust. Another calm step back. Her swings were completely ineffective.

He landed on the floor again. She seized a bottle and jumped over him, knocked a table over, landed with a thud. She kicked the table toward him.

Thom moved just a tiny bit slower that time. It almost tripped him.

She rose to her knees and chucked the bottle at his head. It cracked into his shoulder, and he flinched—the barest reaction. Elise brought the glass bottle down like a club. She saw him duck out of the way. Another miss.

He spun and twisted behind her. He didn't trip on the fallen table. She reached for him, flinging her free hand out, and her fingertips brushed silk.

She knew a moment before he disappeared again that he would reappear on the other side of the table.

Her sword was there when he stepped back.

Thom looked down at her fist pressed tight against his side. The blade jutted from his back.

Blood rushed in Elise's ears, a roar of white noise that drowned out her breath. Satisfaction surged through her. She saw nothing but Thom's pale, surprised face, and the genuine shock in his black eyes.

"Good," he said, and her satisfaction vanished. Thom stepped away from her. The blade exited his body as smoothly as it had entered, and he didn't show any signs of pain. Her fingers went slack with shock. She almost dropped her falchion. "Clean your blade if you want to keep it."

When she didn't immediately move, he plucked it from her unresponsive hand and wiped it off on his shirt. He lifted the sword to study it in the bar lights.

Once he was satisfied it was clean, he returned it to her. She missed twice before sheathing it.

"What are you?" she whispered again.

"I am very many things. I have been sent to assist you."

"Sent by whom?"

He pointed to the ceiling again. "You are not the only one who wants Him gone," Thom said. "How do you kill something immortal? Truly immortal? When man has no weapon that can touch it, when no wound can injure it, when it possesses no soul to exorcise…what do you do?"

"You stay the fuck away. That's what you do."

"But there is a solution. An ugly solution, no doubt, something intolerably wrong—but you are the key. You are the…"

"Don't say it again," she interrupted.

Thom inclined his head in acceptance. "You have been marked as different. You must be able to kill that which cannot be killed. You are the one who will end Him."

She shuddered, shutting her eyes to block out the sight of him. But that couldn't block her memories. "I've tried before. I don't know how."

"Not yet," he agreed, his voice heated. For the first time, she saw real emotion in him. It was uncomfortably similar to the desire in Anthony's eyes when she stretched naked in his bed. "But you will. When you do…"

He leaned toward her as if for a kiss.

She didn't wait to see what he had planned. Elise swung a hard right hook, and her fist landed on the wall. Thom was gone.

EIGHTEEN

MR. Black was not a good man, but he did have some honor—perverse as it may have been. Elise had told him she wanted to be there when he used the bowl, so he contacted her about it a few short weeks later.

The message arrived on her anonymous voicemail service, which she had just established using the money she earned for retrieving the bowl. She hadn't even shared the number with anyone yet.

"Hello again, my dear," said Mr. Black on the message. "I have put together a little something at my house using your kind donation to my private collection. Seeing as you expressed interest in it, I hope you'll join me for the activation next Saturday. I'll send a car. Don't be a stranger."

Elise played it again for James that night. He had sequestered himself in his room for three weeks to craft paper magic, and his Book of Shadows was bulging.

"Donation," he repeated with a scoff.

Thanks to the generous payment, they had moved from their stuffy motel to an upscale hotel. Their suite had two bedrooms, two bathrooms, and room service. Elise had never stayed somewhere so plush. She was actually bathed, well-fed, and had put on some muscle.

But she was not one to sit idle for long. Waiting for James to assemble his spells was killing her, especially when she knew Mr. Black would soon make his move.

"Will you come with me?" she asked when she finished dressing and emerged from the bathroom, fresh-skinned and smelling of peach soap. Elise latched her mother's cross necklace at the back of her neck.

James flipped through his Book of Shadows as if checking its progress, but she thought he might have been hiding a smile. "Of course."

Their reservation was under a pseudonym, but a car was indeed waiting for them when Saturday morning arrived. James stayed in the lobby as Alain parked and got out to open the back door.

"I will check you for weapons," he said.

Elise took a big step back. "Don't touch me."

"You cannot see Mr. Black armed. It will only take a moment. Lift your elbows."

Reluctantly, she obeyed. He gave her a short pat down with the backs of his hands, missing the slender notebook in her back pocket, and then nodded. Elise didn't have any knives for him to find anyway. She didn't need blades to kill.

He waved her into the car.

"It is a long drive," he said in French as he took position behind the wheel again. "Make yourself comfortable."

She sat stiffly in the back and didn't put on her seatbelt.

They took a direct route out of the city and exited onto a rural road that wandered through lush green hills. Elise didn't try to see if James was following. He had tagged her with a tracking spell and would be miles behind them.

Alain had to go through two gates to get to Mr. Black's property, which was set in the very center of a huge field of grapevines. It felt strangely empty—there was no harvesting equipment or workers. The manor was huge and sprawling. It looked like a plantation taken directly from the South.

Mr. Black stepped onto the porch to greet them. "You made it!" he exclaimed, as though it was a surprise to see her.

Elise got out of the car, and he took her hand like he was escorting a debutante to a ball. She recoiled. He didn't seem to care. "Not comfortable with contact, are we? My sincerest apologies. I'm so thrilled you could join us. Just so thrilled."

"Where is it?" she asked.

"Straight to the point! Won't you let me give you a tour first? I don't get many visitors, and I love an opportunity to show off. You understand."

She nodded reluctantly. Each step she took toward the front door made pressure build in her skull, as though her brain was swelling. Her blood pulsed in her temples.

The gate was complete, and it was near.

She felt drawn toward the east wing of the house, but Mr. Black led her in the opposite direction. "This way!"

He had done well for himself indeed. Elise hadn't met many other kopides, but those she had lived in squalor. The life of a demon hunter wasn't one that lent well to being a productive member of society. But Mr. Black's choice to settle down and start his businesses had obviously borne fruit. His floors were polished wood, the architecture was spacious, and each of his rugs must have cost at least half of what he had paid her to retrieve the bowl.

She glimpsed more fields through the arched windows in a kitchen lush with marble fixtures.

"Is there a point to this?" she asked, rubbing the back of her neck to try to relieve the pressure.

Mr. Black beamed. That broad smile somehow made his handsome face a shade uglier. "Just showing what's possible when you put your mind to it, my dear. This has all been built with my hard-earned money, from foundation to rafters to those pretty pillars you see out back. Such good fortune is humbling."

That was a word for it. He made a big show of leading her into a wine cellar, picking out a bottle, and pouring two glasses for them. He held one under her nose. It smelled woody and peppery, more spicy than sweet. "Do you like it?" he asked, pushing it into her hand. "We grew it ourselves. Come, my dear, take a look."

He led her upstairs again to French doors at the back of the house, where a patio overlooked a field of terraced grapevines. The hill sloped steeply down, and the haze of the sun cast violet shadows on the vines. There were no more houses behind them—just rolling hills, golden brush, and a distant lake.

It was easier to breathe outside, but it had nothing to do with the fresh breeze that stirred against her legs. There was a palpable difference in tension when walking over the threshold. Alain must have cast wards all over the manor to retain the power of the gate.

Elise scanned the doorway. The marks were small enough to be unnoticeable to anyone who wasn't searching for them. A thin stripe crossed the patio, curved around the bushes, and vanished at the end of the wing.

"The equipment for producing the wine is in the shed out that way." He waved casually toward the east, drawing her attention back to him. Shading her eyes, she saw a sprawling building that could have passed for a small factory. "We're no major operation, but we make do. There was a time I would have been able to work the fields myself, but..." He lifted his hands. The skin was rough over the knuckles from fighting. "I'm not as young as I

202

used to be. Don't you think it's a shame we should only know such wealth when we're too old to enjoy it?"

Elise gave his broad shoulders a skeptical look. He may have been old for a kopis, but even in his fifties, he was in good condition.

"Sure," she said.

His smile grew fixed. "Of course you don't. You're young, and you're the 'greatest.' Your legacy is secure." A strange light filled his eyes for an instant, but the moment quickly passed. "There's plenty more to see. The main feature is yet to come."

Mr. Black ushered her inside. Elise dumped the wine in a potted plant when his back was turned.

He took her into his study. James would have been jealous. Every wall was covered in oak bookshelves, and there were statues in each corner that wouldn't have been out of place in a museum. A lockbox sat next to his desk. When he caught her looking at it, he nudged it under his desk with a foot.

"Let's be frank, Miss Kavanagh. You know why you're here."

"You said you were going to kill Him," Elise said. "I could help."

Mr. Black nodded and sat behind his desk, steepling his fingers. "Surely you must wonder why I would have such lofty aspirations. Killing a god. It's no small task. Have you heard the legends? The power that can be gained?"

"I have no interest in power."

"Charming. Really. Very charming. And humble—but that won't take you far." He leaned on his desk to give her an intent stare. "There's some way to harness that power. It involves the artifacts—including the bowl you retrieved—and ethereal beings. But I'm not sure how. Since you're so humble, I'm sure you don't care about eternal youth,

203

immense strength, control over the domains of Heaven and Earth...?" He trailed off, waiting for a reply. Elise only glared. "No? You don't want to live forever?"

"I just want to stay away from Him. I don't care what it takes."

Mr. Black studied her for a long, silent moment. The smile faded. "Why you?" he murmured. "What makes a young girl so special?" He didn't give her a chance to respond. He pushed his chair back and stood. "I have a book that might interest you. See here, my dear."

He led her to a glass case at the back of the room. It held an ancient tome bound in leather and wood. Mr. Black lifted the glass and handled the pages tenderly, touching only the very edges as he flipped to a bookmarked section.

"This is where I learned of what could be gained in His death. It's a record of prophecies. Look—this one is from the days of Apollo and Pythia. History says that he spoke the future through a mortal vessel for the benefit of farmers and kings, but some scholars believe it was truly about love. Isn't that touching?"

"No," Elise said.

"Imagine that. A god so enamored with a mortal woman that he needed to possess her body and mind. Think of the legacy that woman would leave behind."

She glanced at the exit to the room. He seemed pleased by her discomfort.

"There's a precedence for it, you know. See these prophecies? Hundreds of years old. They speak of Durga, a living weapon of Shiva, and Mahishasura—a demon god. She was so beautiful and desirable that he ripped apart the world to have her. And you know what she did?"

"She killed him."

"That's right. She killed him." Mr. Black turned a devilish grin on her. "Do you know much about Durga and Pythia?"

She stared at him blankly.

"The power of woman over man is an amazing thing. It's the stuff of legends."

"Where is the gate?" Elise asked.

He shut the book. "No curiosity. Shame. Very well; let's move on."

The east wing was populated by guest bedrooms, each of which was as mundane as the last. They weren't as well-maintained as the rest of the house. There was a layer of dust on the fixtures, and a faint, musty smell of places no human had been in months. Mr. Black didn't take long to pass through it.

But the further they moved down the hall, the heavier the pressure in Elise's skull grew. Something was humming. She took the notebook out of her back pocket and clenched it in her fist.

"I've converted the largest of the guest bedrooms to accommodate my…shall we say, unique art collection?" He chuckled. "Not that I need to deceive you, of course. You know what I have. Don't you?"

Elise nodded once, lips sealed tight.

Mr. Black stopped in front of the last room. The hallway felt darker at the end, even though the windows had been opened to the hot summer air.

"Here we are. The *piece de resistance*, in a manner of speaking." He pushed the door open and stood back for Elise to go through first. She set the notebook on a table before entering.

Mr. Black hadn't just converted the room. He had knocked out the walls between several of the bedrooms, as well as the ceiling between the first and second floors. It created a cavernous space that took up almost the entire wing. They had somehow fit a mechanical crane inside. The flooring was removed, too, and poured concrete sat

205

exposed.

And on top of that stood a finished gate.

It hummed when she walked into the room as though the stone recognized her. The graceful loop of the arch almost reached the top of the second floor. Sinewy lines banded it from bottom to top. The stone appeared to be braided together.

The bowl she had retrieved formed the capstone of the arch, and the air around it vibrated. Elise swallowed a swell of nausea.

"Beautiful, isn't it?" Mr. Black asked.

She had to take a long, deep breath before she could respond. "It's a monstrosity."

"Yes, I could see why you might think that. You've been through one of these before. Haven't you?" Elise gritted her teeth and didn't respond. "Does it surprise you that I know that? No? But I know a lot about you, my dear —even more than you would expect. I've done my studying."

She paced around the gate, scanning the symbols carved into the floor around it. Alain had been busy. There were twelve parallel lines of magic runes like the ones outside the house, most of which she didn't recognize.

"Will these kill Him when he passes through?"

Mr. Black gave her a wan smile. "No, I'm afraid not. Killing God isn't so easy. I've learned a few fascinating things about ethereal artifacts these past months, though— would you like me to share?"

"No."

He ignored her response. "All this isn't really made of rock. It's ossified bone. There are animals on the heavenly planes you can't even imagine—these mighty beasts that walk on air and exist beyond time. Truly amazing. And the angels slaughtered them to build with their bodies."

Alain was pacing, too, staying opposite Elise on the

marks. She didn't cross the line. Every time she took a step, the gateway pulsed. Her palms itched.

When she passed by one of the windows, a shape flitted past the bushes. She only saw it for a half second, but she knew it was James. He had honed in on his notebook and found her. He flashed by a window further down, tagging it with a paper spell before moving on. He had prepared three dozen fire runes just for the cause. Once they were triggered, the entire home would be set aflame—including the east wing, judging by his trajectory.

Only Elise had seen him. Mr. Black went on, waving at the gate with a wine glass as he spoke.

"The truly terrible part is that these creatures would be eternal if not slaughtered, like all angels. Did you know that's one of the things the Treaty of Dis only gave to angels? Immortality? They're so very difficult to kill. And the greatest angel—the one you might call 'God'—can't be killed at all."

"You said you were going to kill Him," Elise said.

"I did, didn't I? But that's another one of the things I learned about angels. No human can kill God, but we can summon Him, and contain Him...and with the right gate, use His power." Mr. Black's eyes glowed with a hungry light. "Maybe even become immortal."

"So this has always been about immortality."

He drained the last of his wine and set the glass down. "You're still young. Powerful. The greatest, they say. You have no clue what it's like to feel your body dying."

Alain started to move for Elise. She quickened her step to stay on the opposite side of the gate. For a moment, she glimpsed him through the twin pillars of bone, and the air was distorted between them. The air vibrated with flashes of light.

"See that symbol on the top of the gate, my dear? That's a mark. You should recognize it. It takes three marks

207

to open a gate and cross from one dimension to the next. It's somewhat of a safeguard against the wrong people using it. There's one mark on the gate, and one mark per angel. So it takes at least two angels to cross over with the help of a gate. Or…"

Alain darted around the circle, fast as a bullet. Elise didn't expect it.

He snatched at her, and she stepped aside fast enough that his swinging hand caught her necklace instead of her arm. The chain snapped. Her mother's cross vanished into a hole in the floor.

His second attempt to grab her succeeded. His fingers dug painfully into her bicep.

"Or one gate and one Godslayer with two marks," Mr. Black finished. The word shocked through her.

Elise twisted out of Alain's grip and made a break for the door, but the older kopis was in the way. Mr. Black blocked her with his body. She swung a punch, but he ducked.

She heard the click of a gun behind her.

Elise threw herself to the ground before Alain could fire, sweeping a leg out to hook it behind the witch's ankle. He dodged her, and Mr. Black was suddenly on top of her, pinning her to the ground with his hand at her throat.

There was no hint of the Southern gentleman in him when he struck her across the face hard enough to scatter her vision with black stars.

"The crane," he said.

Alain disappeared, and she heard the whirring of a machine a moment later.

She threw her weight into him, shoving Mr. Black onto his back. He grabbed her calf and forced her to the ground again when she tried to stand.

He fisted her shirt, lifted her head an inch off the ground, and punched her so hard her skull bounced. The world fuzzed around Elise.

Mr. Black sat up. Her limbs were too heavy to respond. He smoothed graying hair off his forehead. Gestured to Alain beyond the line of her foggy vision. Stood up, kicked her in the ribs. She folded around the blow as pain blossomed in her side.

"'Greatest,'" he said scornfully. "A travesty."

Blood pulsed through her veins, clearing her head with the speedy recovery of a kopis. But it wasn't speedy enough. A metal hook descended toward her face.

Elise took a deep breath, jumped to her feet, and made another dash for the door.

Her throbbing head made her too slow. Mr. Black caught her in a bear hug, and it turned out he was exactly as strong as he looked. Despite his age, he was easily Elise's match—except that he had a good fifty pounds on her, and in such close quarters, size would always win out.

She stomped on his instep and drove her elbow into his gut. He grunted, but didn't let go.

Alain forced her wrists together, pinning both of her arms under his while he wound rope around her hands. Then he peeled the glove off her right hand, and she spit in his face. Phlegm slapped in his eye.

"Get the other one," Mr. Black said.

She tried to twist her arms away, but there was nowhere to go. Alain removed the other glove.

"No!"

Elise clenched both fists shut. It was like trying to close her hands over crackling balls of electricity. Her skin tingled and burned from fingertip to wrist.

The marks on her palms had minds of their own. They longed to be united with the symbol on the gate, and the harder she fought to keep them contained, the worse it burned.

"To the crane, please, Alain."

209

The aspis went to the control panel again and swung the crane six feet clockwise, within Mr. Black's reach. He let go of Elise long enough to grab the hook and loop it through her ropes.

Alain flipped a lever. The crane lifted with a squeal to drag her arms over her head. Gravity strung her body into one long line. And then her feet were off the ground, and she was swinging toward the gate.

She jerked to a halt an arm's length from the capstone. The stone vibrated, giving a low buzz that dug deep into her skull, and it was hard to breathe or think or move. Her spine and shoulders ached from the suspension.

"Wonderful," Mr. Black said, dusting off his hands as though he had just cleaned something filthy. "And now the wards, please."

Alain knelt by the curved lines of symbols and touched them, whispering words of power.

Light flamed to life around the gate. Heat flushed into the air, sweeping Elise in a torrent of flame and power. The marks on her hands were too strong to control. An electric shock of pain lanced down her arms.

Her left hand popped open and wouldn't close. Blood trailed down her wrist.

"No," she ground out through gritted teeth.

Where was James?

The fingers on her right hand trembled, and the gate glowed with life.

From her point of view near the top of the gate, Elise saw something stir beyond the line of light glowing from Alain's binding spells. Wisps of black smoke curled under the door to the hallway.

Mr. Black hadn't noticed. "This would go much faster if you relaxed," he called.

Alain crossed the other side of the power circle and touched it again. It pulsed with light. "It is ready. We can open the gate."

"Miss Kavanagh, would you be so kind?"

"Turn around," she yelled back.

He spun and saw the door. "What the—?" Mr. Black flung it open, and black smoke poured into the room. He coughed and threw an arm over his face. "Alain! Fire!"

The witch drew his gun and plunged into the hall.

Her right hand burned and her fingers twitched. The gate's hum had grown louder with the sense of her presence, and the air within rippled and swirled.

She could hear her name. Someone was calling to her.

Elise...

And then her right hand opened.

Her palms pressed together in a position of prayer. Blood spurted from the marks. Power erupted between Elise and the gate to form a thick cord of energy that shocked her deep into her bones.

Suddenly, there was no noise. No shadow. She floated in a white void with no arms, no dangling legs, no skin or body or marks.

A wistful, distant sigh pierced the emptiness.

Elise...is it really you?

Her eardrums rocked with the voice. Her skull split in half. She was falling apart, and it was all she could do to scream and keep breathing and stay within her mind. It could have been seconds or years or no time at all.

Oh, Elise...

Eternity stretched in front of her: the severe, frowning face of her father the last time she saw him; a cold expanse of Russian tundra; rain spattering against glass as a train rushed her through green pastures; pale white hands stretching toward her, stroking her cheek, touching her hands...

But just as suddenly, the void vanished.

Someone was screaming, and it wasn't Elise. She

211

gasped and choked on smoke.

Fire consumed the east wing of Mr. Black's manor.

She blinked watering eyes, struggling to focus through the fire to the fight below her. The circle of power had failed. James straddled the lines with several paper spells clutched in each hand, and flames shot up the walls and devoured the exposed beams of the ceiling. Alain was unconscious at his feet.

"You idiot! Don't you realize what you've done?" Mr. Black shouted, but his voice was lost in the crackle of his burning home.

Elise recovered enough to swing her legs forward and then back, throwing her entire body in a wide arc. Then she flipped her feet up, kicked off the gate, and levered herself to crouch on top of the crane. Lowering her arms felt painfully good.

Where her foot had connected with the gate, the ethereal stone cracked. The bowl split.

Wrapping her knees tight on either side of the crane's arm, she reached over and clawed at the capstone with both hands. There was barely enough slack for her to reach. Even though it was old and crumbling, she only managed to wrench a small piece free—hardly bigger than a fingernail.

It was enough. The gate stopped humming and glowing.

With an almighty groan, it began to collapse.

One pillar separated from the second. Elise had half a second to realize that it was falling toward her before it crashed into the arm of the crane.

Her stomach flew into her throat as she tumbled toward flame.

The crane smashed into a wall, and she was flung off the top of it. Her arms were nearly wrenched from their sockets. She cried out. Her legs dangled a few feet off the ground.

The fire crawled toward her, consuming the remaining floorboards inch by inch. Plumes of smoke and burning air swept up her body as the second pillar collapsed into the opposite wall and shattered windows.

Wind blasted more heat toward her, and she kicked her legs up, trying not to get burned.

"James!" she shouted.

He glanced over his shoulder at her, mouth opening in surprise—and Mr. Black seized the opportunity to lunge.

Both men went rolling across the torn floor and vanished down a hole.

Elise groaned, twisting her wrists in the ropes again. They rubbed against her slick, bloody skin, but the loops were too tight to slip free. "Come on," she grunted, twisting her arms as hard as she could. The flames licked at her feet.

And then James staggered out of the smoke. He held a knife that looked like it belonged to Mr. Black.

He stretched on his toes to slice the ropes at her wrist. Elise collapsed, and he caught her. After having her wrists bound for so long, her arms tingled and burned with pinched nerves.

"Are you okay? Can you walk?" James asked.

She nodded. He set her on her feet.

"Mr. Black? Alain?" she said.

"Unconscious. Hurry!"

They found the door to the hall more through luck than by sight. James's spells had done the trick. Each of the external walls was consumed in fire, and they had to crouch low to keep breathing.

When she moved for the entryway, he pushed her in the opposite direction.

"This way out!"

They found an open window in one of the bedrooms—

213

likely the way James had entered—and climbed onto the lawn. Sucking in fresh air was a huge relief to Elise. But she didn't stop to enjoy it. She ran for the front door.

"Where are you going?" James asked, halfway down the path. "Elise, don't!"

She shoved into the building again and ran for the burning study, covering her nose and mouth with the crook of her elbow. Ash swept into her eyes, sending tears cascading down her cheeks.

Elise didn't need her eyesight to find the lockbox she had spotted on the earlier tour of the house. She remembered the position of the desk—kitty corner to the door, opposite the passage to the kitchen—and pushed blindly through the smoke to find it.

She heard James calling her from the entryway and ignored him, searching blindly under the desk with one bare hand while the other was still pressed to her side in a fist.

Her fingers touched metal. She closed them around the handle.

The lockbox was heavy and awkwardly large, but she hugged it to chest and barreled out the office again anyway. James looked relieved to see her, but he didn't waste time asking where she had been. He grabbed her arm and hauled her outside.

The roof of the entryway collapsed behind them, sending billowing clouds of dust exploding out the door.

All the smoke she inhaled caught up with her two steps later. Elise fell to her knees, lockbox cradled in her arms, and hacked something thick and black onto the grass.

"Are you okay?" James asked, kneeling beside her.

She nodded without speaking.

Elise turned to take a last look at Mr. Black's manor. The entire manor was consumed, as were half the trees and

214

grass around it. The level of power required for such magic was staggering.

He gave a guilty smile. "I had to make sure," he said.

Elise recalled the gate and the voice and felt no shame. "Good. Help me up."

She shifted the weight of the lockbox under one arm, and James slung her other arm over his shoulder, bending over to lift her to her feet. Together, they staggered down the path to the gate.

She was never sure if it was her imagination or not, but she thought she heard Mr. Black screaming behind them.

It took them three weeks to figure out how to open the lockbox.

First, James and Elise moved to another city—and another country, as a matter of fact. They ate good food, drank water until their throats no longer burned, and enjoyed the comforts of a nice hotel. And then they set their minds to the task of the box.

The combination dial wasn't the difficult part, nor were the double keys on the back. Spending months scrounging for survival and stealing to eat had taught them a few unsavory tricks for opening things that were meant to stay closed. Yet even when the tumblers were in place and the dial was broken, the lid still wouldn't open.

"Magic," James said, showing Elise a rune on the bottom of the box. "That damn Alain Daladier was a master of the binding spells. If anyone could contain a deity behind magic walls, it might have been him."

"Can you undo it?"

"Maybe. I'm not sure."

So for weeks, James worked. Elise bulked up on protein and bought lots of spare gloves.

215

And then, one Thursday morning, he gave an excited shout. Elise hurried inside from their balcony, where she had been staring at Vancouver and doing her best to think of blissful nothingness. She had finally grown comfortable enough with James to ignore him and relax, which more than she could say about anyone else.

Elise stopped on the edge of his circle of power, which took up most of the hotel room. He was seated on a cushion with an array of crystals and a poultice that reeked of dragon's blood.

"Well?"

"I think I've done it," James said. "Watch."

He passed a pearl over the rune, and the lid swung open. He looked inside. His mouth dropped open.

Elise's heart beat a little faster.

"What is it?"

With one hand, he pulled out a stack of cash. With the other hand, he pulled out a diamond necklace. "I think everything is about to get a lot easier," James said.

She forgot that she wasn't supposed to break the circle and jumped on him.

They hugged, laughed, and counted their cash.

It was the first time they were genuinely happy together, and it was far from the last.

NINETEEN

TWENTY

JULY 2009

ELISE found herself walking by the river as morning dawned instead of returning to her car. She should have gone to bail James out of jail and check on Betty, but the idea of going to Stephanie's house was unbearable. That woman would blame her for everything. And she would be right.

She could still hear Thom's voice whisper from the recesses of her memory.

You are the one who can kill that which cannot die, he had said. *Godslayer...*

Elise stared at the river as it bubbled past, sloshing over rocks and forming eddies in the shallows at her feet. The pink light of clouds at sunrise painted the surface with shifting shades of crimson and violet. Further upstream, someone was already lounging in an inner tube and drinking a beer—getting an early start on summertime laziness. They bobbed toward her. She stuffed her hands in her pockets and headed downstream.

When she found a quiet spot under the bridge, she sat down on a rock and pressed her forehead to her knees.

When was the last time she slept without dreaming of that damned gate? Days? Weeks? It felt like she might never sleep restfully again.

The weight of everything pressed against her. The spider-demons. Those staring angels. Thom's forbidden knowledge. All the things she tried to escape by retiring.

"There is no escape," she whispered to the water.

A homeless man stirred under the bushes nearby, poking his head up to give her a slit-eyed stare. When he saw her bruised face, he dropped back under his makeshift tent. Wonderful.

Her phone rang. She didn't check the number before answering. "What?"

"Is this Elise Kavanagh?"

"Who's asking?"

"I'm Portia Redmond. We met at my house party the other night." Her voice was so soft and quavering that it was hard to hear her over the rushing water. "I need your help."

It took Elise a moment to put a face to the name. "Portia. Right. What's wrong?"

"I have one of the missing pieces of the gate, but I don't want to see that man. That witch. He can't know about this. Thom and the Night Hag would only attempt to exploit it."

"I'm in a contract with them. Why would you trust me?"

"You're a kopis," Portia said in a soft, pleading voice. "Unlike Mr. Black, you're neutral. I know you can help me."

It was hard to argue with someone who sounded that pathetic.

"I can be there in an hour."

"Thank you," she said, and she hung up.

Elise climbed the riverbank to street level and retrieved

her car from the parking garage. She sat behind the wheel for a few minutes without moving. She couldn't seem to work up the energy to put the keys in the ignition.

She had several hundred dollars of cash in her pocket and extra tanks of gas from the trip to the desert. She didn't have to go to Portia Redmond's house. Elise could head east at breakneck speed and lose herself a few states away. Or Mexico was only a long day's drive away. She hadn't been there since she retired with James.

Even though she had her fair share of enemies in Mexico, nobody had the power to destroy her life like Mr. Black. And best of all, nobody would have ever heard the word "Godslayer."

The brand on her shoulder itched.

She started the car. Her enemies wouldn't care if she was hundreds or thousands of miles away. Distance meant nothing to them. Someone would find her. They always did.

Elise made the drive to Portia's house and found the gate unlocked when she arrived. It was cracked open. Every light in the house was turned on, even though daylight had arrived. Another party? There were no cars outside.

She parked in front of the patio and got out, alert for movement in her peripheral vision as she knocked on the door.

It wasn't fully closed. It swung open.

Elise stepped into the entryway. The smoke from burning incense wafted around the hall, masking the scent of lethe that should have been hanging around after the party. That stench never came out of upholstery.

A small speaker mounted on the wall played "Für Elise" at top volume. The piano strains drifted through the entire house. James had thought it was funny to choreograph a student performance to that song when she still handled the grade school dance classes, so she knew it by heart. And she still hated it.

Unease crept over her. Elise stretched out her senses.

There was nothing infernal or ethereal in the area, but there were a lot of ugly human things that could be waiting, too.

"Portia Redmond?" she called, raising her voice to be heard over the music. "This is Elise Kavanagh."

No response.

The party room had been restored to what she assumed was its normal condition. Cushions and hookah pipes had been replaced with elegant couches and house plants. The curtains were parted, the windows were cracked, and a summer breeze ruffled a fern's leaves.

Something creaked on the second floor—a door opening from shifting air pressure.

Elise mounted the stairs. Beethoven grew louder until she couldn't hear herself over the pounding piano.

Light spread in front of a door at the end of the hall, broken only by the dappled shadows of a plant swaying in the breeze. The wind picked up and the door closed an inch again. Her hair was blown back from her face.

She stretched out a hand to push the door open, but something on the knob caught her eye. A smear of blood.

Elise drew her sword as the piano crescendoed.

She kicked the door in.

The room was motionless beyond the swaying of the trees outside Portia's windows. A thin trail of blood led to the bed. It was big enough to sleep five people, covered in plush pillows, and drenched in a sticky black puddle.

Elise felt nothing as she surveyed the body resting neatly atop the comforter. It belonged to a slender woman with her brittle hands folded neatly over her chest, and she thought she recognized Portia's jewelry, even though she had no head. Her wrists were slit, and if the staining on

220

her dress was any indicator, they had pierced the femoral artery as well. The scent of iron and meat was rich in the air.

Anger crept in a few seconds later.

"Damn it," she muttered, sheathing her sword in the spine scabbard again. She couldn't even find it within herself to be disgusted now that she had seen the slimy mass that had once been David Nicholas. A decapitated corpse was downright cheerful in comparison—and definitely more the style of Mr. Black than the Night Hag.

So he had her phone tapped. Or maybe Portia's phone. Either way, he had been listening, and he had gotten there first to leave a message.

She searched the room for Portia's missing head. It had been set on top of a dresser next to a vase of roses and a half-empty bottle of wine. It was a tidy tableau: No blood splatters, or even an errant smear. All the blood was contained on the bed. Portia would have been drugged before they dismembered her. Her makeup was garish in the daylight.

A sealed manila envelope with Elise's name written on it in looping calligraphy was propped against the vase. Her wrist brushed against Portia's neatly-coiffed hair when she picked it up.

A letter and a few photos tipped out of the envelope when she opened it. The note had been typed with careful precision. Not a word was crossed out or rewritten. But the hammers had struck so hard in some places that they tore the page.

Good evening my dear:

So sorry to have missed you this afternoon. Given the state of the nearly-assembled gate, I hoped our long-awaited reunion would be imminent, but a complication arose. It seems one of my suppliers is trading with a competitor. Shame to lose an old friend to such disloyalty! Rest assured I've taken care of my

221

supply chain issue. Everything is back on track. You and I will meet again soon.

In the meantime, I hear you've made a new friend; a certain fragile old businesswoman in direct competition with my interests. How well do you know your friends? Trust is so important in any relationship, don't you agree?

Find attached some pictures of interest. I'll spare you a narrative.

Dreaming of the time our paths will cross again,

Yours truly, Mr. Black.

She examined the glossy, eight-by-ten photographs underneath. The first one was of one the same daimarachnid breed she had hunted in the desert. The second was unmistakably of David Nicholas with the Night Hag surrounded by more of the spider-demons. They were deep in conversation and didn't seem to realize they were being photographed.

The question of how Mr. Black could have gotten pictures from inside the Warrens was not as pressing as the implications.

Clarity descended on Elise. Her pulse accelerated.

She examined the final picture. The almost-finished gate filled the right side of the frame. The image had obviously been taken by a digital camera, because the waves that came off the stone were powerful enough to distort and pixelate half the image. Nevertheless, a huge form lurked beyond it—something with eight thick telephone pole legs.

Elise crumpled Mr. Black's letter in her hands.

"It's a trap," she said to Portia's head. "He just wants me to kill the competition." The corpse didn't reply, but her silence was a compelling argument on its own.

The Night Hag knew Elise still had a piece of the gate. That was why she had sent the spiders into the studio, and it also explained how they had gotten in. James had bound the wards with Elise's blood. Now that she was marked with the overlord's brand, none of those wards would work against her.

It also meant she had tried to kill Betty. The reasons why didn't matter.

The Night Hag had to die.

Sudden footsteps pattered in the hall outside the door. She whirled.

A man stood in the doorway. He had bronze hair that brushed his shoulders and an elegant way of moving that brought to mind flags rippling in a breeze. An angel. But not just any angel—the one the Night Hag had building her gateway.

Elise waited for him to attack. But he didn't move.

"What do you want?"

He spread his fingers out to show he had no weapons. "My name is Nukha'il. The Night Hag sent me to watch you."

"That's not a job I would volunteer for," Elise said. "You know what I did to him?"

"Have mercy on me." He sank to his knees and bowed his head so sheets of shimmering hair fell over his shoulder. "I know who you are and what you can do. We whisper your name and carry it through light and shadow. You are—"

She raised a hand before he could say it.

"Shut up. Right now."

He crawled toward her, and she reacted on instinct. She drove her knee into his face with a crack. Angels didn't bleed like humans did, and he didn't cry out. His elbows hit the floor. His head hung between his shoulders.

"Why would you want mercy from me?" Elise demanded, voice cracking. "Don't you know that He's after me? Don't you know I've killed dozens of you to escape Him before?"

223

When Nukha'il looked up, she aimed the falchion at his face. But he didn't fight back, and his expression was not as subservient as his posture. The hands he stretched toward her were clenched into fists. "I know, and don't care. Mr. Black has clipped my wings and made me a demon's slave. The things the Hag does to me for amusement... I don't want to know this life anymore. I hate the earthen planes. I hate them! I need your blade to give me mercy."

Her blade wavered. "I won't kill you."

Surprise sparked in his gaze. "I'm not asking for my death. I'm asking for theirs. That demon, Mr. Black, his aspis—all of them dead at my feet."

Elise nodded and sheathed the falchion. "That's the plan. You don't have to beg."

"Restore my wings. You have her brand; you can release me. I can liberate the other angels and collect an army one hundred strong. We will kill them all together." He clawed at the necklace on his throat.

A hundred angels. That would be an incredible army. With that many ethereal creatures at her back, she could take down a lot more than the Night Hag. She could take down civilizations. And the whole time she marched, the angels would stare at her with those desperate eyes.

Her stomach twisted in on itself. "Sorry. I don't ally with angels."

"Then let me go, at least. Free me to exact revenge. *Please.*"

Elise hesitated. She didn't want to have anything to do with anything ethereal—not those ruins, not the things that lay beyond, and definitely not angels.

He gave her such a wretchedly hopeful look when she stood over him that she almost reconsidered her decision. But when she spoke, her voice was hard, and it didn't waver. "Don't follow me. Stay here until sundown, and don't tell the Night Hag I saw you."

Horror dawned in his eyes. If Elise could remove the collar, then she could also give him orders. The muscles in his back flexed as though he was going to stand, but he didn't budge. He couldn't.

"Mercy," he whispered.

"I'm all out of that for the day." She took a step away, but paused. "You should know that Itra'il is alive."

He sucked in a hard breath, gripping his chest as though his heart hurt. "She's *alive*?"

"Yeah." Elise brushed past him. "Sorry."

The police allowed James a courtesy call when eight o'clock rolled around. He drummed his fingers on the desk by the phone for almost five minutes before deciding what number to dial.

It took Anthony two hours to show up with a stack of money fished out of James's safe at Motion and Dance. He stared around at the police station like he couldn't quite believe he was there.

"Thank you, Anthony," James said. "I can explain all of this."

"Yeah, I think you better," Anthony said. The beaten old Jeep waited outside in the parking lot. It was a welcome sight after a night trying to sleep on concrete. "Where should I take you?"

"The parking gallery, please. My car was left there overnight. You can go back to work afterward."

"It's fine. I should check on Betty anyway." He put the Jeep into gear and shook his head. "You know, I've seen some weird stuff since I started dating Elise. Zombies. Giant spiders. Exorcisms. But when I'm halfway through rebuilding the transmission on a VW and I get a call from

225

you—*you*, of all people—asking me to bail you out of jail…
that's got to rank at the top of my 'shit I never expected to
deal with' list. You don't even *like* me. Why didn't you call
Elise?"

"And that would be part of the story. I'll tell you
everything. Later."

It was the longest, most awkward ride possible back to
the parking garage, even though they were only a few
blocks away. And true to his word, Anthony followed
James all the way to the suburbs north of Reno.

"So?" Anthony demanded as soon as they met at the
front door of his house.

James sighed. "Is now really the time?"

"I missed half my shift at the shop because of you. This
is a *great* time."

His upper lip twitched. "Fine. Let's go inside, at the
very least." It was a small mercy that Stephanie was
nowhere to be found, and that Betty was still sleeping on
the couch. James brewed a pot of coffee, uncomfortably
aware of Anthony leaning against the opposite counter
with his arms folded and an expectant look. "Do you take
cream?"

"No, but—"

"You would take an explanation. Yes. I get it."

"I was going to say I take sugar, actually. But sure.
How *did* you land in jail?"

"Elise. Elise got me arrested. Happy?" He poured two
cups and sat down at the kitchen table, which was topped
with rare Indonesian agarwood to match the paneling on
the island, at Stephanie's insistence. James massaged a
hand over his brow. "Of course it was Elise. That should
go without saying, shouldn't it?"

"It's not like she's not a criminal," Anthony said,
grabbing his mug. He didn't sit down.

"Your defensiveness is charming. It's lovely not having

226

to be the one doing it, for once. I hope you get to enjoy many, many years making excuses for Elise."

"Do we have a problem?"

James barked a laughed. "No. Of course not."

"Good, because whatever you think, I just went through all the trouble of calling Milo into work to cover for me and opening a magical safe with one of Elise's gloves. I'm going to catch so much shit for leaving early. And you—you and me—" Anthony gestured between them with the mug, "—if we've got a problem, then I don't know why I would have bothered."

James pinched the bridge of his nose and shut his eyes. It was hard to open them again. He was going to pass out for a few years as soon as he got horizontal. "Then why did you bother coming to get me?" he asked dully.

"Because you're Elise's…" Anthony wiggled his fingers in what was probably supposed to be a rough approximation of casting a spell. "I thought she had to be dead or something, if you were in jail."

"She's not. Not until I get at her, anyway." James snorted at how offended the younger man looked. "That was a joke."

"If you're going to—"

The front door opened. Elise appeared in the space between the formal dining room and the kitchen like a ghost. Yellow, splotchy bruises covered the entire left side of her face. It wasn't as bad as her expression—that exhausted, miserable look of someone who hadn't slept or eaten in a week.

She looked so terrible that James forgot to be angry. He shoved his chair back and stood.

Anthony pushed past him. "Elise!" He wrapped her in a hug. Her arms stayed limp at her sides. "Jeez, are you okay? What happened?"

She handed him an envelope wordlessly. He removed a

227

couple of pictures. James wanted to see them, but he remained frozen by the kitchen table instead. Elise's expression was telling enough. Whatever was in those photos would be very terrible, and very likely mean a fight.

Instead, he studied her as Anthony studied the photos. It was the first time she had set foot in James's new house, and she looked like a snake surrounded by mongooses. Her upper lip curled as she took in the nonporous countertops, the backyard, the framed photo of James and Stephanie waiting to be mounted in the hallway.

"Are these those spiders that we fought?" Anthony asked. Elise put a finger to her lips and shook her head. "What? Why are we being quiet?"

She pointed at James and Anthony, then at the floor. The message was clear: *Stay here.* And then she drew her sword and moved to the back door, peering into the yard. It hadn't been landscaped yet, although stakes with yellow flags marked where empty dirt was destined to become brick paths and grass.

"You don't need your sword. Stephanie isn't here," James whispered.

Even that couldn't make her laugh. She slipped into the living room, and he took the photos from Anthony.

James didn't recognize anyone in the pictures. The old woman had a distinctly inhuman appearance—the Night Hag?—and he was sure that the spiders were the same demons that Elise had been hunting in the desert. But that wasn't what gave him pause. The gate in the third picture made a chill wash over his body.

"What is that?" Anthony asked.

James dropped the envelope and followed Elise.

She was kneeling under one of the bay windows to glare at the neighborhood through a crack in the blinds. Betty was so buried under blankets and pillows that only the top of her blond head stuck out. She didn't stir when James crouched by Elise.

He tried to see what she was seeing through the window. Trees baked in the hot summer sun. His new neighbor gardened in a pair of purple Crocs.

And then—a flash of movement. Something darted past the back fence.

Elise hurried out the front door, which she had left cracked open. By the time James got to his feet, grabbed his notebook off the coffee table, and followed her onto the front step, she was wiggling onto the roof. All he saw were her feet kicking as she disappeared.

He swore under his breath and stuffed the notebook in his belt before leaping to grab the gutter.

The ceiling tile blazed under his hands. Stephanie had insisted on a white roof to reflect heat, so walking on it was like being trapped atop a range set to ten. He jerked his scalded fingers back.

Elise's hair was just visible over the slope of the roof. She was already crouched on the other side.

He squatted beside her. "What—?" he began, but she cut him off by pointing.

The house James and Stephanie bought was a recent addition to the neighborhood. The only thing at their back was empty hillside, which had been leveled into terraces and marked for future development. From their elevated position on the roof, they could see over the hill, and all the way to the highway. But Elise wasn't pointing that far.

His eyes fell on a hulking shape behind the fence. A daimarachnid.

"The Night Hag said she would have you guarded," Elise murmured. "I thought she meant by the Gray."

"Those photos—the old woman—"

"That's her. She's had the spiders this entire time. She's the one who tried to kill Betty."

The daimarachnid scuttled to the corner of the fence, and Elise pulled James behind a gabled section of roof. It was a half a degree cooler in the shade underneath. Sweat dripped from the back of his neck down his spine. "It's logical, in some sick fashion. How do you cement the allegiance of a reluctant warrior? Do you give them promises of safety and money, or do you take away the people to which they already hold allegiance?"

"Why not both?" Cold fury glowed in Elise's eyes. "We're killing her today. Right now. And I'm starting with that spider."

Without warning, she leaped to her feet, rushed around the gable, and launched from the roof.

James couldn't help it. He gave a little shout of shock and fear as she plummeted to the other side of the fence. It was barely a half second of warning, but it was enough—the spider attacked while she was still on her knees.

She brought up her sword. It connected with the mouthparts of the daimarachnid with a meaty thump.

Elise cried out.

The fence blocked his view, so his mind was immediately flooded with a thousand horrible thoughts of huge bite wounds and pulsing venom. James dropped to his belly—the roof burned even through his t-shirt—and slid down feet-first.

But when he got to the other side of the fence, the daimarachnid was already dead in the dirt. Elise stood over it, sweaty and panting with ichor caking her shirt to her chest. Relief swamped him. "I thought you got bitten. Those spiders—you know they're venomous."

"Yeah, I know. We have to move fast. The Night Hag is going to feel its death, and we have to get there before she realizes what that means."

She took a step toward him and staggered.

James tried to catch her. Elise's arms were so slick with

230

the demon's juices that she dropped to the ground anyway.

"What—?"

"It's fine," she said, but then he saw the ragged flesh on her thigh, and he realized that she had been bitten after all.

He wiped some of the blood away with his fingers for a better look at the wound. From somewhere in the musty depths of James's memories of academia, he recalled the word "necrosis." It should have taken hours to develop, especially with Elise's robust immune system, but there was nothing normal about bites delivered by demons. The injury was already as big as his fist and blackening around the edges. It didn't bleed so much as ooze.

She grabbed his wrist when he pulled the Book of Shadows out of his belt. "Save it."

"We can't leave that," he said. "I have a spell—"

She pushed him back and shook out her leg. "I said I'm fine. It just burns. We've got to kill an overlord and shut an ethereal gate, so I can't let you drain your magic."

"How do you plan on fighting like that?"

"With this," she said, picking up her sword and sheathing it again. Her cheeks were pale. "Now help me push this body over the fence before someone sees it."

TWENTY-ONE

ANTHONY WAS WAITING at the back door when they shoved the daimarachnid into the yard, and he hurried over to help them drag the body under the shelter of the house. Elise wished she could see how Stephanie reacted to finding a dead demon in her yard. That would have been a popcorn-worthy conversation.

She limped into the kitchen and took one of James's dish towels out of the drawer by the sink, where he always kept them. The spider bite burned like a cigarette jammed into her thigh.

"We have three major problems," Elise said, wetting down the towel and pressing it to the wound. "First: We just killed the spider guarding James, and Mr. Black is still out there, so he could jump on us at any moment. Second: We have to kill the Night Hag. And third: She's about a half mile under the city, so we have to get in and out without dying."

To Anthony's credit, he barely blinked. "Okay. We'll go together."

She lifted the rag to inspect her wound. The flesh was shiny red in the center where her skin sloughed away. She squeezed bloody water into Stephanie's stainless steel sink and wetted it down again.

"You can't fight like that," James said.

232

"I just need bandages. Anthony, wake Betty up. Tell her we're getting out of here."

He looked startled at the order. "Betty? Really?"

"We're not leaving her alone." Elise cast a disdainful glance around the kitchen. James might have organized it, but everything else was obviously Stephanie's doing. Betty was right. The house reeked of bitch. "Where's the bathroom?"

James pointed her down the hall. She limped through the formal dining room and helped herself into the guest bathroom. They had seasonal towels and decorative soaps in the shape of frogs. She grimaced.

"Just let me heal you," James said from outside the door with exasperation. "This is ridiculous."

She hopped onto the edge of the countertop. There was no bathtub where she could rinse her leg off; they had opted for a glass block shower instead. "I would need an antivenin before you could heal it properly. Tylenol? Advil?"

He opened the medicine cabinet and tossed her a bottle. She turned it over to read the label. Percocet. Nice.

She chewed a couple of pills and palpated the edges of the wound with her fingertips. It felt like getting bitten anew. James watched her splash water onto the wound with a deep frown.

"If you say 'I told you so,' I'm morally obligated to slap you," Elise said.

He threw his hands in the air. "What's the point? You won't listen to me. You turned to demons for help and won't let me heal you, so obviously, you don't want anything to do with me these days!"

"You're the one who decided to move away from the studio we bought—together—without telling me. When you try to decide which one of us doesn't need the other anymore, you should think about that. Where are your

233

bandages?"

"We don't have any."

"How can you not…? Never mind. Old t-shirt?"

James left and returned a moment later with a Motion and Dance polo shirt and a pair of scissors. Elise cut it into strips and bound them tight around her leg. The painkillers were starting to take the edge off.

"I want to say, for the record, I think—"

She held up a hand to cut him off. "Does Stephanie make you happy?"

"We just killed a daimarachnid behind my house and are about to attack a demonic overlord. Is this the time for such a conversation?"

"Yes."

Anger flashed across his face. "Well, believe it or not, I don't have to confer with you to make every decision. So tell me what you want to hear, Elise. Do you want me to say that she makes me miserable? Would that satisfy you? Because you seem to have this sadistic urge to make me suffer alone, and if telling you that will make you leave me to live my life, then so be it!"

The question that had been bothering her for weeks—months—leaped out before she could give it a second thought.

"Why aren't I enough?"

His face was inscrutable. "What?"

Elise shrugged and focused on cutting more strips. "You're all the companionship I've ever needed. Going to college, getting a job, trying to make other friends…it kept me busy when I wasn't hunting anymore. But I don't need Betty or Anthony. I don't need *any* of it."

Just you.

The last part was left unspoken, but it hung between them. He swallowed hard. "When you went missing over a decade ago—when the coven summoned me to find you

234

—I had a life of my own. I had a home and plans to marry. Do you ever think about that?"

Anthony's open, imploring face came to mind. *Do you ever think about the future?*

"No," she said. "I don't."

"Well, I do. I'm almost forty. I can't get back all those years I've lost. You don't want a spouse? A home? Children? Fine. But most people don't find comfort in a splatter of blood and the company of demons. Some of us need other people. Intimacy. A real life." He waved a hand at the house surrounding them. "And while you're seeking satisfaction at the end of a sword, I…" He finally noticed her expression and trailed off. "I'm sorry. I forgot you can't —you know."

Her mouth twisted. "Anthony asked me about…" Elise mulled the words over. Just thinking about it made her sick again. "Marriage. Kids."

"After three months of dating? Ambitious." He made it sound like a joke, but he wasn't smiling. "Does he know?"

She washed her hands in the sink with soap and water, then swung her leg to test mobility. It wasn't pretty, but it worked. She couldn't expect anything better. She also couldn't seem to meet James's gaze.

He stepped forward, reaching out to touch her shoulder, but changed his mind. He sagged against the counter beside her instead.

"Death's Hand killed me, Elise. When I think back on that night—hell, on the thousands of nights like that one— I feel my age. You will not be able to save me every time. We were right to retire."

She tipped her head back to study him in the mirror. His reflection wasn't nearly as tired or aged as hers, even though she was twelve years younger. "You were the one who wanted to do it again."

"Once. Just once. Only because we needed to."

"Once for you, maybe. But that once was enough to ruin everything for me. I don't have any choice now. Everyone knows where I am, and Mr. Black has taken everything." She stuffed her hands under her arms, hugging her ribs tight. Her feet dangled over the side of the counter. "I can't get out of this. Not anymore."

"He hasn't taken your friends. Or me."

"No. You did that yourself." James flinched as though she had punched him. A sick sense of satisfaction resonated through her. "So...does Stephanie make you happy? Really?"

"Yes." He almost sounded sure of himself. "Yes. She does." James brushed the braid over Elise's shoulder, and his fingers paused on her skin. It looked like he wanted to say something else, but the sentiment stuck in his gaze without making it to his lips.

"Fine," she said after a protracted silence. "Good. I'm happy for you." She didn't bother making it sound like she meant it.

"What is that, Elise?"

She had to twist around and look at her reflection to see what he meant. She had forgotten about the Night Hag's brand on her shoulder. It had mostly healed and left a fresh pink circle marked with eight radiating lines.

She didn't have time to answer. Someone knocked at the door, and James dropped his hand.

The door opened another few inches, and Anthony's reflection joined theirs. "Betty's awake," he said. "We can go."

Elise's leg buckled under her when she jumped off the counter, but she ignored James's attempt at giving her a hand. "Great. We'll take the Jeep."

"Family field trip," James muttered. "What joy."

Getting into the Warrens was the easy part.

Craven's was mostly empty in the afternoons other than the demon employees, who weren't surprised to see four heavily-armed humans march through on a mission. They did, however, give them a very wide berth. Nobody tried to stop them as they ascended to David Nicholas's former office.

His door placard was conspicuously missing, which left a blank beneath the "general manager" sign. Elise felt a faint twinge of guilt—but only a twinge. She made sure it was empty before letting everyone inside.

Where his office had once been filled with trash and bowls of masticated chewing tobacco, now it was nothing but a cavernous room overlooking the game floor. She found a light switch behind the desk. The overhead fluorescents cast the room in harsh blue light.

"What is this place?" Betty asked. Going on the offense had put a pink glow on her cheeks and a gleam in her eye.

"This is where the manager worked. There's a back path down to the club here."

Anthony cupped his hands around his eyes to peer at the tables on the floor. The dealers must have known David Nicholas was gone. They chatted and smoked around empty tables with their uniforms undone. "Where's the manager now?"

Elise glanced at James. He was flipping through his Book of Shadows and pretending not to listen.

"I killed him."

Betty's mouth opened in an "o" of surprise.

A quick search of David Nicholas's desk yielded a key ring and a dusty flashlight. She unlocked the door he used to get to Eloquent Blood, propped it open with her foot, and studied each of her friends as they passed through. They didn't look like much of a team. Anthony was greasy

237

and exhausted. Betty wheezed when she walked. And James was still pretending to be absorbed in his Book of Shadows. She wasn't much better. She couldn't put any weight on her bitten leg.

They made it halfway down the stairs to Blood without seeing anyone. When they passed the ground level, Neuma rushed toward them.

Her shorts and pink tank top were so different from her normal clothes that Elise didn't recognize her until she smiled. She wasn't even wearing makeup. "Elise!" The half-succubus suddenly noticed everyone else, and her smile faded. "What's going on?"

In the corner of Elise's vision, Anthony had gone rigid. Even in her lazy day clothes, Neuma's sex appeal was enough to instantly decimate the brain cells of any red-blooded human in her vicinity. Fortunately, she didn't have the charm turned on.

There was no point in lying. "I'm going to kill the Night Hag."

Her face went slack with fear. "No—oh, no, you can't do that!"

"I've got two swords, two witches, and a shotgun. I'm not feeling bad about my odds," Elise said. Betty grinned at being included in the list of weapons.

"It's not like that!" Neuma grabbed Elise's hands and lowered her voice so the others wouldn't hear. "You're *branded.*"

"It'll be fine."

"Even if she doesn't kill you on sight, which she totally can, the Night Hag owns *everything* in the city. You know what happens if she dies? Have you seen what happens in a territory without an overlord?"

She freed her hands. "Consider this fair warning. It's about to get ugly. You can stick around to deal with the fallout, or you can run."

The bartender glanced nervously at the others again. "Been nice knowing you, hot stuff."

Anthony watched her ass as she fled up the stairs. Betty smacked him in the arm, and James coughed into his hand.

"Come on," Elise said.

It wasn't much further to the club. There were no waitresses in sight to distract Anthony, and the cleaning crew was absent from the floor as well. Their shuffling footsteps echoed. "Nobody here? This will be easy," Anthony said with a nervous chuckle.

Elise wasn't as optimistic. They would only get as far as the Night Hag wanted them to go. She had to have realized her daimarachnid guard was dead and connected it with Nukha'il's failure to return. If she was letting them pass unobstructed, it was because she wanted it that way. But she didn't need to scare everyone by saying it.

"Stay close."

The elevator into the Warrens stood open. The bulb had even been replaced. It didn't flicker anymore.

"So what's the plan?" Anthony asked as they approached it.

Elise blinked. "Plan?"

He gave that nervous laugh again. It was starting to get annoying. "It's not like we're going to walk into some demonic overlord's evil underground lair and expect to kill it without a plan...right?"

"Actually..."

"Just a moment, please," James said. He led Elise around the corner of the DJ booth. He glanced at the place the cage had stood the night before and pulled a face. "I know you didn't want me to say that I told you so—"

"And I still don't."

He folded his arms tight across his chest. "I know what that scar on your shoulder means." The brand ached as though it knew they were talking about it. "You can't confront the Night Hag like that. She can kill you with a thought."

"I know. That's why I thought we would piggyback."

"Are you certain that's a good idea?"

They hadn't joined in an active bond since the spring, when Elise used their shared power to exorcise a child. It made both of them stronger, but only briefly. And sharing their powers always came with the risk of burnout.

"I'm not sure it will even work when I'm branded," she admitted. "But having an aspis is supposed to protect me from things like getting killed with a thought, so it's all I have. If it doesn't work, this could be a really short fight."

"We don't know if joining while you're branded will make you impervious to her, or make her impervious to us."

"I know."

He grimaced. "Then I won't do it."

She massaged her temples. Pressure was gathering in her forehead, and she wasn't sure if it was because they were so close to the Warrens or because James was stressing her out. "I know you're mad at me…"

"That's a word for it."

"But what other choice do we have?"

Elise glanced around the corner. Betty and Anthony were just a few feet away, pretending not to listen. When they realized she saw them, they turned away with nearly identical expressions.

"I'll do my best to shield you, but it's too dangerous to piggyback. I'm sorry, Elise." James marched toward the elevator. She had no choice but to follow him.

Fitting four adults into a small metal cage was cozier than Elise liked to get, but with awkward maneuvering, they managed to shut the door and flip the lever.

Something hard and intangible pushed against the

240

back of her skull as they descended. Even the Percocet haze couldn't block it out. A sense of unease crept upon her. The pressure in her skull was growing stronger, and she thought she recognized it now.

It wasn't the feeling of a powerful infernal presence—it was ethereal.

The silence in the elevator was unnerving. Even Betty seemed to have run out of things to say. She gave an occasional cough that rang out in the too-quiet air, but she wasn't smiling anymore. Anthony gazed at the darkness above the cage. They could only see the walls a few feet above them before they were swallowed by shadow.

"So demons use mine shafts. Why am I not surprised?"

Nobody responded. He rubbed the back of his neck and stared at his feet.

When the elevator finally reached the bottom, Elise held up a hand to indicate that they should wait. A soft hum filled the hall. Betty shone the flashlight around the rock walls, but there was nothing to see.

"Maybe the Night Hag isn't down here. It's awfully empty," Betty said.

Elise shook her head. "She's here."

They walked down the long, empty hallway. Nothing was guarding the entrance into the chamber where the gate had been constructed.

Elise edged around the door. The gate had been finished, the empty crates had been carried away, and the working demons were nowhere in sight. Only a single figure stood in front of the door in a long black gown. It looked like the Night Hag was taking a solitary vigil.

"That's the overlord—the old woman by the gate," Elise said, pointing into the cavern. "I don't know where Thom is, but he has to be around. Watch for him. They say he's a witch, but he's much more powerful than that."

"What's he look like?"

241

"Like a supermodel. You'll recognize him if you see him."

She took another long moment to study the cavern and the gate. Instead of having the bowl fragments at the capstone, the Night Hag had redesigned it so that it was at the base instead. It wouldn't require wings to open the gate. Elise could walk down, touch the stone, and pass through to the ethereal ruins…if she wanted to. But she didn't plan on letting it get that far.

Elise gestured. They edged down the path with their backs against the wall.

She didn't make it six feet before the Night Hag looked up. Betty gasped.

The overlord wasn't alone after all.

Nukha'il knelt on the floor on the other side of the gate, hidden by its shadow. He glared at Elise with bitter fury. His face was swollen and bruised from a thorough beating, and chains at his wrists pinned him to the floor.

"This is a trap, isn't it?" Anthony asked.

An instant later, something massive dropped from the ceiling and pinned her to the ground.

Her injured leg couldn't take the impact. Her body struck dirt, and Anthony jumped back with a shout. A daimarachnid reared over her.

Elise drew her sword too slow. One of its legs crushed her arm to the dirt.

It didn't try to bite her. Instead, its mouth descended on her throat and snagged the chain of charms almost delicately.

The spider broke the chain and jumped off the ramp.

James grabbed for the charms and missed.

"No!" Elise shouted, scrambling on her knees to the edge, but it was already gone. It took the charms to the Night Hag like a dog fetching a bone.

"You have been very helpful!" called the overlord as

242

she picked out the bowl fragment and threw the rest of the charms aside. "Shame that you should bite the hand that feeds. You are an incredible weapon. I would have loved to wield you."

She extended a pale, slender hand and inserted the pebble into the crack.

Elise felt like she had just jumped off a bridge. Her pulse thrilled. Her stomach leaped into her throat. Sudden wind whipped her hair around her face, battering her body, and all she could do was dig her fingers into the ground to keep from getting ripped off the side.

The gate was complete.

"Bring them down!" ordered the Night Hag.

A dozen more daimarachnids emerged from the other side of the cavern and scuttled toward the ramp.

Elise tried to get to her feet, but her leg completely gave out. She struck the ground on one knee. Pain arced from hip to shoulder, and spots of blood dotted the bandages.

"James!"

He was beside her in an instant. "We should run—"

The spider-demons were rushed toward them. Every rustling motion echoed off the high cave walls. She grabbed his arm, dragging his face down to her level.

"Piggyback," Elise said. "*Now*."

"Elise—"

"Just do it!"

The blast of the shotgun roared above them. One of the daimarachnids had skipped the slope and climbed beside Anthony and Betty instead.

James swore and held Elise's face between both of his hands. A bolt of power shot through her. "Hang on," he said. She felt him open himself to her. Magic pulsed around them. He extended it to her, pale eyes glowing, and she opened herself to take it.

243

And then they both blacked out.

TWENTY-TWO

ANTHONY THOUGHT HE coped pretty well with the whole demon thing. He didn't have a nervous breakdown after the zombie attack, which was pretty good considering he hadn't even believed in ghosts before that. When he went camping with Elise, he took a spider down on his own. Mostly. And he'd become pretty good with the shotgun. As far as "people who can't turn paper into fireballs" went, he would definitely say he was a useful team member.

But nothing could have prepared him for the moment Elise and James went limp on the ground and left him alone with his wheezing cousin, a demonic overlord, and a gateway into an angelic city.

He stared at their bodies.

"Oh no," Betty said.

They didn't have long to be shocked. A dozen daimarachnids reached the bottom of the ramp, which gave them about twenty seconds before getting overtaken. Anthony pumped his shotgun and stood over his cousin while she examined their friends.

"She's not responding!" Betty cried, jamming a knuckle into Elise's breastbone. The pain from that should have been enough to wake the dead.

He stepped around her, angled the shotgun down, and

fired off a shot. The spider-demon in the front lost its eyes in a cloud of blood. It collapsed and tripped the spider right behind it.

Anthony didn't get a chance to fire again.

"Bring them down."

The spider-demons lifted James and Elise's bodies in their mouthparts. Their gentleness was surprising.

But the demons didn't try to be nearly so gentle with Anthony and Betty. They drove into the back of his legs and shoved him down the path. "Hey!" he protested, twisting around to aim. They rewarded him with another, harder shove. He lost his balance and fell onto all fours.

The shotgun flew from his hands and dropped over the side of the path.

The spider-demon that had pushed Anthony seized him with its forelegs to lift him over its head. Its grip dug into his back and sides. When he was seventeen, he had body-surfed at a music festival after too much weed, and it felt a lot like that—except nobody in the mosh pit had pincers. He stared at its glistening eyeballs as it hauled him toward a woman he was pretty sure planned to kill him.

"It's okay, Betty, we'll be okay!" he yelled, trying to comfort his cousin. When she didn't respond, he twisted in the spider's legs to see what she was doing.

Betty was still at the door, kicking and punching and generally making herself impossible to grab. "Fuck you! Yeah! And fuck you, too! Ouch—hey!" Two of them finally jumped and pinned her to the ground. They dragged her down the slope. "Let go of me, you ugly bastards!"

At any other time, he would have laughed.

Each step of the spider beneath him was uneven and jolting, like riding a horse with too many legs. The demon holding Elise drew level with him. The hilt of the falchions jutted over each of her shoulders, and blood dripped from underneath the gloves. Her arms and legs dangled

246

uselessly. So much for hoping she was only pretending to be asleep.

"Anthony? Anthony!" Betty wailed.

"Don't worry, it's going to be fine. We can—"

"Optimism. How sweet," said the Night Hag as the spiders dropped all four of them in front of the dais and stepped back to form a loose circle.

Anthony eyed Elise's swords. They were the only weapons left now, but he hadn't even touched them before. He played baseball in elementary school, though. How much harder could it be to swing a sword?

Before he could decide if he wanted to make a move, the Night Hag descended to examine him like he was a piece of dog shit on her kitchen floor. Her nose wrinkled.

She snapped her fingers, and a beautiful man appeared at her side. He had full lips, long black hair, and no shirt. Anthony found himself gaping and had to shake free of it. The new guy had to be Thom.

"What is this?" she demanded. "What are they doing here?"

"They are friends of Elise's."

"Idiots. Amateurs! You would think a kopis would know better than to bring children with her!"

"Hey!" Betty complained.

The overlord ignored her. "At least she came at all. Strip her gloves and open the gate."

"I'm afraid I can't do that," Thom said.

She spun on him. "Are you challenging me?"

"I have obeyed your every other order, but I will not expose her hands." He hooked his thumbs in the waist of his slacks. "Make of it what you will."

Several tense seconds passed.

Surprisingly, it was the Night Hag who looked away.

"Nukha'il!" she snapped. "Come here!" The chains fell away from the man on the other side of the gate. He stood slowly, as though he had been forced into a kneeling position for so long that he could barely move. He joined her on the dais. His wrists, rubbed raw by metal shackles, looked like they had delicate bird bones inside. "Grab the kopis. Remove her gloves. Open the gate. Do I have to spell it out for you?"

He glared, but he stepped down from the gate without arguing and knelt to grab Elise. Betty shielded her body.

"Don't touch her!"

He shoved Betty with one hand. It was the smallest of gestures, but she went flying as though he had thrown his whole body into the punch. She cried out. Anthony barely caught her before she hit the ground.

Nukha'il scooped Elise from the ground, propping her awkwardly against his shoulder so he could peel off one of her gloves. Crusty blood made the material stick to her hand, but when he ripped it free, Anthony saw that the black symbol wasn't black anymore. It glowed with the same faint, silvery light as the gate. Fresh blood dribbled from the center as if she had been stabbed.

"Hurry," the Night Hag said, gesturing impatiently. "Do it now." With an arm slung around Elise's waist, he lifted her hand to the gate.

Anthony had to do something. Before he could reach the first step onto the dais, he caught the beautiful witch watching him. Thom gave an almost imperceptible shake of his head. The intent was clear: *Don't do that.*

Nukha'il pressed the mark on Elise's hand to the mark on the stone with his fingers spread behind hers.

The glow went out of the stone.

He stepped back, leaving a bloody handprint where Elise's fingers had been.

Anthony was suddenly face down on the floor and had no idea how he had gotten there. He felt the pain an instant later—a splitting in his skull so much worse than having a wrench dropped on his head, worse than getting smacked in the nose with a baseball bat in Little League, worse than being tackled by spider-demons. It blinded him with white light.

He couldn't see. Couldn't think.

"Anthony!" Betty gasped, dropping at his side. "Oh my God, what—?"

The Night Hag was cackling, but Anthony couldn't focus on her. He could barely see past Betty's feet. "It works! Now, my angel, go through the gate. Make sure it's safe."

"No," said a soft voice that had to belong to Nukha'il.

A cry of pain.

"I am getting sick of all this defiance!" she spat. "Go through the gate! I will kill you if you don't. Make your decision."

Anthony squinted at the dais. There was so much light pouring from the stone arch that he could only make out the shadowy backs of the overlord and her minions. Why wasn't Betty screaming? It hurt so much.

Nukha'il dropped Elise. She tumbled down the steps and rolled to a stop beside Anthony.

"As you demand," said the angel in a low growl.

With an arm lifted in front of his eyes, he passed through the pillars and disappeared.

Everyone was focused on the gate. Anthony saw his moment. He took one of the falchions out of Elise's spine sheath, gritted his teeth against the pain, and got to his feet. Betty gaped at him as he ran onto the dais.

The overlord heard him coming and turned. He drove the falchion into her stomach.

Black blood spurted from the wound. The Night Hag cackled shrilly. "It stabbed me!" she said to Thom, turning to face him as though Anthony wasn't even there. "That little boy *stabbed* me!"

249

He shrugged. "That happens."

She shoved Anthony off the dais. The overlord was stronger than she looked, but not strong enough to throw him. He stumbled back to Betty as she jerked the falchion out of her stomach. "And to think I just finished improving this body. What a waste of time."

She wriggled her fingers into the stab wound and began to pull. Her flesh tore away like rubber. There was something underneath, something black and crimson and not quite blood.

Her body shuddered. She heaved. The skin on her face loosened. The mouth-hole stretched until all her teeth were visible in a skull's grin, and then they fell out one by one in sparkling shards of bone.

A huge, slippery limb pushed from the stab wound. It slid out like a tree branch birthed from her gut and felt around for the floor. When it touched down, the tip of a second limb joined it and ripped the hole wider. Her entire ribcage was bared as a third leg pushed through, and then a fourth. Each was as thick as Anthony's body.

The Night Hag's flesh sagged. Her arms and legs emptied into wiggling sacks.

A hulking spider rose from the remains of her human form—larger than the dais, larger than the gate itself, far larger than the semi Elise had hijacked. Anthony fell onto his back. The Night Hag loomed overhead.

Red eyes glistened on a brown and tan head. Brands blazed down her belly and legs. Her flesh was mottled with patterns meant to blend in with one of Hell's deserts.

Anthony had seen the picture of the giant spider next to the gate. But he hadn't imagined it would be quite so *big*.

"Uh," Betty said. She couldn't seem to process any bigger words than that.

They exchanged a glance. He didn't have to read her

mind to hear the unspoken motto they usually shared in jest, but now with complete sincerity: *What would Elise do?*

There wasn't time to strategize. He let his mind return to their week in the desert—he killed his spider by running it over with the Jeep, but he would need a really big Jeep for this one—and thought of how Elise always went for the eyes, the joints, the comparatively soft underbelly.

The underbelly on this thing was about two feet over his head.

"This really sucks," Anthony said, and then he grabbed the second falchion.

"Kill the humans," said the Night Hag. Somehow, she sounded completely normal, like there should have been a woman standing in front of the dozen smaller daimarachnids.

Oh yeah. The other spiders.

Anthony swung the falchion into the mouth of a demon rushing Betty. She threw her hands over her head with a shriek. Ichor splattered on both of them.

It stumbled back, but a second spider took its place immediately. He swung again, and again. There were so many of them. He couldn't tell which legs belonged to which body. The only way he knew he hit anything was that the blade would stop, something would shriek, and venom would splatter burning hot on his hands.

"Get out of the way!" Betty shouted.

"What?"

"I said, move it!"

Anthony sidestepped.

Something hot blasted past the side of his head and set fire to a spider-demon.

All those wiry hairs ignited simultaneously. The hard carapace shriveled as it screamed and flailed and kicked. All the other spiders stopped to stare, too—like time came to a complete halt as one demon burned to death.

Something inside its shell popped as its innards cooked.

It flopped onto its side and stopped moving.

He whirled on Betty. She was clutching a notebook decorated by pink flowers and an ephemeral white unicorn.

"I told you I can cast magic missile!"

"Perhaps I spoke too soon about children," said the Night Hag.

Her leg swung over Anthony's head as she took a huge step. It only took one to reach them. The stink of rot and age overwhelmed him. Each one of her fangs was half as tall as he was. She hunched over, bringing that giant mouth toward their faces.

Anthony wrapped an arm around Betty's shoulders and launched into a run.

The pincers snapped shut where they had been standing a moment before.

"What else do you have?" he asked, swinging and hacking their way through the crowd of spiders. They all were trying so desperately to obey the Night Hag's orders that they stepped on each other, toppling and clumsy.

"Uh—just a second, I don't—"

"We don't have a second!"

She flipped through the pages and ripped one out from the back.

"Okay! Here!"

Betty ducked around him with a sheet of perfumed pink paper between her thumb and first finger. Her lips moved, but Anthony didn't hear anything.

The air popped.

A firestorm blasted around them and blew through the crowd of demons. The three daimarachnids closest to them caught fire like the first one had, shrieking and twitching and falling all at once.

Anthony had never been scared of Betty before. Never.

Even when they were kids, and she was five years older, and her idea of babysitting was to literally sit on him. But watching the demons burn made fear thrill through his stomach.

"I traced that one straight out of James's Book of Shadows," she said. Her lips were pale. Her knees buckled.

Anthony had to let her fall. A particularly ambitious daimarachnid climbed over its burning friends, scuttling toward him like an attack dog. He dodged to the side and sliced, but missed. It twisted. Pain whipped through his calf as one of its pincers scraped him through his jeans, and then those fangs hooked on his shoe and jerked him to the ground.

He kicked it in the face and sent it flying. But another one took its place and knocked the falchion from his hand.

It was hard to throw a good punch from the ground, but he sure as hell tried. Hitting the daimarachnid in the face was like hitting a brick wall. His knuckles split open on contact. It reared back an inch—only an inch. It was enough. He lifted his knees, planted his feet on its hind segment, and threw it over his head with its own momentum.

Betty got to her knees and ripped another page out of her notebook.

Another word of power. Another silent explosion.

The spider that had been on top of him splattered.

The paper dissolved under the force of its own magic, and she wiped her hands clean on her shirt. "Oh my *God*. I didn't know—I don't—oh my God!"

"Freak out later!"

Anthony grabbed the falchion, getting to his feet again in time to take the impact from another daimarachnid. There were still almost a half a dozen—plus the big one over the gate, who seemed to be watching them with amused silence.

He stabbed the falchion through the top of a spider-demon's head with enough force for it to come out the other side. The tip of the sword buried in the dirt and pinned the demon down.

"I don't think I have anything else," Betty said, dissolving into a coughing fit.

"Help us!" he cried to Thom on the dais.

The witch was examining his fingernails, reclined against the gate as though it wasn't throbbing with immense, uncontrollable energy. Thom's eyes skimmed over Anthony's body, and something like approval flashed across his face.

"Oh, fine." Thom stepped down to Elise and brushed his fingers across her brow. He winked at Anthony. "You're welcome."

"What are you doing?" the Night Hag demanded.

He vanished. And Elise didn't move.

"Anthony!" Betty cried.

She was pinned by one of the smaller daimarachnids. He wrenched the falchion out of the ground, kicked the demon off Betty, and pulled her to her feet.

The Night Hag's leg swept over him with another step, and the lowest joint caught his attention. The armored shell was split so she could move.

He drove the sword up with all his strength. It buried into her flesh. Fluid sprayed from the Night Hag's leg. The giant spider jerked away with a screech, but Anthony followed her. He hacked at the joint like he was splitting firewood at his aunt's house—hairy, twitching firewood.

Elise's falchion got stuck in the exoskeleton and ripped from his hands.

She slammed him against the wall. "I am having a bad day," the Night Hag said in a low, cooing voice that came from nowhere. "And you are not helping anything." And

254

then she bit.

Elise woke up feeling very strange.

Her skin didn't sit right on the muscle. Brilliant spikes of light filled the empty spaces in her skull. Her tongue tasted like ozone. And the air—so many new colors surrounded her. A not-quite-silver, a blue that wasn't blue, and so many shades of gray that she didn't see with her eyes.

It was the same thing she had seen on the chains binding Nukha'il, but it was magnified a thousand times and painted across the entire world. The light was brighter and the shadows were deeper.

Elise was seeing magic.

"James," she groaned as she sat up, clutching her forehead in both hands. Her leg didn't hurt anymore, and when she peeled off the bandages, she found blood staining unbroken skin. And one of her gloves was gone.

Her aspis was sprawled motionlessly beside her, and she grabbed his wrist to feel for a pulse. It beat steady and strong in his veins.

That was when she realized that Betty and Anthony were missing.

Elise riffled through James's shirt to find the Book of Shadows tucked in his belt. "Sorry about this," she muttered, getting to her feet to look around.

The gate was open. Pale light flowed from its center, warping the air so she couldn't see through to the other side of the cavern. That explained why her glove was gone. But instead of the painful roar she experienced last time a gate was opened, this one chimed. It was a soft, musical note, like a chorus waiting in the white beyond.

It didn't hurt. In fact, nothing hurt. She felt…good.

255

Maybe a little too good.

But there wasn't time to figure out what changed. An infernal presence was strong on the other side of the glowing dais, and Elise reached up to draw one of her swords.

Her hand met empty air.

She spun to search the floor. Her swords were nowhere in sight.

"Great," she muttered.

Elise stepped around the dais. There were more pillars near the wall, although they were black instead of white. Where had they come from?

Her gaze traveled up the long columns.

Her jaw fell open.

There was a huge spider in the room. It had Anthony pinned against the wall. And four or five smaller daimarachnids milled around them.

One of her swords was right in front of the gate. Elise dived for it. Getting so close to the gate made her entire body vibrate, but it wasn't nearly as agonizing as before.

The giant spider moved to bite Anthony. "Hey!" she yelled.

It looked at her. "Oh, wonderful. It's you." Elise recognized that voice. She was too giddy to be surprised that the Night Hag had turned into a spider.

"Yeah. Me." Elise lifted the Book of Shadows. "Betty!"

Her friend looked up. Elise threw the notebook, and Betty caught it. Her eyes lit up. "Should I—?"

"Make a miracle happen!"

The Night Hag rushed Elise, limping on an injured leg. As soon as it landed in front of her, she jumped onto it and scaled the spider's body, dragging herself atop the head. Elise nearly slid off the top when she thrashed, but her fingers caught a ridge near one of the angry eyes. It swiveled around to glare at her.

She levered herself onto her knees, lifted the sword over her head, and plunged it into the Night Hag's eye.

Betty spoke a word of power.

The air boomed as the symbols on the sword blazed. All eight eyes erupted at once.

The Night Hag roared. Elise lost traction. Her sword tore free.

It was a long way to the ground.

Anthony caught her. She had the presence of mind to drop her sword to keep from stabbing him, but his arms barely softened the blow. His elbow connected with her stomach. All the breath rushed out of her as they both hit the ground.

The spider stomped blindly toward them with a wailing shriek. Elise jumped out of the way of a crashing leg, pulling Anthony with her. She shoved him toward the wall.

She didn't even see the second leg coming at her.

It smashed her to the ground. Elise threw her arms over her head, trying to shelter herself from the thrashing limbs, and felt ichor shower onto her shoulders from the stab wound. Elise was an instant from getting crushed.

The light in the gate suddenly grew again. Nukha'il appeared at the top of the dais with a flash, looking winded and confused. "Nukha'il!" she shouted.

He glanced between Elise, under the stomping feet of the giant spider-demon, and the Night Hag herself.

A huge foot flew toward her.

Nukha'il darted in—a pale blur in the darkness. Cold hands grabbed Elise's. He dragged her out of the way.

"Get against the wall!" Betty yelled, standing over James's body.

Elise didn't ask why. She threw Nukha'il toward the side of the cavern and covered his body with hers.

Magic coalesced in a nimbus around Betty's head. Her

257

hair stuck straight out in every direction as though she had been struck by lightning. There was paper clutched in both of her fists. Steel-blue light crackled around her. Elise had never seen James's magic before. It was so much darker than she expected.

Betty threw the paper at the Night Hag.

The spells hung, momentarily suspended, in midair. Then they rested against one of her telephone-pole legs.

She pointed.

The room filled with light and heat. All moisture vaporized from Elise's skin. Her clothing charred instantly as the tapestries behind the gate caught fire.

The Night Hag screamed.

Elise ducked her head so she wouldn't have to see. But there was no way to tune out the roars of pain and fury as she thrashed in her final death throes.

It felt like she screamed for hours. Days.

Eventually, they trailed into sobs, and then there was nothing but the echoes of crackling fire. The Night Hag had fallen by the dais. Her body was a black husk, and red embers glowed within her carcass. Entire tapestries had disappeared in a puff of smoke.

Both Anthony and Betty were covered in ash, but unharmed. Elise let Nukha'il sit up. He stared around with shock, as though he couldn't imagine a human causing such devastation.

"My Lord," he said.

Elise's mouth was too dry to speak. She worked her tongue around in her mouth to create saliva before saying, "Good miracle, Betty."

With a shaky laugh, Betty sank to the ground and pressed her face into her knees. Elise crawled over to her. "I'm okay," she mumbled without getting up, "I'm okay. Is James...?"

"He's still breathing. He's fine. What about you?"

258

"That *hurt*," Betty whispered. Her hands were closed so tightly around the remaining scraps of paper that her knuckles were white. Elise carefully opened her fingers.

"Relax. That's James's magic going through you. You'll be fine." Elise made herself sound confident, even though she wasn't sure that was true. What happened when a weak witch channeled power of James's caliber? She had never seen it before, but they were probably lucky Betty was still awake, much less alive.

Nukha'il dusted himself off and came to stand beside Elise. The magic on his necklace had faded, but not gone out.

"Free me," he said. There was no supplication in Nukha'il now—only defiance.

Elise stood. "Why?"

"I helped you. Free me."

She nodded. He turned around. Her fingers tingled as she pressed the latch open, and the metal fell to the floor with a clink.

A sudden swell of ethereal energy rose around him. Nukha'il sighed and rolled his shoulders. "Thank you," he said. "Finally."

"What will you do now?"

"Find Itra'il and move on. I have wasted too much time in servitude."

With a small bow, he turned to leave the cavern. Elise watched him go. The presence of an angel always left a sour taste in her mouth.

"Elise?" Anthony's call drew her attention back to him. He was gaping at the Night Hag's body. It seemed to have lost half its mass in death, but it was still terrifyingly huge. "Should we do something about the gate?"

"Sure. Why don't you stay here for a second, Betty?" Her best friend nodded against her knees. She was pale and trembling. Elise collected her swords, sheathed both of them, and joined Anthony by the fallen overlord. She was impressive, even in death. "She's dead, Anthony. We don't have to keep an eye on her."

"I just can't believe…" He blew a heavy breath out of his lips. "That was terrifying."

He probably was hoping for words of comfort. Elise didn't have any.

She turned to face the gate. The light inside whirled and swirled. She stretched a hand toward the broken fragment that had come from her necklace, but getting too close made her fingers burn.

"Here," Anthony said.

He plucked the stone out of the gate, and with a resounding clang like a heavy iron door shutting, the light went out. It sounded like the very gates of Hell swinging shut. But it was so much worse than Hell—and so much more satisfying.

A huge weight Elise hadn't realized she had been carrying lifted off her chest. She sagged against his arm.

His fist clenched around the rock, brown eyes burning bright. "What now?" he asked.

Now she would take that rock and throw it into the deepest reaches of Lake Tahoe. Now she wouldn't worry about anyone reaching those ruins again. Now the overlord and the brand on her shoulder were gone, and the city was hers. Now…

Relief thrilled through her chest, foreign and strange. She seized Anthony's shirt in both hands. "Now this," she said, pulling his head down to kiss her.

His empty hand pressed against the small of her back, crushing her body to his. It felt good. She could have done it forever, if they had the time. Forever turned out to be just a few short seconds, but when she broke free, Anthony pressed his forehead to hers.

"Wow," he murmured. "That good, huh?"

"Yeah. That good."

He laughed and swept her up in his arms, spinning her around. "Jesus, Elise! Thank *God* you woke up when you did. I was sure we were going to die!"

"You didn't do too badly on your own." She leaned on his chest when he set her on her feet again. "Remember when you asked if fighting was a little exciting in the desert?" she whispered, low enough that Betty wouldn't be able to hear. She didn't feel like being teased. Not when she was so relieved. He grinned.

But Betty wasn't even listening to them.

"Hey, lovebirds! I think James is waking up!"

Elise broke free of Anthony. "Of course he missed all the good—" she began, facing her friend, who had pillowed James's head in her lap.

Motion loomed in the darkness beyond Betty.

Alain entered from the hallway above, flanked by twin angels. They were statuesque and pale with the silvery ghost of wings sweeping from their shoulders. Both had swords that flamed with ethereal light.

And the witch's pistol was drawn and aimed at James.

"Watch out!" Anthony shouted.

Three things happened at once.

First, Betty saw Alain and lifted one of James's paper spells, bold challenge glowing in her eyes. Elise could see the confidence in her face. The surety that she could wield that kind of magic. But shifting to take the spell from his Book of Shadows put her directly between the gun and James.

Second, Elise shoved her boyfriend out of the way and drew her sword. The stone dropped from his fingers and clattered across the floor.

Third, Alain squeezed the trigger.

The explosion echoed in the great underground chamber, like two gunshots in quick succession. His muzzle flashed.

Betty fell.

Alain swung his arm and aimed at Anthony. He fired again.

Elise had moved fast to get him out of the way, but not fast enough. Her boyfriend shouted. Blood spurted on his leg.

She leaped over Betty's prone body, which had folded protectively over James, and buried her falchion hilt-deep in Alain's stomach.

He was still unbalanced from the second shot and couldn't protect himself. The impact of body against body brought her to a halt face-to-face with the witch, so close that she could smell the beer on his breath and see the hate deep in his eyes.

Her free hand bit down on his arm, digging her nails in until he dropped the pistol.

But he was smiling. Why was he smiling?

"Mr. Black sends his regards," he hissed. His tongue was stained with his own blood.

The angels whirled with motion—not to attack Elise or defend Alain, but to snatch the stone from the ground and slam it back into position on the gate. The ringing of chimes roared through the chamber as the gate swept open once more. Wind lashed Elise's braid around her head.

She withdrew the falchion. Alain stumbled back, gripping his wound. Off-center. She may not have hit anything important, but it would slow him. Blood dribbled through his fingers.

Still he laughed, shrill and delighted, and when Elise turned she saw why.

Betty had been shot in the face.

She was slumped to the side on top of James. Her forehead was a ruined mess, though the injury was only as wide as a coin. From this side, the wound almost looked

262

too neat to be fatal. But there was nothing in her eyes and her muscles were slack. Elise had seen the emptiness of death more than enough to recognize it without needing to check for a pulse or the rise and fall of breath.

One corner of Betty's lips was still spread in the tiniest smile.

Dead.

A ringing filled Elise's ears, drowning out the gate and the heavenly choir and even her own heart. She was frozen to the spot. Her fingers suddenly didn't have the strength to hold her falchion.

Translucent feathers swirled around her. An angel wrapped his arm around Alain's midsection. He mouthed words Elise couldn't hear: "Go! Now, go!" And both angels, with the witch in tow, leaped through the gate.

Her knees connected with the ground. She didn't realize she was scrambling over to Betty until she took the woman's shoulders and turned her gently onto her back. Something warm and sticky met her fingers. The exit wound at the back of Betty's skull was low, almost at her spine—Alain had shot from above and gone all the way through—and it dribbled down her neck.

Her blood was sprinkled on James's cheek like tears flicked on his skin.

"Betty," Elise whispered, taking her friend's hand. Her fingers were still closed around one of James's spells.

Someone was screaming.

Anthony limped over and collapsed. He was shot, too, but Alain had only hit him in the thigh. Shock turned him white and shaking.

"Betty—Betty—oh my God, Betty, you can't—"

His fingers clenched too hard on her shoulders. She was dead weight when he shook her.

"Stay with her," Elise said.

Anthony turned wide, helpless eyes on her as she

stood. "Where are you going? You can't leave us! Betty needs help, she has to—"

"Betty is dead."

Her voice broke on the last word. Elise took up her sword with blood-sticky fingers and sheathed it. "Elise—"

"When James wakes up, tell him I've gone through," she said.

She felt calm. Composed. Total clarity descended upon her in a silent, crystal moment of realization: Alain and the angels had gone to the other side. She was going to follow him, and she would kill him.

Elise stood in front of the gate. It seemed so much bigger now that she knew she had to pass through it. The darkness beckoned to her with slender fingers.

Elise…

That voice. It had been calling to her for weeks.

Now she would answer its summons.

She glanced over her shoulder at Anthony, James, and Betty. So much blood. She clenched her jaw, tightened her fists, and took a deep breath.

Elise jumped through the gate.

TWENTY-THREE

THE FIRST THING James realized when he reached consciousness was that he was very cold and laying just a few feet away from the Night Hag's doorway—which was open. Light radiated from it in colors he had never seen before. It would have transfixed him if he had been alone.

But the second thing he realized was that Mr. Black was standing over him.

He groaned, trying to push himself away on instinct. But hands clapped down on his shoulders and hauled him to his feet before he could go anywhere.

The cool hands burned against his skin. He tried to pull away, but the angel was too strong for him to break free. Even if he could have, there were more angels waiting to stop him. James made a quick head count. Six of them. Where ethereal beings were concerned, it was virtually an army.

"So glad you could join us," Mr. Black said, drumming his fingers against a notebook tucked under one arm. The Book of Shadows. Fantastic. "I thought I'd have to throw you over my shoulder to jump through."

James tried to remember how he had ended up in the cavern and what happened. When had the gate opened? Why was there a dead spider the size of a small house on the other side? And where was Elise?

Then he looked down at where he had been laying. Someone was on the ground not far from him.

"Oh no," he whispered.

Betty had been laid out with her hands folded on her stomach and a shirt tucked under her head. She might have been sleeping, if not for the bullet wound.

He clapped a hand over his mouth and turned away. It seemed somehow obscene to gaze upon the body of Elise's best friend. Maybe if he didn't see her, it wouldn't be true. Maybe she would sit up and be fine again.

"Look at her," Mr. Black said. "Look."

James didn't want to obey, but he couldn't tear his eyes from the wound on her forehead and the bloody line running down her nose. He thought of all the times he had snapped at her for doing something absurd at the esbats, and her musical giggle, and he felt like he was going to vomit.

He turned on Mr. Black. "You're sick," he said, voice trembling with fury.

"Actually, that would be the mark of my friend Alain. Isn't he a good shot?" Mr. Black stepped close to James. The old kopis was three inches shorter than him. "I'll admit I was a tad offended when you burned my home and destroyed the gate. In fact, I've thought about very little else in the years that have passed."

"We didn't kill anyone."

"No, but you sure as God tried. Now, I hope you spend the rest of your life thinking about this…" He swept a hand toward Betty. "Like I've thought about you. However short that 'rest of your life' might be."

He tossed the Book of Shadows aside. It disappeared into the darkness, and James watched it go with longing.

"Elise is going to—"

"Shut up. I'll consider myself threatened and save you the effort." Mr. Black took out a pocket watch to study it.

266

"Alain should have everything ready now." He pointed at the gate with his cane. A silver cuff glimmered at his wrist. "You first, Mr. Faulkner."

Elise would have argued. She probably would have fought him, and seen how many angels she could take out before they brought her down. But James was not nearly so brave. He couldn't stop staring at the neat little hole in Betty's skull.

"You've made a big mistake," he said.

He prodded James in the knee with his cane. "Walk faster, please. We're on limited time."

There were only three wide steps to reach the dais on which the gate had been built, so there was little time to examine where he was going. James knew quite a bit about angels and their ruins, and this was not a gate to an ethereal dimension—that much he could tell. He suspected it would take him to the mysterious angelic city rumored to be under Reno. It was enough to get his academic heart racing.

He tilted his head back to gaze at all the shifting colors and shapes within the gate. He stretched a hand out and felt the vibrations in the air. He had never felt it like that before. Something had changed.

Mr. Black cleared his throat. When James didn't immediately move, he prodded him again.

Bracing himself, he stepped through the gateway.

When he reappeared a few seconds later, he was on all fours on a street corner. His glasses fell off the bridge of his nose. They cracked when they struck the cement sidewalk.

"Damn it," he muttered. His stomach wanted to reject everything he had eaten that day. He took shallow breaths and focused on holding it down.

He studied his surroundings through a fall of bangs. The angels had appeared around him on their feet. They were as calm and composed as though stepping through interdimensional gateways was an ordinary part of their day. For all he knew, it might have been.

Then he looked straight up.

He lost his battle against his own heaving stomach and vomited.

When he was done, he didn't dare look up again. One glance had been more than enough. The mirrored cities were too much for any mortal mind to process.

James trembled as he sat back, wiping his mouth clean. The angels watched him, showing no signs of concern. They looked so different to him now. His body reacted to them—a clenching of his gut, a tickle in his skull. It was like a whole new sense had opened for James.

And then he realized what had changed.

He could *feel* Elise.

To an extent, that was nothing new. He could always sense her. She was like his phantom limb, and sometimes he felt a little twitch that said Elise was thinking about him. But this was something new. He could hear her voice, like tuning into a fuzzy radio station.

Anthony shot him…going to regret that…damn it, Betty…

He glimpsed an image of a bloody skull and brain. James couldn't make sense of it. He gripped his head in both hands as the images and voice grew stronger.

I can't do this…

James tried to see over the heads of the angels, but they were taller than him—a novel experience. He couldn't see anyone on the street. It didn't sound like he was hearing with his ears anyway. He was hearing her inside of his mind.

And being close to the angels made his palms itch.

"Elise?" he said aloud. She didn't respond.

He put his broken glasses back on his face. The left eye was fragmented into two, warping the buildings. It was not nearly as dizzying as the mirrored cities.

268

A moment later, Mr. Black appeared on the other side of his angelic guards.

The air warped, and he dropped a few inches to the cobblestone street. He lost his balance and fell with a cry. The cane flew from his hand.

James seized the moment.

He stumbled to a standing position and ran. He made it about three steps before his heaving stomach brought him to his knees again.

An angel swept in and took his arm. It was a beautiful woman, elegant and slender, and he tensed with the expectation of being dragged to his feet. But she only offered him a hand. "Be careful," she murmured. Coppery hair fell in soft waves around her shoulders.

After a moment of hesitation, he let her help him up. Something in her face was open and trustworthy. "Let me run," he whispered urgently.

She shook her head. "We have a plan. Wait."

By the time she guided him to their landing spot, Mr. Black had stood. Sweat drenched his brow as he clutched at his chest. "No," he gasped. "Where did he go?" He spun, staring wildly at the ghost city around them. "Where is he? Alain? Alain!"

James didn't see anybody on the street. "What are you on about?"

The kopis dropped his cane and seized James's shirt in both hands. "He's gone. Alain is gone. I can't feel him!"

"Perhaps he's not here," James said.

But he suddenly knew that wasn't true. He saw the bloody skull again, and could hear the faint blast of a shotgun. *Anthony shot him...*

Mr. Black shook his head. "No! He came ahead of me! That can only mean he's..."

His mind caught up to what he was about to say an instant before he said it. Horror dawned on his face.

269

Alain was dead. James couldn't find any satisfaction at the realization.

Why could he hear Elise's thoughts?

Mr. Black dragged James down the street. The angels drifted after them without being ordered to do so. "Impossible," the older man muttered. "He can't be dead."

Have to find Mr. Black...

The thought didn't belong to James.

The angels followed him with those beautiful, expressionless gazes. They flanked him to either side as if he might run from them. Where would he go? The only way out would be to go through one of those gateways.

He closed his eyes for a moment, letting Mr. Black's hand lead him on, and caught flashes of imagery in his mind's eye. Even though he couldn't see Elise, he felt like she should have been standing next to him.

An elevator. More angels. Parking garage.

She was close. He was certain of it. But he had no idea *why*.

He opened his eyes to search for her again. If she was that close, he was sure he would have been able to see her. He scanned the roofs of the nearby buildings as Mr. Black dragged him along.

Angels moved atop the nearest structures surrounding the dark gate. They were spreading long lines of cloth ribbon in rows. One strand had been laid across the street, and James took the opportunity to examine it when they passed. It was covered in magic symbols, like the pages in his Book of Shadows.

"Paper magic?" he said. "That's impossible—I've never shown anyone how to do it."

"Some of the spells you used to burn down my home never ignited." Mr. Black bit out every word, shooting a glare over his shoulder. "Alain studied them. Deconstructed them. His aren't quite the same, but they do the trick, and—my God!"

The exclamation made James look up. They had turned a corner to see a parking garage—the same parking garage he could see with his eyes closed, but from another angle. A ritual space had been established at the corner near a street light.

Alain's body was a few feet away with blood and brain drying on the wall behind him.

"*Mon ami*," Mr. Black murmured.

Before James even realized the older man was moving, Mr. Black swung his cane. It cracked against James's skull.

His ears rang and his vision blurred. But he was ready for it when Mr. Black swung again.

James caught the cane and tried to wrench it from his grip. They struggled. James was a good twenty years old and several inches taller—it shouldn't have been a fight at all. But even an older kopis was much stronger than the average human.

Mr. Black shoved him to the ground and seized a fistful of cloth ribbon.

"She killed him," he said, voice thick with tears. "My aspis—my companion—"

"Karmic justice," James said.

"Justice? *Justice*?"

He didn't even see the strike coming this time.

The force of the blow made James black out. It was only for a few moments, but that was enough time—when he roused again, he was dangling upside down over the shoulder of an angel as they ascended in an elevator. He watched the hazy mirror-world slide outside the window.

When the door opened, the angel carried him outside and threw him to the floor.

James stared up at the towering column of the gate. It was so much bigger than anything he had seen before. The very top almost brushed the real city, and light swirled between the pillars like a tear in existence. The symbols at the base were already glowing. It was almost open. All it needed were the matching marks.

Mr. Black knelt over James with a fistful of ribbons, blocking his view. "Activate it."

James's eyes traced the path of ribbon. The angels had completed the circles—all nine of them, each one slightly smaller than the last and nested within each other. It encompassed the entirety of the gate.

He could see the spells for entrapment in the line, which had been Alain's specialty. It was relatively harmless—if one considered trapping a god harmless.

"I won't do it," James said.

"Hold his arms!"

An angel pinned him down. There was no fighting against its grip.

Mr. Black threw the rope of ribbon around James's head and tightened it on his throat. Pressure crushed against his esophagus. He gagged and gurgled, tongue bulging from his mouth.

"Activate them!"

James would have said no again if he could speak. He fought against the restraints of the angel's hands to no avail.

And Mr. Black pulled harder.

His skull began to fill with white noise. The older man's face blurred in his vision. Elise's voice echoed in the back of his mind: *He's here… where is he? James?*

Such pain.

He stretched out a finger to touch the ribbon as Mr. Black tightened the ligature.

The symbols flared to life.

Magic flowed from him into the ribbons, stretching out over the city. James moved through his magic. He raced through every line and saw the angels with their hopeless stares as if he walked past them himself.

And he saw Elise running toward Mr. Black's back.

She jumped on the other kopis, knocking him off James. They bumped into the angel. The pressure vanished from his throat and arms.

Freed.

James ripped the ribbons off his throat, sucking in a blessed lungful of air. Anthony raced from the stairwell. "Stop the magic!" he cried, waving his arms.

But it was too late to take it back. The entire city was aglow with the symbols on the ribbons.

Elise and Mr. Black rolled across the roof, trading blows. They ended up on their feet on the other side of the pillar, just beyond the barrier of the ribbon.

She lunged toward him, but Mr. Black side-stepped her, moving out of the way as though she had telegraphed her move. She swung again. His arm struck hers, knocking it aside.

Mr. Black slapped her other hand when it rose to strike him. He twisted, capturing her arm, and bent her elbow the wrong way. She cried out.

He finally gave a hard shove, launching Elise over his head, and she stumbled over the line made by the ribbons. "Finally," he spat.

"Don't start celebrating yet," she said, striding toward him again.

But when she reached the ribbon line, it was like striking a wall. The shock of it resonated through James. She couldn't pass the magicked runes.

"I've envisioned this moment for years," Mr. Black laughed. "Years! And what a satisfying moment it is."

Anthony tried to rush the barrier of ribbons, but an angel snagged him in its arms, holding him back. "Elise!" he shouted.

She faced the gate.

Elise…

This time, it wasn't her voice that James heard, but another entirely—something great and terrible that rang through his entire being, vibrating down to the marrow of his bones.

She held up her ungloved hand. Blood streamed from the symbol again.

The marks *wanted* to open the gate.

Her legs moved of their own volition. She stepped toward the pillar, rooted deep in the concrete of the parking garage.

She fought it. She fought it hard. But there was no way to stop the inevitable march.

Before she even touched it, the gate began to open.

A gust of wind roared across the top of the parking garage, ripping through them and nearly blowing James off his feet. Electricity sparked and danced in the air around the pillars. A rumbling shook the entire structure, from the top of the gate to the very earth, and the angels backed away as white light erupted from the arch.

He flung up a hand to shield his eyes, but it did nothing for the painful brilliance that burned through Elise's skull.

Her hands were stretched toward the pillar, dragging her forward inch by inch.

James and Elise's eyes met through the light. He knew she could see and feel the way he did, sharing every thought and sense between them. Something had happened when they piggybacked. Something wrong. She shared his sore neck. He felt her grief at Betty's death, and the marks on her palms burned on both of their hands. He felt the pull as strongly as she did.

And he felt the moment she made a horrible decision.

"He can't have me," she said. "I'll never go back to Him."

"No," he whispered. He didn't have to raise his voice for her to hear it.

Elise drew one of the falchions. "Sorry, James."

She plunged it into her gut.

Pain ripped through him as though he had been stabbed, too. A scream tore from his throat. He fell to his knees. At the same time, Anthony yelled—but it was all so distant, so meaningless. James's palms burned and the gate throbbed and he could feel the blade scraping bone.

Mr. Black ran to the edge of the ribbon. "No!"

Elise hit her knees. Fell onto her side. Released the sword. The power rushing through the gate immediately faltered. Her vision dimmed, and she felt *satisfied*.

He didn't stop to consider the ramifications. He shoved past Mr. Black, jumped over the ribbon line, and fell to his knees beside Elise. She swatted weakly at his arm, as if to push him back, but there was no strength in it. She was bleeding out too fast.

His Book of Shadows was still in the Night Hag's cavern. There was no time to cast a spell. James was one of the most powerful witches in the world, and yet his kopis was dying in front of him, and there wasn't anything he could do. "Goddamn it, Elise!"

She smiled to see him. "Hey," she said. Her vision snowed.

Elise's eyes unfocused. Her chest hitched.

He ripped the second glove off her hand, baring both bloody marks, and pressed them to the angelic stone.

Energy shocked through them. A mighty bell chimed.

The gate opened.

TWENTY-FOUR

DYING WAS A lot more painful than Elise expected.

She had given the subject a lot of thought over the years. Kopides seldom lived past thirty, so it wasn't a question of whether she would die a violent death or not—it was a question of *when*.

Since fights were seldom painful while she was in the midst of it—the adrenaline and endorphins took care of that—she expected the act of dying to be relatively painless, too. She thought she would go into shock. She might even be dead before she knew it was going to happen.

All of that was completely wrong.

The sword hurt as it was punched in, and it hurt just as much coming out the other side. Elise felt a twinge of sympathy for all the demons she had killed in that fashion.

But then she was falling, and she didn't really feel much of anything except the pain.

There was a commotion around her. People yelling. The towering bone pillars of the gate beginning to shake. She could see it all through James's eyes—including Mr. Black's horror as he rushed to the edge of the circle.

Good. Let him despair.

The blood loss caught up with her a few moments later, making the last vestiges of rational thought fade. A gray haze filled her vision.

Scraps of random thought flitted through her mind. She wasn't in the angelic city—she was buying the studio with James, bumping her shoulder against his and enjoying the glow of companionship. She was meeting an incubus in her new office, hoping to acquire her first client. She was taking a test with Betty in a lecture hall at the university. She was sinking deep into the snow…

Cold.

She was so cold.

Elise remembered running.

Her bare feet slapped against white cobblestone as a pale dress streamed behind her. Angels flanked her to either side. "Help me!" she had cried, and they rushed in to take her hands. She was a little smaller, in those days. Thinner and less muscular. Younger. But not weak.

"He will be so angry when He realizes you've gone," one of the angels told her. "He will tear apart the world to find you. He will destroy *everything* to bring you back."

"Let him," she said.

So they ran—Elise and twelve angels.

She had only been sixteen years old. She hadn't deserved what He did to her. She didn't deserve to be trapped in a black garden where light and hope did not exist.

There was a gate then, too. The angels took her there.

She had put her bandaged hands upon it. Her palms bled, the gate opened, and she jumped through to the other side.

Those were the facts. She understood that was what happened. But she didn't remember anymore.

Hazy memories. Scraps of time drifting on the wind.

She could see the pale hands reaching for her and hear His voice as He shouted for her.

Elise!

And when she awoke again—only for a moment—it was in the depths of snowy winter with James kneeling over her.

At the time, she thought he was another angel who had come to rescue her from His grip. She had been trapped for months—month upon month of torture, insanity, and pain under the guise of loving care. It only ended when James took her away.

She tried to forget. It was better to forget.

The concerned face of her aspis loomed overhead. "Goddammit, Elise," he muttered from a million miles away. He was turning her over, helping her face a sky filled with white light.

She wished he wouldn't look so sad. She reached up to touch his cheek, but her hand was too heavy.

"Hey," she said. She wanted to add, *It's okay.*

Feathers drifted through space.

It was so very cold.

James saw the instant that Elise lost consciousness. Her eyes went empty. The lids fell shut.

A moment later, the world flipped upside down.

For a horrifying moment, he dangled from the roof of the parking garage and stared at the real city beneath him. His stomach rose into his throat. His feet lifted from the cement, and he clutched Elise's limp body to his chest as if he could save her from the fall. But then pressure built within the barrier of the ribbons that pinned him in place.

A fissure appeared in the air between the gate's columns like a lightning bolt suspended in midair.

It split open.

Black, yawning darkness waited on the other side of the gate. It was pure nothingness, colder and emptier than the void of space. Like staring into the nonexistence of death.

He is coming.

Although He was pure energy—and inconceivable to the human mind—James knew the instant that He stepped through the door. Everything within the ribbons turned to white fire. The air scorched his flesh. He folded himself over Elise to protect her, but she was burning, too. All the oxygen vanished. James tried to suck in a breath—and failed.

The magic on the ribbons flared with power, straining to contain Him.

Beyond the ribbons, Mr. Black had fallen to his knees. He mouthed words that James could not hear.

James gathered Elise in his arms and struggled to stand. She should have been light. He always thought of her as hollow-boned, like a bird, and through a thousand rehearsals and a hundred thousand dance lifts, he never had to fight to lift her. But now he couldn't breathe. Couldn't think.

Ridiculous thoughts to have in the face of their greatest enemy.

His muscles trembled. "I have Elise," he gasped. He felt the voice in his throat, and the spasm of his lungs as they struggled to breathe, but his words were sucked into the abyss. "Now heal her!"

The light faded as he rushed toward unconsciousness. James fell, unable to support Elise's weight.

Heal her…save her life…

He wasn't sure if it was his thought, or if it belonged to the vast entity surrounding him. The light faded as He realized he was trapped. He wouldn't cross the gateway

279

into a cage.

"You can't go until you heal her," James croaked, doubling over. "You can't…"

Another figure moved behind Mr. Black's shoulders. It wasn't one of the enslaved angels. It was a man that burned with inner light, despite the overbearing light of God, with broad silver wings stretching behind him.

He landed at Mr. Black's side and seized his arm.

James didn't need to hear him to read his lips: *Burn in Hell*.

The angel smashed Mr. Black's silver cuff.

The outermost ribbon ignited, flashing with flame and turning to ash. The pressure eased off James. Oxygen rushed into his lungs. All sound resumed.

Mr. Black's influence lifted from the angels on the rooftop. A couple of them looked around as though they had just woken up. The one who had been holding Anthony sank to his knees and began crying.

The rest went insane.

The angels attacked each other. From the other side of the ribbon barrier, they were an indistinguishable mass of seething bodies. James couldn't see any detail through the brilliant light, for which he was grateful—but there was no way to drown out the sounds. Screams tore the air. Slick crunches and thick splats punctuated every cry.

"Anthony—run!" James yelled.

He rushed for the stairs at top speed, fists pumping and feet pounding against the cement. He jumped over the rail to the level below. Mr. Black followed suit and bolted —but much slower.

His motion caught the attention of the angels that had gone mad.

They flew at him with wings that were beginning to blossom again and fell upon him before he could take three steps. They dragged him to the ground just a few feet away from James. He saw everything.

Teeth sank into Mr. Black's shoulders. Clawed fingers dug into his belly. The suit was stripped from his body, and then the flesh from his bones in a spray of blood.

An angel tore the jaw free of his face. Hands pressed against the sides of his face and crushed his cheekbones. One eyeball bulged, then exploded. White matter splattered against the invisible barrier over the ribbon. The attackers dug elbow-deep in his body to yank viscera free.

James saw the copper-haired angel descend and remove a female from the fray. Her lips were stained with Mr. Black's blood.

"Itra'il!" he cried.

She struggled against him, but he lifted her into the air as though her kicks and punches meant nothing. Another angel took her place over Mr. Black's body as both disappeared into the glowing sky.

The rest of the ribbons caught fire and disappeared. A line of blood spilled across the place the barrier had been a moment before.

James wasn't going to wait for the angels to notice.

He threw Elise over his shoulder and ran for the stairs. Nothing stopped him. Every ribbon was broken and his path was clear. Carrying her body made him even slower than Mr. Black had been, but the angels were so preoccupied that it gave him a few seconds' head start.

They reached the top of the stairwell before the angels began alighting on the wind. Massive wings whipped behind them, only a shade darker than the light from the gate.

James didn't watch.

There was no sign of Anthony as he rushed through the streets with Elise hanging over his back, and he didn't dare search for him. Angels swooped overhead with wailing screams.

281

The windows on every shop had shattered when the gate opened, leaving shards of glass scattered on the sidewalk. His every footstep crunched. There was nowhere safe he could hide from the angels with the shops open—and he didn't dare pass through one of the gates.

But the river wasn't far. He could hear it roaring less than a block away.

James rushed around the corner, across a brick plaza, and down white stone steps toward the water. Angels wheeled around the buildings. One passed so low that it ruffled his hair. Feathers snowed around him, loosening from ethereal wings that had sprouted anew, but he didn't look up to see if they were coming for him.

The Truckee had risen on its banks to swallow the walkways that surrounded it. James's foot slipped and he sank knee-deep in water. It was so cold that it burned.

He sloshed through the shallows to shelter under the bridge as another angel shrieked past. James set Elise's body on a narrow strip of rocks and climbed beside her, crouching under the low shelter of stone. She stayed dry, but he was wet to the hips.

James peered out at the blazing white sky. He couldn't see the gate from their hiding place. Was it still open? Had He gone back, or was He in the city?

There was no way to tell. He turned his attention to Elise.

Her skin was colorless. James pressed his hand to her throat and found her pulse sluggish—and slowing.

Something splattered on the opposite bank.

James moved to shield Elise, but it wasn't an angel, and it didn't move to attack. It was a lumpy red mass—what remained of Mr. Black's body. The angels had dropped it on them. His blood clouded the water.

He scanned the sky. The angels spiraled overhead with no indication of dropping. Everything was bright and colorless, as though He should have been close. James had been so certain that He wouldn't be able to resist Elise. It was the only way to heal her. "Come on, where are you?" he shouted to the sky. "Why won't you heal her? She's going to die!"

Something shifted behind him. James turned, expecting to see Him. Instead, he saw the shattered husk of Mr. Black getting to his feet.

It should have been impossible to move. The muscles had been ripped from his right leg, leaving the bones exposed from hip to ankle. There were deep teeth marks in his femur. The cavity of his skull dripped onto his shoulder. Parts of his spine were missing.

But still, he stood. And what remained of his face was trying to smile.

"Hello," he rasped through a flapping esophagus.

Another voice echoed behind Mr. Black's—one greater and far more terrible.

Hello.

That single word felt like having a stiletto driven through his ears. It resonated in James's chest. For an instant, his heart did not beat.

Mr. Black's arms stretched out.

"You've brought her to me. Thank you."

Thank you.

James's teeth vibrated in his skull. A sharp pop against his cheek told him that a filling had exploded. The scar on his shoulder blazed with white-hot pain, and it took all of his strength to respond. "She's dying. You have to heal her —I know you can do it, you can do anything—"

Mr. Black splashed forward, and his bleeding fingers stroked Elise's shoulders. Shredded skin hung from his wrist. A fingernail was missing. "Yes. I will take care of her."

She's mine, mortal.

283

This time, the voice did not just hurt James. It stirred Elise.

Her eyes opened to slits. She looked up and saw Mr. Black. Their bond was so strong that James could see through her eyes as though they were his own, and she did not see a corpse. Instead, He looked like a glowing man, taller and brighter than the sun, with endless voids where His eyes should have been. He smiled for her.

She knew Him.

And she mumbled a single word: "Thom."

A shadow moved over them. The light was eclipsed by a mighty darkness—a black fog that oozed from the empty windows and doors of the angelic city.

"No!"

The responding echo was weaker than it should have been.

No…

A new man stepped from behind the bridge.

Thom had changed since they met at the police station. His hair extended into shadow, vast and infinite. Fire burned in his eyes. He was as beautiful as Mr. Black's body was hideous, and when he turned to appraise the situation, James saw a sweep of translucent black wings at his shoulders.

"I've been summoned. What is this?" he asked, his tone far too mild for the situation.

"Get away," said Mr. Black's body.

She's mine.

"Is that so? I don't believe that's true—yet." Thom tapped his chin with a finger. "You were already barely in this dimension, and now you've taken a tangible body. What a terrible idea. You didn't give that decision much consideration at all."

You know who I am.

"Yes."

You are not my match.

"No, of course not. Not when you're in your true form. But this…" Thom waved his hand at the body. "As I said— terrible idea."

He rushed toward Mr. Black.

Shadow clashed with light, and James's mind completely refused to process what he saw. It couldn't handle the information. His vision blanked, and his ears filled with a dull buzz.

When his senses cleared a few seconds later, he saw Thom seizing Mr. Black's shoulders and lifting Him into the air.

They blasted through the sky, receding into a pinpoint between the parking garage and its mirror. Both Thom and Mr. Black's body vanished through the dark gate.

The air was rent by the sound of a door slamming shut. It resonated through the entire city, sending a wind sweeping along the streets that kicked up glass shards and blasted away the light.

All the pressure vanished. The distant chimes went silent.

It was over, and He was gone.

Elise was still pale and unmoving, and the wound on her stomach wasn't bleeding anymore. He didn't have to check for a heartbeat to know she didn't have one. He felt it in the way his own heart shattered. "No," he said, smoothing a hand over her forehead. "Please, Elise…"

He searched inside himself for something from her. A hint of thought, a memory, a single neuron firing… *Anything.* But he had nothing. His mind was empty where Elise's presence should have been.

The angels were gone, and the air was still. A twilit fog settled where the light had been. The riverbank felt very lonely.

Anthony must have still been somewhere in the city.

285

He would want to say goodbye to Elise, too. But there was no time for that, and it was probably better that way. It had always been the two of them—Elise and James versus the forces of Hell and Heaven. It seemed fitting that it should end that way, too.

He pressed his forehead against hers. It was cool and clammy. "You're always so damn difficult," he whispered.

"This is touching. Shall I give you a few minutes?"

Thom stood knee-deep in the river with his thumbs hooked in the waistband of his slacks. It was a bizarrely casual position for someone who had just flung a god into another dimension. His skin steamed.

Anger choked James. "You let her die!"

"Such melodrama. All that activity in your lateral orbitofrontal cortex must be exhausting."

"*What?*"

Thom pushed James aside and took Elise in his arms. He gazed at her with an expression that could only be called adoring. "So it is true," he murmured. "She is the Godslayer. Such a thing exists."

"She *was* the Godslayer."

Thom snorted. "Elise isn't dead yet. Her brain has oxygen, and a heart is an easy thing to restart. I won't permit her to die. Would you like to go back to Earth?"

"How? The gates are all closed."

"That's not a problem."

James started to agree, and then remembered that Elise hadn't come into the city alone. "There's another man. Anthony…"

Thom shifted Elise in his arms so he could touch the red choker at his throat. "I will bring him, too. Do not concern yourself."

He snapped his fingers.

286

TWENTY-FIVE

PASSING BETWEEN DIMENSIONS a second time was just as difficult as the first. The instant James reappeared, he vomited across the dusty stone floor of the Night Hag's cavern. There wasn't much left in his stomach. Two short heaves, and he was done.

The underground chamber was too dark after the brilliance of the angelic city. He blinked green shapes out of his eyes as he tried to make sense of his surroundings. Anthony was sprawled a few feet away, unconscious but breathing. Beyond him, Betty's body was still resting—paler than the last time he saw her, but untouched.

Where was Elise?

He stood and spun, searching for any sign of her between the silent gate and the spider's body, but all he found were pages from his Book of Shadows scattered across the floor.

A sigh whispered through the room. James looked up.

Thom drifted from the top of the cavern, black wings spread wide. The span was so great that they brushed the distant walls. Elise was curled in his arms with her head tucked under his chin. She was still unconscious. It was the only time she could look so unguarded and innocent. James felt nothing from her—no dreams or emotions—but as Thom grew closer, he saw the rise and fall of Elise's chest.

His bare feet touched the dais. He settled to the earth, and his wings folded behind him. They vanished. The glow of his skin faded. "I see your apprehension," Thom said to James. "Don't worry. She only sleeps."

James took an unsteady step toward the dais, stretching out his arms. "Give her to me."

"You want her now? You, who was so eager to hand her to her greatest enemy just moments ago?"

"She was dying."

"And now she is healed without a mark of blood on her body. You are welcome for the favor, and to make it better, I will do another—I will retrieve her falchions and return them. But later. Even I must rest when traveling between dimensions." Thom quirked an eyebrow. "So. You attempted to surrender your kopis to a mad god. I don't know her as well as you do, so perhaps I am wrong, but tell me what she would choose if she were conscious: life in His garden, driven to madness, or the peaceful void of death?"

"Elise doesn't always know what's best for her."

"How fortunate that you do."

He hesitated. "When she wakes up...will she remember...?"

"Nothing. She will have no clue you tried to surrender her unless you share that fact, which I don't recommend if you treasure your relationship with her."

James tried not to look relieved. "Give her to me now."

Thom stroked the hair back from Elise's face. "There are many great mysteries in this world, James Faulkner, but few of them puzzle me after thousands of years. Yet when a deity chooses to elevate one of mankind above the rest, I can only marvel at such a decision. What makes this one special? Why should any of you be special when your lives are as short as a beat of my black heart?"

288

Thousands of years? He struggled to think of a response. "Elise is certainly unique," he said cautiously.

"'Unique' is inadequate. She has been touched by God and bears two marks. Why?"

"Do you expect me to have an answer for that?"

"Perhaps not. You are only human." Thom knelt and rested Elise on top of the dais. James crouched over her in some semblance of protection, though he was very sure that anything that could drive a god back to his kingdom would not be impressed by the mightiest of his spells.

"Are we safe? Is He gone?"

"He's not on Earth, if that's what you're asking," Thom said. "The angels whose minds have been destroyed by Mr. Black are contained as well, but they live. Safety is subjective."

He sat beside James, completely human in appearance once more. His brown skin had pores, the light touched his hair, and the hand reaching for Elise's cheek had manicured fingernails. "Don't touch her," James said.

Thom ignored his protestation and stroked her hair. "No matter the why, she is the Godslayer. Watch her well, James Faulkner, because she is mine. I will be back for her."

"What the hell are you?" he whispered. "Some kind of fallen angel?"

"Oh no." Thom smirked. "I'm something much worse."

He vanished without another word.

When Elise and Anthony woke up an hour later, night had fallen. She carried Betty's body out of the Warrens to the hospital. It was only a few blocks away. She refused to let anyone help her.

289

What happened after that was a blur. They didn't admit Betty because there was no treatment to be done for a dead body. Stephanie cried when she saw the wound, and James comforted her. Elise didn't stick around to watch.

Time passed. Things happened. Elise watched as if from a very long distance, going through the motions of filling out paperwork and giving them the phone number of Betty's parents and sitting in a waiting room.

Somehow, she found herself sitting with Betty's body. They had put her somewhere quiet and dark with only a single light to illuminate the bed. Her skin was the same color as the white sheet tucked under her arms. Elise stared at her, disconnected from herself, and thought that Betty would probably want to put on some kind of makeup before anybody else saw her. She hated to be seen without makeup. The pale lips and mascara-free lashes looked unnatural.

Anthony knelt at her bedside as tears cascaded down his cheeks. He had started screaming again, after Stephanie told them they could take their time saying goodbye before she was transported to the morgue, but he had been quiet for almost fifteen minutes.

"Do you want to say something?" he asked.

Elise folded her arms tight across her chest. Say what? Goodbye? "Sorry my enemy shot you?" No good words came to mind, so she just shook her head.

He reached out to touch her hand. "I killed him," he said thickly. "That guy is dead, and it's not good enough. She's still..." Anthony dropped his forehead to the bed. His fingers tightened on her wrist. "I don't blame you."

"What?"

"I know this isn't your fault. Betty was too eager. She didn't..." He sucked in a shuddering breath. "She knew this could happen. So I don't blame you. I thought you

290

should know."

The idea of it hadn't even occurred to her.

Elise got up and stood by Betty's head. She gazed down at her friend, knowing it would be the last time, and tried to see past the bullet wound. That wasn't how Betty would want to be remembered. Elise's eyes roved over her plump cheeks, her freckled shoulders, the curve of her body under the blanket. She wanted so desperately to feel a connection between herself and Betty, something that would give her what Stephanie called "closure," but she didn't feel anything at all.

That wasn't her friend. It was a body. The chance for goodbyes had long passed.

"I'll be outside," Elise said.

She went into the hall and leaned back, gently bumping her head against the wall. The curtain wasn't enough to separate her from Anthony's grief. His renewed sobs echoed through the hallway.

Once she was away from the body, she couldn't tune out James's thoughts anymore. With nothing to look at but a blank wall, her mind filled in with what he saw instead. He was in the lobby. There was an older woman with him, and although Elise had never seen a picture of Betty's mother, she had been told about all the bangles she liked to wear and the horrible perm. The woman was sobbing. James held her hand.

Shock had wiped his mind almost as blank as Elise's. Small mercy. She didn't want to have to hear her own thoughts, much less his.

A figure moved at the end of the hallway. Wearing a plain t-shirt and jeans, Nukha'il looked nothing like the angel that had attacked Mr. Black in the city. It seemed he had gone shopping at a thrift store. His wings weren't substantiated, but there was no hiding the subtle, shifting light that followed him.

Elise welcomed the distraction of his presence. "I didn't think I would see you again."

"Itra'il has gone mad," he said. "She is not the woman I knew. But with time..." He trailed off. "She won't be a danger to anyone. I'll keep a tight hold on her."

"Good. I don't want to kill anything else."

The angel didn't react to her threat. He stood beside her and faced the window into the room. The mini-blinds were mostly closed, but Elise could see Betty through the slits. Anthony had his hands folded at the side of the bed. His entire body shook with sobs.

"You lost your friend in this fight. Didn't you?" Nukha'il asked.

Elise nodded, lips sealed tight.

He crossed himself, bowed his head, and whispered a prayer. When he lifted his head, tears gleamed on his cheeks.

"I will carry the pain of your grief in my heart. For your friend, and for everyone else who lost their lives to this fight. But she is in a place without suffering now. You should take comfort in that."

His words didn't warm her. Betty might have been in a place with no pain, but she was also in a place where she wouldn't get to sunbathe, either. She would never sexually harass another colleague in good humor, or finish her research at the university. She would never feel the sun on her face again.

"It's a black place," Elise said dully. "A place with no light."

"Don't you believe in Heaven?"

"I've been to the ethereal and infernal planes, and there are no human souls there. When we die...that's it."

Nukha'il gave her a sad look. "Nobody knows what waits for mortals on the other side. Not even we do." He watched Anthony for a moment without speaking. Elise turned away. "I hope you and your loved ones find peace. I'll pray for you."

She shook her head. "Don't do that."

He briefly laid his hand on her shoulder before leaving. It didn't sting to be touched on her shoulder blade anymore. The Night Hag's mark had faded with her death.

Elise felt a presence at the opposite end of the hall and realized that James was approaching with Betty's mother. There would be more tears. More questions. The same lies she had written on the police reports about gang violence. More grief.

She left before they came around the corner.

James didn't think he would ever sleep again. Yet when he climbed into the bed he shared with Stephanie, he passed out immediately and didn't wake up for a long time.

The sleep wasn't restful. He awoke feeling like he hadn't slept at all.

He waited a day before seeking out Elise. He could tell by the tumult of emotions through their bond that he wasn't welcome. But when night fell again, and a new morning dawned, he couldn't stay away any longer. He didn't have to search. He only needed to close his eyes to see familiar couches, the late-afternoon haze glimmering on dust motes, and the window-mounted air conditioner.

He knocked lightly before entering the apartment above the dance studio.

Elise knelt between two boxes on the living room floor. She didn't look up when he came to stand beside her.

She had a white photo album spread across her legs and stared at the pictures with no expression. Her gaze was unusually opaque, even for her, but the bond had opened an entire new dimension to him. What he felt staggered him. Grief and rage and regret roiled through her like an angry wound.

He had to brace himself with a hand on the back of the couch. "Elise," James said, voice ragged.

"Betty had her wedding album in the fire safe. She didn't have her social security card there, or her passport, but she had her photos."

"Whose wedding photos?"

"Betty's. She got married at eighteen. When we met at college, she was going through a divorce." Elise ran a hand down the page and rested a fingertip on one of the pictures. "I met her ex-husband once. He wasn't a bad guy. They just...grew up. Grew apart. People change. He wanted kids and she wasn't ready."

James swallowed a lump in his throat. "I had no idea."

"There's a lot people don't know about Betty. Even Anthony doesn't know..." She pulled a photo out of the plastic sheet. "Well. It doesn't matter now."

Elise handed the picture to him. It was a solo shot of Betty in front of a trellis of roses with her train stretched across the grass and flowers in her hair. She beamed with none of her usual mischief.

"She looks so young."

"Betty would have been twenty-eight next month. She *was* young. What was I thinking? I never should have let her come."

"Elise..."

She put the picture back and snapped the album shut. Her face was red when she finally looked at him. "I wish I had died."

"Don't say that."

"I killed Betty. There are insane angels running loose in a parallel dimension that could break out at any time. And He knows where I am now, so sooner or later, He will come for me. You should have left me there to die!"

He refused to match her fury. He knelt at her side and stroked a hand down her healed shoulder, brushing the hair behind her neck. "I will always bring you back, Elise," he said, echoing what she had told him just days before. He traced his thumb along her jaw. It made her grow still like a hawk that had been masked. "Always."

She pushed his arm away. "Don't use that on me, not when—"

"I'm sorry."

"You're sorry? For what?"

He rested back on his heels with a sigh. There were so many things he wanted to tell her. Things that a thousand apologies couldn't amend. "For everything."

"It's too late for that." She stuffed the album back in the box and closed it. "Anthony wants to go through what's left of Betty's belongings. I should get her purse from Stephanie's house." Barely-restrained tears made her voice thick.

"Betty was your best friend. You can cry for your friends."

"No. I can't." He tried to wrap his arms around her, but she shoved him away. "Don't touch me." Her chin trembled. She took a deep breath and furrowed her brow as she concentrated on the wall. He could feel her fighting to hold onto her composure.

"It's okay."

James embraced her again. Her attempts to fend him off were much feebler the second time. She finally buried her face in his neck.

The pain poured out of her. The fear of being found. The horror of what Mr. Black had done. The loss of Betty.

Her thoughts faded and out of his mind.

Why Betty? Alain didn't feel enough pain when he died… I hate this…hate everything…

He thought Elise would feel better once she cried, but

he was wrong. Instead, her sorrow reached new depths to fill every crevice of her heart and mind. It was almost too much for him to take.

He pressed his lips to her brow. "It will be okay," he murmured against her forehead.

Elise thought that his breath was too warm in the summer air. The angry murmur of her thoughts latched onto it, seeking something she could control. He heard it, and she knew he heard it. James also knew the question she would ask a moment before she said it.

"What *is* this? What happened to us?"

He had been wondering the same thing since they returned from the city. None of his books talked about such a phenomenon, but he had a theory.

"When I died and you resurrected me, I think it... changed us. We're somehow trapped in an active bond—a permanent piggyback. I've tried to end it several times, but it's like we're stuck."

"Great. Just fucking great. Betty's death is my fault. Your death was my fault. This...*thing*...is my fault." Her mind had gone distant, retreating into a dark recess of memory. "I pushed Anthony away when I saw the gun. Alain wasn't even aiming at him, but I moved to save my boyfriend instead of Betty. If I had gone for her..."

"Then Anthony might be the one who died."

"I should get away from him. I'll kill him next."

"You didn't kill Betty," James said, smoothing a hand down the back of her neck. Her skin was feverish from crying. "Listen to me. You didn't kill Betty."

Her chin trembled. "I might as well have." She drew her knees to her chest and wrapped her arms around them. "God, it hurts. How do you feel like this all the time? How do you handle so much emotion?"

"What?"

"This is yours," she said with a hard sniffle. "This...

296

crying thing. All this grief. This is your weakness, not mine."

He took her hand, and he could feel it from her perspective as well as his own. James didn't just feel the supple leather of Elise's gloves. He felt the roughness of his skin, too. "Have you considered that you might not be getting it from me? You loved Betty. It's natural—not weak —to grieve for those we love."

Elise dropped his hand. "This isn't me. It's not." She swiped the tears off her face and straightened her back. "I'm going to help Anthony make arrangements. Betty wanted to be cremated, so there's…" She swallowed. "And I'm going to Craven's. They need help, now that the owner is gone."

"What's going to happen to the city without the Night Hag?"

"Reno survived without an overlord's help for years. But the threat of her presence kept challengers out, and I killed the only person who might have taken the line of succession. Now it's going to get messy. There will be territory battles."

"You can take time to grieve," he said.

Elise stood and hugged the box to her chest. There was one other box, too. That was all that remained of Betty's life—two banker's boxes in a half-empty apartment.

He followed her to the front door.

"I don't need time," she said. Her voice was dead again. The tears were gone. "What would I do with time? Wait for Him to find me? Throw myself on the floor and cry? Waste my time wishing that Betty hadn't…"

Her lips sealed shut before the last word could emerge.

James reached for her again, but she pushed away from him, opened the front door, and stepped onto the stairs.

She glared at the horizon. The tops of the casinos

297

downtown were visible just over the trees. There was no sign of the city mirrored above—not so much as a waver in the air.

"Let me help you," James said. "Please."

Elise shook her head. "I can't handle this. Any of it."

She walked down the stairs, and James watched her disappear into the blazing sunlight.